THE FAMILY GIRL

A NOVEL

Katherine Brankin

First edition 2014
ISBN: 978-0-692-42206-9

Published by DMD Books™
Batavia, Illinois, USA

THE FAMILY GIRL

To my boys, I love you with all my heart.

Acknowledgements

My heartfelt thanks go out to my "girls"—you know who you are—for their love, support, wine, and never telling me I was off my rocker when I started this. Especially to HH—thank you for being my first reader, for pushing me to finish, for the courage to publish, and for demanding an immediate sequel. To DB—thank you for teaching me how to put two words together a long time ago when I was a design intern. And to AA—the cards were absolutely right.

Prologue

Arlington, Virginia

To passersby they looked like a father and son enjoying the afternoon sun in the park. But that was not the case. This was their first and last meeting, and both were hoping that their paths would not cross again.

"Look, I was told that you could do this sort of thing… All I want is his research, which was mine to begin with… I made this guy, I pulled him out of that foul hole he worked in and gave him everything. And this is how he repays me? By refusing to give me the final product! That son of a bitch!… I really don't care how you do it, just get me my research. Or make sure that no one else gets it," the young man said to the old one between puffs of his cigarette.

"And you can't do it in-house?"

"Unfortunately for us, the S.O.B. is an American."

"You better be prepared to offer me something other than money for this. I've got money," the old man replied and readjusted the baseball hat he was wearing. He must have not been used to wearing one, for it seemed to bother him and he kept fiddling with it throughout their conversation.

"Full immunity. Past, present, future. You'll be untouchable. It's an offer you can't refuse," the young man replied after a minute and flicked his cigarette on the ground. It landed a couple of feet in front of them and lay there, slowly smoldering.

"Quoting *The Godfather* will not make me take your

offer, nor does it make you a man," the old man answered and readjusted his baseball hat again. He sat deeper into the bench and sighed.

"Listen, I'll give you time to think about it. 24 hours. But you'd be foolish not to take me up on it," the young man finally said and got up to leave. "24 hours, after that the offer's off the table," and he walked away.

Late that night, an old man with a limp walked into a crowed pub and elbowed his way through the crowd to the phone in the back hallway by the bathrooms. He dialed a number and waited as it rang on the other end. The phone was picked up after one ring. The old man smiled.

"Consider it done. Send me the dossier," he said before anyone on the other line could say hello and hung up. He then pushed his way to the bar and asked for a double gin on the rocks. When the drink arrived, he lifted the glass a little in a small toast to himself and took a long sip. A big, satisfying smile spread on his face once the gin warmed its way down the pit of his stomach. Yet, to the bartender, who happened to witness this smile, the old man looked even more menacing than before. The bartender shuddered and moved to the other end of the bar, hoping for the man to leave.

1

January, present time

The ringing startled her at first. Then, an eerie feeling crept over her as she recognized the sounds. It was her satellite phone, given to her by her father to be used for family emergencies only. From anywhere in the world they could reach each other, untraceable.

She scrambled to find the phone, and finally got it on the last ring. "Yes?"

"Lina, it's me. I'm sorry. I should've listened to you..."

She listened without interruption while her older brother talked. By the end, he was sobbing. She stood in the middle of her bedroom clutching the phone, not reacting. Finally she managed to grind out through her clenched teeth: "I'll take care of it."

Evanston, Illinois

"Your daughter has a visitor Mr. Bennett," said the duty nurse at the NICU station. Mark's pulse stilled. This statement could not mean anything but more bad news.

"Who is it?"

"A woman. Your sister? She said she's in between business flights and only has a couple of hours for a visit."

Mark's heart started to beat again. Slowly. Uncertainly. He hadn't talked to or seen his sister since he defied the family and married. Yesterday was the first time they've spoken since that day. A day he came to regret for the rest of his life.

He walked down the corridor to the room where his newborn daughter was fighting to survive along with other preemies. Through the glass door, he could see a fur-clad woman standing next to her crib. 'And the devil does wear Prada,' he thought. The hydraulic doors opened silently as he approached. The woman turned her head.

"You have a beautiful baby," she said.

"What are you doing here? Why didn't you call?"

"I had to meet her, Mark," Catalina walked over to her brother. They stood there, in the door jam, silent, awkward, each looking each other over. She reminded him of their father with the same cold steel blue eyes. So cold was the look that he felt shivers down his back. She thought that he looked haunted. 'No shit, after living with those bitches, you'd be haunted too,' she smirked to herself.

"My mother-in-law had a heart attack, Lina," Mark finally whispered.

"Things happen. I'm sorry for your loss. Both of them," she replied. And with those words Catalina leaned over and embraced her brother.

"It's done. The will, everything. Daddy's on his way to help with the follow through. Don't fuck this up and you'll finally be free. That bitch should've driven into a tree a long time ago," she whispered into his ear. "All you have to do now is take care of your daughter and listen to the Family." She released him. "I'm going to miss my flight. I won't be able to make the funeral. Neither, at this point," she said out loud, mostly for the benefit of nurses buzzing in and out of the room.

She turned around to look at the sleeping baby one more time, then started walking out the door. At the door she paused and turned to Mark. "Girl's a Bennett, she'll make it. Say Hi to Daddy for me." And with that she was gone.

Mark just stood in the NICU room for a long time, silent, motionless. In his head he was reliving the last year. His late wife turned out to be a mean jealous woman who, out of fear that he'd finally leave her, tricked him into getting her pregnant. She was also a reckless driver who had so many accidents that her license was revoked. And yet she still drove herself even though her rich mother provided her with a car and a driver. Last week, while being 30 weeks pregnant, she plowed into a tree. She died in the hospital, on the operating table, as her child was being delivered. Mark had to make a choice: save the baby or her. He chose the baby. Which meant that his mother-in-law lost her only child. The apple didn't fall far from the tree in that family, as Mark's mother-in-law was truly a monster. Enraged over loosing her only child, she proceeded to immediately seek custody of the baby even though she didn't want her. She just wanted to hurt Mark. Desperate to keep his child, he broke down and called his sister. Deep down, he knew what he was truly asking her to do when he asked for her help.

He finally walked over to his baby's incubator and put his hand through. As he was stroking the baby's head he noticed a clock on the wall. His hand froze, and he shuddered. Sometime in the last twelve hours, his younger sister assassinated his mother-in-law. And he ordered the hit.

2

Boston, Massachusetts, two years ago

When the call from ICtech finally came, Elliott Wilson Ph. D. was not surprised. He waited for this moment ever since he started his project. He published papers in the right publications, joined the right circles, attended the right conferences, left enough breadcrumbs on the web. All to draw their attention. His efforts were finally paying off. He imagined every night how the first conversation would play out. Wondered what would they offer. He even had time to come up with a plan. A plan that would make him independently rich and free to lead the life he truly desired.

He was surprised, however, by who was actually calling him. The voice on the other end of the line was young and impatient. The man introduced himself as Jason Ellis with the Strategic Investment Team. Wilson had researched ICtech thoroughly and this guy was on the bottom of the totem pole. Which meant that he was this Ellis's meal ticket. That might work to his advantage.

They had several conversations on the phone before Ellis came to see Wilson's lab and the research. He was impressed; the end product would be very valuable to the intelligence community. Ellis asked how much money Wilson would need to complete his research. Wilson gave him a sum and added that he preferred to set up his new lab in England. He explained that his wife was English, missed her family, and he would work much more efficiently if she was closer to them. Out of his hair, so to speak. He left out the fact that his wife's family was extremely wealthy and he wanted to be closer to the money. They came to the final agreement several weeks later. A week after that, the first deposit was made into his account.

That night Wilson celebrated by getting drunk and cruising the streets for hookers. When he finally came home, he woke up his wife and told her that they were moving to London. He also told her that if she thought that she could divorce him while in London and run to her family, he would find her and beat her to death. He then locked himself in his office and worked out the last details of his 'get rich' plan. He remembered how Ellis's eyes lit up when he explained the project, and could practically hear the sounds of cash registers opening in the man's brain. Only Wilson did not intend to share the wealth. Getting a call from ICtech only proved that he was on to something valuable. He figured that it would be even more valuable to someone on the other side of the fence.

Wilson sat in his office, scheming and drinking, watching his large computer screen and periodically toasting to the image it displayed. On the screen, a 3D model of a complex organic compound's molecular structure was slowly revolving.

3

Zurich, Switzerland, June, present time

An impeccably dressed woman walking into Credit Suisse on Bahnofstrasse was a usual occurrence. This one sported a short blond bob, Fendi dress and jacket with half sleeves, Louboutin kitten heel pumps, and large sunglasses. It looked like she just finished dropping a small fortune at Chanel and Louis Vuitton, as she carried several heavy bags from the stores. She asked a security guard to locate the bank manager for her and deposited herself into a chair to wait. The unusual happened when she provided the bank manager, Herr Lehmann, a numbered account and asked what it held. The bank manager ushered her into his office, quietly telling her that there were certain security procedures to complete. In the office he called her Mrs. Wilson and asked for an ID. She happily produced it, informing the bank manager that she was simply following her husband's instructions. She spoke the Queen's English. The bank manager asked her a couple more questions. The questions seemed to be ordinary, but all were part of an elaborate security check. Lehmann was well aware of the fact that Dr. Wilson was found dead a week ago under rather embarrassing circumstances. The woman answered all his questions without a pause. Satisfied that the woman in front of him was indeed Mrs. Wilson, the bank manager finally explained the contents of the account. It seemed to be a large safe deposit box.

"Would you like to access it now, Mrs. Wilson? Do

you have the key with you?" the bank manager inquired.

"Oh, yes, please. This is the last of my late husband's business and I would like to finish this as soon as possible. As you can see, I have moved on," she pointed to her rather large collection of shopping bags.

"Please follow me then."

The steel box was larger than she anticipated. The guard deposited it on the table in the private waiting room and left her alone. She produced the key from inside her bra and opened it. The contents were not what she expected. She pondered what to do with them and then decided to leave them all the way she found them, save for a silver flash drive that looked like a cigarette lighter. The flash drive could prove lucrative down the road. She stashed it into her purse and locked the box, then buzzed for the bank manager. He appeared almost instantly, as if he was waiting to be summoned.

"I would like to continue with this arrangement," she informed him.

"Same duration?" Herr Lehmann inquired.

"Yes. I would like to ask you for a favor, however. Should anyone inquire about the account, would you call this number?" She handed him a folded piece of paper. "The person on the other line will know what to do." She bid him good day and left. Lehmann slid the paper into his trouser pocket and proceeded into his office. This wasn't the first mysterious numbered account he managed, however it was the only one with a unique request to be stored 'until the Milky Way meets Andromeda.' For his banking purposes, it meant indefinitely.

4

Washington, DC, a week later

The sun was trying to invade the lushly appointed bedroom through a tiny crack in the shade. The sliver of light was slowly making its way up the bed and into Catalina's eyes. She stirred for a moment, aware of the invasion and turned to the other side. She was not ready to get up yet. She hadn't been home in a couple of weeks and although her last five-star hotel had every luxury, her bed at home was much better. She smiled as she remembered dropping a small fortune on bedding, shopping catalogs and designer stores. She buried herself deeper into the down plush and fell back to sleep, still smiling.

Catalina lived in a row house on Washington's Massachusetts Avenue, also known as Embassy Row. Five years ago she did a favor for a small African country that used to own her home and asked for it as payment. Embassy Row, the meticulously maintained street with old European charm, captivated her attention for quite some time. She left the country's flag on the front so the neighbors wouldn't be too alarmed to the change of residents.

The house went through extensive renovations to suit her unique needs. Fire retardant walls and shatter-proof windows were installed along with state of the art security systems and a vault in the basement. She wasn't paranoid, she was cautious. She didn't want to sleep with a gun under her pillow in her own house. Thus the vault, as it housed her arsenal, enough to wage a full-scale war on a small country, along with a mountain of cash in multiple currencies and a bag of krugerrands.

Her home was well appointed with designer furnishings and boasted an extensive art collection. Every single wall was covered in art; in her library the paintings were leaning on the bookshelves on the floor, since she ran out of room. If anyone would wonder about the thickness of the walls or the glass in the windows, she could just say it was to protect the art. Not that anyone ever came to visit. Her neighbors suspected that she possessed a small museum, but only because it took three days to deliver and install all the art. She used dealers all over the world, but her favorite was a little bespectacled Russian by the name of Victor Babinsky and who operated a tiny gallery in New York. He carefully curated her ever-revolving collection, always knowing when was the right moment to sell a particular piece. Catalina always purchased her art after a job and, since she was never emotionally attached to her possessions other than shoes, always sold a piece at its peak. Art was the best investment she ever made.

The beam of light finally succeeded in waking her up. Catalina slowly slid out of bed. She took a long shower and shuffled downstairs to the kitchen for breakfast. The kitchen took up the back half of the first floor. Cooking was her other passion. She took classes at Le Cordon Bleu in Paris once, while she was lying low after a job. She spared no expense in appointing her kitchen with double Sub Zero refrigerators, a huge 60-inch Wolf stove along with an additional wall of ovens, microwaves and warming drawers. The cabinets were cherry to complement the Brazilian cherry herringbone-patterned floor that ran throughout the entire house. The counters were granite in a warm sandy shade. The color scheme was reversed on the huge island. The base cabinets were white with chocolate granite. The side of the island facing the wall ovens was designed for baking with a huge slab of marble to roll out dough. She installed freezer drawers under the marble to keep it cool. The island also housed two dishwashers, a huge sink and a wine fridge. When she sat down with her kitchen designer, she asked for a kitchen that can handle several chefs catering a large formal dinner. Since the house was on Embassy Row, the designer never assumed that this kitchen would never see a gathering of people and the only dinner it will produce will serve one. Assassins were anti-social creatures, they lived longer that way.

She was alone in the house today. Antonia, her Sicilian housekeeper, was spending the day at a spa. Catalina always arranged a spa visit for Antonia every time she returned home. It was Catalina's way of thanking the housekeeper for her impeccable service. Antonia ran the household with an iron hand: it was always spotless, all of Catalina's needs met, all secrets well kept. The only time Catalina would lift a finger around her house was to either cook—she cooked every meal when she was home—or to clean her arsenal. Antonia provided Catalina with a peace of mind, order, and companionship.

Antonia, an attractive 52-year-old brunette with fabulous curves, had no immediate family left and Catalina was her whole world. Catalina's father, Frank, sought her out in Sicily after Catalina mentioned a need for a housekeeper. Both Antonia's husband and son were gunned down by the Family's rivals, she had nothing to live for. In return for Antonia's loyalty and service to his daughter, Frank guaranteed that the thugs that destroyed her life would be severely punished. Two days after Antonia moved into Catalina's house, the thugs met their Maker. They died a slow, horrific death, and Antonia felt avenged. It was Frank's last kill.

Catalina made herself an omelet with smoked salmon and dill, a slice of white toast, and a cappuccino. Since the day was turning out warm and sunny she decided to eat outside. Her back garden was yet another spectacular space. Antonia designed the garden herself, being once a farmer's wife, to give Catalina a slice of paradise. There was not a weed in sight and not a leaf out of place. She plopped down on a chaise and proceeded to enjoy her meal.

Her state of contentment was short lived—disturbed by a ringing cell phone that she automatically shoved in her bathrobe's pocket when she got up. She groaned as she looked at the screen, the ID said 'Mother'.

"So... did you fall off your diet while on your trip?" the voice on the other line was male, not female, as Mother was the nickname of her handler who had an annoying habit of 'mothering' everyone. "Some gourmet apple pie perhaps?"

Even though they both used burn phones and encryption software, they always talked in code and it was always food related. She instantly knew Mother wasn't talking about her contract, but a side job she pulled while in London and that the target happened to be a CIA asset.

"Gourmet pie, huh? Was not aware of that, tasted rather ordinary." The CIA angle was missing from her surveillance package that was presented to her.

"Oh, cut the crap! What did you get for breakfast?" Mother wanted to know how she spent the money.

"I got an omelet. It was all organic and full of veggies. And you know how much I love my omelets." Catalina spent the money on a Fabergé egg.

"Omelets, you don't need anymore omelets," Mother groaned on the phone. Catalina had a soft spot for Fabergé and Mother knew that most of the eggs in her collection were obtained through questionable sources. But she never took a quickie just to get one. "Alright I'll bite, how big was the omelet?"

"It's the biggest omelet I've ever had. What's up?" she was changing the subject.

"Well, I hear that the gourmet pie had undercooked apples and the chef is very worried."

"Mother, the pie came personally recommended. I didn't know it was on the menu. "

"You have to come in for a weigh-in, dear. I usually don't care if you fall off the wagon, but this one I need to know."

"I'm not going anywhere, I just got in. Want to chat, you'd have to come here. I'll cook."

"In an hour," and he hung up. He just told her that the asset was developing something for the CIA and that they were now looking for his killer.

"So much for relaxation," she said to no one and slipped the phone back into her robe. She sighed and finished her breakfast. Then she looked up at the clear sky and sunshine. This morning was not beautiful after all.

5

Exactly an hour later, Mother was at her front door. She saw him on CCTV and opened the door before he even knocked. Mother grunted out a hello and walked in.

For a man well into his 80s, he was an imposing figure. Tall, burly, with close cut white hair and beady black eyes. In his prime he used to bench press 400 lbs, but now the workouts gave way to heavy meals and too much good booze. These days, he also was walking with a cane due to a recent hip surgery.

For a second they gave each other a once over, then smiled and embraced. Catalina's usual cold look in her eyes melted a little. Besides her father and her baby niece, Mother was the only other person she cared about.

"I'm doing steaks for lunch. Is that OK with you, or are you on a diet?"

"What are you, Martha Stewart?" Mother shot back, looking around as they made their way to the kitchen. He knew about her art collection but never believed the Family rumor of how extensive it was. Until now. And he was starting to think that the rumor was far of the mark. Which was making him really nervous.

"Please tell me that you buy more than one piece at a time." He noisily pulled out a bar stool and lowered himself on it.

"What, trying to figure out if I owe you any commission?" Catalina quipped back as she slid a pan full of steaks under the broiler. "It depends. When I started, I would only get one at a time, but one day I came across a series of Degas that just begged to be together. After that I didn't count anymore. But when I get a job I don't shop for art until after. It's my little reward." She failed to mention that this was only half the collection, the liquid one she was to part with if needed; the rest was on the way to her new villa in Sicily.

"Your father considered his bank account a reward. Does he know about this?"

"Yep, knows, saw it, even designed security for it. Salad?" she moved toward the fridge and started unloading every possible thing that could go into a salad.

"Have you got a beer in that monstrosity of yours? Can't have a salad on an empty stomach." She handed him a cold one and a glass. He refused the glass. She didn't insist. "How long before the steaks?"

"About 15." She started to chop veggies for the salad with precise measured strokes.

"Have you talked to your father lately?"

"Last night. He's OK, but bored out of his mind. I think he's starting to regret sticking around to help Marcus." Her chopping stopped for a second when she mentioned her brother, then resumed. But Mother, who never missed anything, noted the hesitation. He wondered if there was something he didn't know.

They ate their lunch in the dining room. It was appointed with Ralph Lauren furniture and the china cabinet was stocked with Tiffany china and Baccarat crystal. There was no art on the walls.

"Ran out of nails?" asked Mother looking around. "No art in here."

"Look above the table," she pointed to the chandelier. "And when you're done gawking at that, you can gawk at the middle of the table." The chandelier was a Chihuly. The handblown glass was in various shades of blue and, by the way it fit into the space, Mother realized that the piece was commissioned. The girl spared no expense. About a dozen Fabergé eggs occupied the middle of the dining table.

"Where's the new one?" Mother asked.

"It hasn't arrived yet," she said and added more salad to his plate. In truth, her new possession was sitting in her vault, waiting to be transported 'south' as Catalina liked to say. The villa in Sicily was like her Cayman bank accounts, safe, secure, and out of anyone's reach.

They ate silently and didn't start talking until after both of them finished their espressos. He asked about her last job, the one he orchestrated, she gave him full report. Then they sat silent for a little longer before she started to talk.

"The dossier described him as a wife beater and an adulterer among other things. That's why I was hired. His wife was English, nobility. It said that she tried to report him, but the police were told to back off. I'm now assuming CIA had something to do with it. He had to go," she stated with a slight shrug.

"How much?"

"It was cash." She was avoiding the question.

"How much?"

"The price of the egg. That was my price. They paid for the egg, it was delivered."

"How much was the egg then?" He was not backing down.

"Enough. It was very special. Cash only." She was standing her ground.

"You sure this wasn't a corporate hit? That you didn't get played?"

"No," she straightened her back and looked straight into Mother's black eyes. "I'm sure of it."

"The only way to be sure is to meet the client," replied Mother. And then it hit him. She did meet her client. "Spill, Catalina. *All of it.*"

"It was her father. He's got ties to MI6, that's how he tracked me down. He tracked me to my hotel. He left the package with the ever-helpful concierge, who is most likely on the MI6 payroll. I charmed a security guard to make me the copy of the footage from the lobby, that's how I know who he is. He wanted a messy departure and proof. He left a burn phone number for response. When I called with my terms, he didn't hesitate. Just asked me to promise that his son-in-law would take a long time to die... He did."

"By any chance, did the guy talk while you were having fun?" Mother asked, cautiously optimistic.

"Oh, he sang like a canary. Only not about his wife. And, to make you happy, I've got it all on video. It's in the vault, I'll get it for you." She got up from the table and started walking down the hall.

"Hey!" yelled out Mother after her, "what did you give them for proof?"

"His prized possession. His dick." And with that remark she disappeared down the stairs.

6

Somewhere in Chicago's Western Suburbs, Illinois

Five in the morning on a weekday was Frank's favorite time to people watch. He did it from the comfort and privacy of his kitchen, watching his neighbors through CCTV cameras discretely installed in front of his and his son's houses. He called the unfolding ritual 'the ant march'. One by one, the husbands filed out of their homes, some slowly dragging and half asleep, some chipper and very awake, almost all with Starbucks coffee mugs in their hands and heavily laden computer bags. They all wore the same outfit: chinos in various shade of beige, polo shirt and some kind of ID card hanging on either a belt or around a neck. Their hands were busy clicking away on the latest iPhone. The husbands would get into their Accords or Camrys and pull out of their driveways always not paying attention to each other and always nearly missing the garbage cans by the curb. They were all heading in one direction but no one car-pooled. They all worked in the city and commuted by train. The train station didn't have adequate parking to handle the recent explosion of residents, so the ones that were willing to get up before dawn got what little spots available. They all had similar jobs in either IT or sales, and all would activate whatever electronic devices were attached to their persons and start pounding away on the keys the moment the train would pull away from the station.

The rest of the street would come alive a bit later when

it was time for children to go either to school or to numerous activities they were involved in. This period was dubbed by Frank as 'The Caravan March' because almost every family owned a minivan. Honda Odyssey was the 'in' vehicle in this area. Some families still held on to SUVs, the larger the better. The title of the Behemoth however was held by his son's vehicle, a GMC Yukon Denali with all the trimmings. The car was so large that it wouldn't fit into the garage. Frank was against the purchase, until he found out that it was the one car that his late daughter-in-law despised. Upon that discovery, he paid for the purchase himself, in cash, sporting a huge grin on his face.

Frank and Mark occupied homes next to each other. Mark's was on the corner lot; Frank owned a double lot next door. He fenced in both properties within a week of purchase to the maximum allowed specs. The fence was eight feet tall, privacy, and came up all the way to the front walls of the homes. Someone down the street tried to complain to the city saying that a fence like that ruined the neighborhood. A week later their yappy little dog disappeared and the rumor spread around that it was coyotes that got her. An eight-foot tall fence no longer seemed an unattractive nuisance.

This was a new construction subdivision in West Suburban Illinois, a place where you still could get a huge house for a somewhat decent price. The land used to be all cornfields, but now all that was growing on it were shopping malls and cookie cutter houses. Frank bought both houses together; they were builder models and had all the upgrades. Mark's house even had a finished basement, something everyone was dreaming about in this subdivision but didn't get because it was 'extra'. Well, Frank had plenty of extras and liked none of them. He missed his house in the Caribbean, a house he designed to fit his every need and desire.

By the time his street fell back into its slumber, he was on his second pot of Kona coffee. He was getting ready to go next door to take over the baby duties when his cell rang.

"What do *you* want?" Frank barked recognizing the number.

"Is that how we talk to friends nowadays, Franco? And I thought you missed me," mused Mother on the other line.

"What do you want?" Frank repeated, knowing this was not a pleasure call.

"Oh, Franco…" Mother had to choose his words carefully, as to not to upset the old friend. "She burned herself cooking last week. Got a little careless. She needs to stay out of the kitchen, somewhere relaxing with less exotic restaurants. I told her she should come and stay with you."

"Send her on a trip of Italy," Frank rubbed his forehead.

"I can't do that, she'll be cooking even more! She's such a talented chef, there will be offers from all the kitchens. She needs a break."

"Fine. But the moment she gets restless, I'm sending her back."

"Done." The line went dead.

Frank pocketed the phone and left the house through the back door. When he was half way down the lawn to his son's house, he paused and signed. Looked like his daughter got a bit careless and now needed a safe place to lay low. For some reason Sicily was out of the question, Mother wanted her State-side and was also afraid that if she goes to Sicily she would just go back to work ticking off Family contracts. Catalina was coming to stay with him for a while. He wasn't looking forward it. 'There goes the neighborhood,' he thought.

7

SAD Office (Special Activities Division, CIA), New York

The windowless room of black operation Darwin was littered with papers, files, and all kinds of hi-tech surveillance equipment. One wall of the room was covered with a multitude of different size screens, dominated by the two 60-inch plasmas in the middle. Both of them were now silently glowing blue. The team just finished watching their prized goose finally lay the golden egg, and they couldn't even take the credit for the handiwork. It seemed that their target—Dr. Wilson, a brilliant chemist but also a narcissist—had spilled his guts, on video, before being assassinated for none other than being a very bad husband. He was one of ICtech's investments, bankrolled by the off-books CIA funds. But unlike their other investments, this one failed to deliver the final product. Instead, Wilson was trying to sell it to the highest bidder in the Middle East. The ICtech man who deemed Wilson a profitable investment was worried about his bonus, and CIA was worried about national security. Wilson had become a threat. They were itching to take him out, but could not confirm if he actually completed his work. And they wanted his work. Black op Darwin was created several months ago to monitor Wilson and to grab the final product, what ever that might be, as soon as he was finished. After that he was to be labeled a terrorist and was to be quietly eliminated.

Now, it looked like he did indeed finish and was now offering it in exchange for his life. However, according to the mysterious ICtech source that provided this video, the assassin that did the job was not interested in Wilson's research. It was still out there.

"So... *this* was interesting," Jim Campbell, Special Agent in charge of operation Darwin, finally broke the silence as he slowly turned away from the screen to face his small team. Jim was tall, well built, with a chiseled face, dark, shortly cropped hair and intelligent brown eyes. He was one of the top agents in SAD. "I want this new intel verified before we make any moves. Lets make sure this is legit, not some desperate attempt at survival. Find the safe he kept referring to. Search his lab and flat again, maybe we missed something last time. And find me whoever pulled that trigger!"

The team sprung into action, pounding away on keyboards and dialing phones, only to be interrupted by a probie agent bursting through the door. He was out of breath and hysterically waving a piece of paper.

"Our UK asset finally came through with Wilson's autopsy report." The agent triumphantly slammed the paper on the desk in front of Campbell, and tried to catch his breath.

"Breathe, McCarthy, breathe," Campbell patted the young guy on his back. "What's all the fuss about?"

"There must have been a proof of death request," McCarthy got out between spasms. "Wilson's missing a body part."

"You ran all the way here over a missing finger?"

"He's not missing a finger... Sir... He's missing his penis... Sir."

Everyone in the room cringed upon hearing this news. Even though Wilson was a scum, he was still a man, and that was no way to go for a man.

"How poetic," Campbell mused. He pondered this

new development for a moment. "Gentlemen, who wants to bet that this was done by a woman?"

8

Chicago's Western Suburbs

The drive from DC to Chicago averaged 11 hours. Catalina made it in seven. She sadly left her house before midnight and was pulling into her father's driveway shortly after breakfast. Frank wasn't surprised, but still decided to give her some grief over driving so fast.

"Who do you think you are, Michael Schumacher?" he teased, pulling his daughter into an embrace as soon as she opened the front door.

"Nope, he drives a Merc. I can't help it; the car handles better over 60. I was careful, I can't get pulled over." The last statement meant that she didn't pack lightly.

"Didn't Mother tell you to leave your toys behind? I've got everything here."

"I doubt you have everything. Where would you store it, the shed? And I just took the necessities. Is there room in the garage for me so I can unload without the audience?"

"We'll have to reshuffle, but I'll get you in. Let's get this over with. And, I store my toys in the basement, " Frank grabbed his keys and stepped outside.

His driveway was now decorated by a beautiful BMW 435i xDrive Coupe in metallic gray. When choosing her personal car, Catalina went for the cliché. Bad guys loved BMWs for their speed and agility, and the manufacturer said it was only an indication that they build great vehicles. She chose soft gray Dakota leather and light walnut trim for the interior. It made the car appear more feminine, while packing a beast under the hood. The vehicle suited her.

With her BMW safely tucked in Frank's garage, Catalina walked into the house through the garage door. The room she entered was a mudroom/laundry room, with limestone floors and cherry wood cabinetry. On one side there were cubbies for coats and shoes, one cubby per person, each cubby labeled with a name. She noted that she already had a cubby assigned to her. Across from the cubbies were huge bright red front-loading washer and dryer. Catalina looked at the brand: expensive. She smiled a little.

Past the mudroom was a little hallway that led into the foyer, a little powder room, opening up to the main living space: the family room and kitchen. More cherry. The kitchen had cherry cabinets, Brazilian cherry floors, cherry stools by the island and cherry chairs surrounding a round table. Even the table was topped with a thick slab of cherry wood even though it had black legs. There was a small staircase leading upstairs directly from the kitchen. The cherry theme continued into the family room with cherry custom cabinetry topped with a 60-inch Sony plasma TV. The only place that avoided the cherry was the fireplace: it was floor to ceiling limestone. The family room had a two-story volume ceiling and Frank had installed two huge ceiling fans that looked like the propellers of a WWII bomber. An enormous brown leather sectional occupied the majority of the floor space. A square leather ottoman, scaled to match the size of the sectional, served as a coffee table.

Catalina stood in the foyer, then slowly turned around to get the complete layout of the first floor. There was another staircase that led upstairs, all decked out in more cherry. A door lead to the basement under the staircase.

The lower three feet of the foyer, the staircase and the hall-way upstairs were covered in wainscoting. Painted white. 'Thank God that's not cherry too,' noted Catalina to herself. She then proceeded through the open French doors into what appeared to be Frank's den, directly across the stairs. A massive wood desk, littered with stacks of newspapers, and an equally large green leather office chair were positioned to face the front window. There was a computer in the middle of the desk, but Catalina noticed it was not even plugged in. Frank still got his news and communications the old-fashioned way: through the newspaper's front page and classifieds. She realized that there would not even be a WiFi signal in this house, she would have to go to Mark and tap into his most likely.

The foyer also opened into a large room that was both living and dining. The room was smaller than the family, which seemed odd to Catalina. In her house she actually used her living room and dining room for their intended purposes and this combo room seemed too small for everyday use. Frank decorated the space with a small cherry dining set and couch and chairs that were upholstered in black and white fabrics. The couch served as a room divider and was facing the window. The coffee table and the end tables were also cherry.

"Cherry? Really? I thought you liked light woods and modern design," inquired Catalina with her father after her survey of the first floor. "You even have cherry wood blinds!"

"It was a builder's model, they put in all the cherry. All this was considered an upgrade so they shoved everything and anything into this house to get people to spend more money. Once you see this, you want the same in your house. I bought it as is," replied Frank with a shrug of his shoulders.

"And the furniture? It's not you."

"Well, I cased the neighborhood after I looked at the house for about a week. People were moving in then, I noticed a couple of trucks from some place called Ethan Allen so I figured this is what was expected in this area. So I went there and told them that I wanted masculine furniture. You know I don't like fluff and flowers. Their stuff's expensive, but when the trucks arrived they made quite an impression on the street. Same as when you got all that Crate and Barrel furniture for Mark… Want to get your bags now?"

They brought in her stuff and she chose one of the guest rooms as her own. Frank pointed out a private bathroom decorated in limestone tile from floor to ceiling and a rather small walk-in closet. He left her to settle in and went downstairs.

Frank was still chuckling over that fact that she brought her own bedding, along with several paintings and a Fabergé egg when Catalina, wearing a bright orange sundress, finally emerged from unpacking.

"What are you laughing about?" Catalina inquired, finding her father in the kitchen brewing another pot of coffee.

"At least you could've left the art behind, I don't live in a shack. Coffee?"

"Yes, but let's take it outside. The art is for Sofia, but you could hang it in your office for now."

Art for Sofia. So she actually did care about the little girl, he was right. Mark's going to have to eat his own words on this one. Frank handed Catalina a cup of coffee and they stepped outside to enjoy it on the porch.

"So, when does the show start?" Catalina nodded toward the street, referring to the neighbor-watching they were about to do.

"Give it a couple of minutes. Might want to take notes on wardrobe and such, you'll have to do some shopping later."

"Do I really stand out that much? I left Chanel at home, you know."

"This is the Midwest and this is the suburbs. You'll see..." Frank smiled as he took a sip of his coffee.

The show commenced about five minutes later. One by one the neighbors' garage doors started to open up revealing their secret dwellings inside. Most garages were littered with toys, unopened moving boxes and enough sports equipment to outfit several third world Olympic teams. In the middle of all this chaos stood a Honda Odyssey, in various stages of filth. The vans were accessorized on the back with either a fish or a window sticker representing each family member including pets. Most had a soccer ball sticker on the side window as well.

"What's with the soccer balls?" Catalina asked in amusement.

"They're called soccer moms. If you're planning to mess with one, I suggest you come heavily armed."

"That could be arranged."

"Better to stay away as far as possible."

The owners of these vehicles appeared shortly after. They were all women in various stages of what Catalina called 'hideous workout sloppy': a yoga outfit two sizes too small and flip-flops. The peculiar thing was that their hair was all done and they all had enormous expensive shades on. A Coach purse and an iPhone occupied one hand, the other was dragging small children behind. The purse and the children were shoved into the cavity of the van and some women went inside for yet another child, this one strapped into an infant car seat. All this was done while still clutching the iPhone. After doing a quick head count, the women got behind the wheel and peeled out, missing the garbage cans by the curbs by a narrow margin. A couple of them weren't so lucky.

"What's with the phone? Are they all waiting for God to call them or something?" Catalina asked.

"Nope. They're either checking email or on that people site, what it's name."

"Facebook? But they've got kids and they're about to drive."

"That's when they make their important calls, while driving."

"And what's with the bags, did they all go to the store together or was there a truck delivery to the neighborhood?" All the bags had the same 'C' pattern on it, for a moment Catalina thought they were a back-of-the-truck special.

"Oh, that's Coach, they all have it. You'll need to get one in order to fit in."

"No, thank you, I brought something with me. And I'm not wearing yoga pants unless I'm actually going to yoga and I don't!"

"Oh, that? They change into dingy t-shirts and some short pants by the time the husbands come home."

"I take it they don't get any then."

"Well, those 'brown bag' parties are all the rage in here now a days," Frank snickered while taking a final sip of his coffee.

"Oh, God, how do you know? Or has the whole street been bugged?"

"If they like you, they'll invite you. Better yet, they'll ask you to host one, they've been dying to get into our homes since we moved in," said Frank with a wide smile. The horrified look on Catalina's face was priceless.

Behind her large designer shades, Catalina's eyes

continued to slowly—and methodically—scan the street. Frank's porch covered the entire front of the house and it was outfitted with comfortable wicker furniture with deep and soft cushions. Huge hanging baskets and evergreen hedges in the front provided shade and privacy. 'Perfect place for a little surveillance' Catalina thought, stopping her gaze on the cabbage-green house across the street. The house looked oddly picture-perfect with freshly cut grass and over-trimmed bushes.

"What's with that house?" she asked slightly nodding toward it with her chin.

"I was wondering how long it'd take you to pick that one out. That's Mr. Perfect. Strange last name. Didn't bother to check further. Yet. At this point he's more entertaining than anything. Got only one kid, a teenager. Skinny as a rail, very weird, odd friends. Something crawled up the wife's ass, that's for sure. She doesn't work. Goes somewhere every day, at the same time. Working out, I think. Somewhere in that house they've got a mother hidden. Think she belongs to the husband, but not sure. They don't let her out. His garage is absolutely empty and clean as a whistle. The kid cuts the grass every week like clockwork and washes their cars on national holidays. I don't think he's got one leaf out of place on those bushes of his. They're quiet, keep to themselves, don't socialize. No one likes them."

"Interesting…" Catalina decided that before her so-called vacation was over, she would mess with Mr. Perfect a bit.

"Don't mess with him. We have to live here you know. I want Sofia to be accepted and liked." As always, Frank could read her mind.

"What if I get bored? There is nothing to do here, besides soccer apparently."

"Oh, you'll have plenty to do. As of now, I'm off Sofia duty, time for you to bond with your niece. And your brother. Welcome to the 'burbs, honey!"

9

Right after a light lunch Frank took Catalina to Mark's, introduced her to the infant snoozing away in her Daddy's arms; and shuffled up upstairs, grumbling about catching up on long overdue naps. Catalina and Mark were left to figure things out on their own. Mark broke the silence first with the offer for Catalina to hold the baby. Catalina reluctantly agreed. Mark instructed her to sit down on the couch, deep and comfortable, and eased the sleeping baby into Catalina's arms. She stiffened and looked horrified.

"Relax, Zia Catalina. She's a good size now, lots to hold on to. Here, I'll put some pillows under your elbows for support so your arms don't go stiff. Just give her a little embrace." Mark surrounded his sister with pillows and noticed that she relaxed a bit. The baby made a little sucking noise and snuggled deeper into her aunt's embrace.

"I think she likes me," Catalina fully relaxed and settled into the couch. Mark calling her *zia*—which meant aunt in Italian—did not go unnoticed. He was finally embracing his roots.

Frank was hiding out in the hallway upstairs, listening on his kids. He could see them from his hiding spot. They looked so grown-up now. Catalina was 32 now, but looked more like she was in her twenties. She had her mother's perfect features, but had his eyes. Only her eyes possessed a much colder gaze than his ever did. 'Eleven years of nothing but wet work will do that to you,' noted Frank to himself. Marcus was only a year older than Catalina, the same height as she was, but looked like he was pushing 40. The ordeal of the past year aged him. His jet-black hair was graying at the temples and he had noticeable wrinkles on his face. Marcus was a spitting image of his grandfather, Frank's dad, with the same brown warm eyes. Which meant that he would also look attractive well into his old age. Mark picked up running recently, to help him manage stress. He now had a runner's physique and good tan. Catalina was model thin, with a healthy tan she must have gotten in some posh Monaco resort. Frank noted that his children were quite a striking pair. If only their mother could see them now.

There wasn't much talk between his children at first, but then Catalina started inquiring about the baby: her health, appetite, routine. She asked about Mark's job, although she knew all about it since she was keeping tabs on him for the last six months. Even while he was in Sicily.

Six months ago, Frank was called back into the States by Catalina to mop up the 'little' situation Mark had gotten himself into. It was decided that the best plan was to put Mark and the baby into the care of the Family. The late wife and mother-in-law got a private funeral, Frank style—cremation, and disposal into a trash bin where, in his fatherly opinion, they belonged in the first place. Since there were no other relatives on the wife's side, Mark inherited the entire estate, which was quickly liquidated, the money hidden in various offshore accounts. Mark, the baby, and a private neonatal nurse were put on a plane to Sicily. There, under the bright Sicilian sun and the salt air of Mediterranean Sea, Sofia quickly developed into a chubby and healthy baby girl and Mark 'grew back his balls' as Frank called it. They returned four months later with new identities and settled into their new life in the 'burbs. Mark, always being a computer geek, got a job as a securities consultant and was able to work from home. As far as their cover story went, he was a single successful professional who adopted a baby. The fact that Frank and Mark were father and son was never revealed, and the neighbors decided that they were simply an odd gay couple that preferred to be in the closet. No one corrected them. Frank asked Catalina to order Mark furniture that would suit his cover. Frank hired a painter and a window treatment designer to polish it all off. If Mark was surprised when his doorbell rang with deliveries, he didn't show it. While in Sicily, he finally learned that the Family knew best. Unfortunately, in Catalina's opinion, that revelation came ten years too late.

It took a couple of days for her to get the handle on the baby's routine and 'equipment malfunctions' as she dubbed the spitting up, drooling, and occasional target practices during diaper changes. Once, unusually large amounts of spit up, projectiled on her designer casual wear, sent Catalina running to the nearest Gap for a stack of basic tees and shorts. After she was settled into the house, Frank sent her out shopping to Oakbrook Mall for a 'Mid-West suburban' uniform so she won't stand out. She came back with a wardrobe from Burberry claiming that she saw a lot of women with strollers going in there. Frank replied with a question of whether she actually saw them buying anything there since no one in this area was skinny enough to wear it. Frank got all excited about the spit up incident because it finally put Catalina into a uniform of tees and shorts. One thing he didn't dare ask her to change was her footwear. He knew that any suggestion of shelving the Louboutins would earn him a bullet between the eyes, regardless of the fact that he was her father. Mother once joked that the only reason she followed Frank into the business was that it was the fastest way to red-soled stilettos.

Catalina's quick adjustment to the routine and her constant presence in Mark's house left Frank alone and with plenty of free time on his hands. He decided to use this newfound freedom to renew his old contacts and quietly look into the rat's nest his daughter managed to step on. He wasn't buying Mother's side of the story and wanted to shake some trees on his own and see who and what would fall out. He lived, and survived, by one rule: Trust no one.

10

"Sir, London's coming online," said young McCarthy to Jim Campbell, who was standing in front of the wall-mounted plasma TVs, without lifting his eyes off the monitors.

"On screen, please," instructed Campbell. Their London team was ordered to go over Wilson's residence and lab with a fine toothcomb. New York was eagerly awaiting their results.

The picture was fuzzy, with a delay in feed. The operative, whose shape filled the screen, was sitting against the bright light from a window. It made it hard to make out his features. Campbell recognized the man by his voice. The two men worked together before.

"So?" They never stood on ceremony.

"Interesting development: we found nothing," the shape on the screens replied in a deep husky voice.

"What do you mean nothing?"

"Nothing. Nada. Zip. Someone cleaned everything out. His flat was completely empty, his widow moved out. We asked around and found out that she disappeared the day of the funeral."

"Trash? Anything in the fireplace?"

"No trash, and no ashes. Looks like it was vacuumed out."

"And the lab?" asked Campbell. He was getting a very uneasy feeling in the pit of his stomach. His small team was sitting with a bewildered look on their faces.

"Well, we got to the lab at a good time. Caught his only assistant shredding some papers and packing up. He was quite helpful, actually," the voice chuckled a bit.

"Did you just say his 'only' assistant? His financial records with ICtech indicate that he had three."

"Negative. Just one."

"So we can add 'embezzler' to Wilson's resume as well. OK, continue," Campbell made a little circular waving motion with his hand indicating to the man on screen to speed it up.

"Well, this is were it gets really interesting: apparently three months ago Wilson gave the guy a paid leave, he only got back to the lab when he found out Wilson died. He was instructed to shut the lab down and destroy everything. Said that the last thing he did before he went on leave was to place an order for a high capacity flash drive. Lucky for us he was able to find the receipt. I'm sending the details."

"Did he know if Wilson finished?"

"He thinks he did. Said Wilson got paranoid at the end, that's why he gave him leave. Told him to take a long vacation. But there is nothing in the papers that were left in the lab, all that stuff is useless. The guy said that there is nothing that has the complete sequence or any indication if the housing component was designed. "

"Do you know who asked him to destroy everything?"

"Yeah. Wilson's father-in-law. He's a Baron and very well connected, by the way."

"Anything else?"

"Yeah. The assistant actually went on a vacation, to Spain. Said that he might have seen Wilson in Heathrow, boarding a flight to Zurich, but he's not sure."

"Did you happen to get a visual of that yet?" Campbell perked up.

"Working on it." The voice responded.

"Let us do it. Wrap it up and come home."

"Got it," the shape gave a loose salute and cut the feed.

Campbell was still standing and looking at the screens, deep in thought, when he was interrupted by McCarthy.

"Sir, I found Wilson at Heathrow."

"You did, ha?" mused Campbell. He was starting to like the young agent. He seemed to be quite talented.

"He boarded a flight to Zurich, first class. Hopefully we can find him there as well, to see what he was up to."

"How did we miss this trip?" for the past several minutes Campbell was trying to solve that riddle in his head.

"It appears he used a different passport and possibly a prepaid phone. We did not have that passport on the grid before," answered McCarthy.

"All right, everyone! Your new objective is Zurich. I want everything! Find out where he went!" Campbell addressed his team. "I'll be in my office."

His office was small, but it had a window with a view of the Hudson River. Someone once asked him what he had to give to get that view. "A kidney," was the answer. He was severely injured on a mission in Africa about five years ago and lost his kidney as the result. He also lost his field status as well, since missing an organ automatically chained one to a desk.

Campbell's first order of business when he got back to his office was to make himself a cup of Earl Gray tea. He was a self-proclaimed tea snob, keeping a vintage English tea set of bone china in his office and an electric teapot so he could brew loose leaf tea. He walked over to the window and watched the boats go up and down the river while the tea was brewing. Then, with a steaming cup in hand, he finally sat down at his desk and opened his email. There were several from ICtech which he ignored. The sender was starting to annoy him. Campbell scrolled up until he found the email from his London team. It had a photo of a receipt for a flash drive. He Googled the item and found a picture online. The drive was silver, a little over an inch wide and close to four inches long. It looked a bit like a cigarette lighter. It could hold 256GB of encrypted information. He printed out the details. At least they now had something to look for.

The next item he was interested in looking up was Dr. Wilson's father-in-law. The search didn't take long, the man was well documented. He was indeed a British baron and had connections at MI6. That little tidbit intrigued Campbell. He wondered if this man was the one who orchestrated Wilson's demise as well as the swift disappearance of any paper trail. His musings were interrupted by a call from his operations room.

"Campbell," he answered.

"McCarthy here, sir. I think we found what Wilson was in Zurich for. We got a visual of him entering a bank."

"What bank?"

"Credit Suisse, sir."

"I'll be right there." Campbell hung up the phone and got up from his desk. On the way out he refilled his teacup.

11

Chicago's Western Suburbs

The Stroller Brigade commenced their exercises twice a week between dropping off and picking up. When they first started gathering, the route covered their street and went into the nearby park. When Frank and Mark moved in, the route changed drastically to go by their homes and turn around in the cul-de-sac next to Mark's house. The change was due to the enormous curiosity about their new male residents. Every member of the Brigade was dying to get inside the homes and behind the fence. They would slow down their march and crane their necks in hopes of catching a glimpse of the inside through the curtains. However, the windows and curtains were never opened, so all their efforts went in vain.

The Thursday morning power stroll started without a hitch, as always. The Brigade assembled in Melanie's driveway, outfitted in their Nike finest, kids strapped into top of the line jogging strollers. Not that the Brigade jogged, they 'power' walked. They started off without a problem, discussing their window treatment dilemmas and school-teachers' inabilities to properly raise their children.

The slow pass by Mark and Frank's homes was at the end of their route. Two months ago they got a surprise when several white and black Crate&Barrel trucks showed up at Mark's door and unloaded a houseful of furniture. Afterwards, they spent weeks on the Internet figuring out what was bought and how much was spent.

Today held another surprise for them. As they rounded the corner and were about to cross the street for their ritual strollby, Misty noticed that an unfamiliar car was parked in Frank's driveway. The Brigade halted.

"Whose car is that? That's a BMW, that's like 50 thousand dollars! Did Frank get a new car? You can't fit a baby in that, why would he get something so small?" They all started talking at once, only to be silenced by an emergence of a woman from Frank's garage.

She was tall, over 6 feet, well tanned, and built like a model with legs a mile high. Her jet black hair was long and shiny, a product of very expensive salon visits. She wore a loose white tee with a denim mini, espadrilles, and carried a bag they all recognized. She opened the door of the BMW and folded herself into it in one fluid motion. The car purred to life and sped away. A little too fast, in Wendi's opinion. The garage door was left open.

"Who…? That bag…" Debi was too stunned for words.

"That bag is like several thousand dollars!" Melanie huffed with envy. "New Jersey plates on the car."

"She's too skinny. Must be anorexic." Debi recovered. Four children left petite-framed Debi thirty pounds overweight with no chance but plastic surgery for losing the weight. She coped with the gain by telling everyone that she was at a 'healthy 150 and curvy'.

"OK, girls, let's get moving, " Melanie got everyone back into gear and they crossed the street, eager to see what was in the garage.

They slowed down as they approached the house. Unfortunately, the garage viewing provided no results, as it was completely empty save for Frank's Buick and some lawn tools. They signed with disappointment, only to be startled by Frank's appearance on the porch. Unlike his children, Frank was not a tall man. He was 5'8" and he compensated for what he considered a lack of height by being extremely fit. He was still quite handsome even in his mid-sixties. The women always skipped a heart-beat when they would run into him. He possessed a flat stomach, muscled arms and straight legs. Unlike their husbands, there was not an ounce of fat on him. He had wavy salt and pepper hair that he wore pulled back into a small ponytail, was extremely tan and had those piercing steel-blue eyes that would give any woman chills. 'Too bad he plays for the other team,' many of the female neighbors thought.

"Good day, ladies! And how are you this fine morning?" Frank raised his coffee cup as a welcome salute and smiled, perfectly aware of what they were up to.

"Doing fine," sang out Chrissie, mother of twins. "I see that you had visitors..," she was fishing.

"Oh, that was my niece. We haven't seen each other in a while, she came to visit. You should meet her, she'll be bored staying with us guys."

"You should bring her to the barbeque on Saturday, we'd love to get to know her!" Chrissie smiled, jumping on the inside from the prospect of grilling this niece about who she really was and how was she able to afford that bag.

"Have a good day, ladies!" Frank bid them farewell and went back inside. A moment later they noticed that the garage door was closed.

"When did he close the garage?" wondered Misty.

"Oh, he must have those silent rubber rollers on the door. Jon wanted to get them, but they're so expensive, and since our bedroom's right above the garage, the only way I know when he's back from poker is by the door sound," Debi answered.

The Brigade finished out their route, and everyone

went back home, still thinking about the visitor and slowly turning green with envy over the bag. And flying down the I-88 highway, a female driver of a BMW 435i xDrive Coupe with Jersey plates was still grinning slightly from the show she put on for the nosy neighbors. Her gaze, however, remained cold as Arctic ice and never left the road.

12

Eddie Washington was built like a tank. Standing at 6'5", he possessed an extremely muscular and large frame thanks to both regular training and good meals. He had an impeccable personal style that would even make Sean Combs jealous. Catalina and Eddie went back a long way—they were childhood friends. Their friendship developed first out of necessity: they were both taller than other kids, in Eddie's case also wider, and no one wanted to play with the oddballs. Their families also stood out in the neighborhood, Eddie's was the only black family on the block and Catalina's was reclusive with an ever absent father and very stern mother. So Eddie and Catalina stuck together, all through childhood and into college, both attending Boston College. In college, Eddie—looking to quickly improve his cash flow since he was on a scholarship—started running several interesting side business, and they parted ways for a couple of years because Catalina wanted to stay under the radar. They bumped into each other at a New York nightclub several years after graduation, and instantly reconnected, as if the years apart never happened. At this point, Catalina was already ticking off her body count with art purchases and Eddie was building his export/import empire. Catalina was well aware of his product line—their chance meeting at the nightclub was not coincidence. She needed a reliable weapons supplier and figured Eddie would not deny an old friend. He didn't, she became one of his best customers. In time, she introduced him to the Family. Eddie was received well and the benefits were mutual.

This current meeting was out of character for Eddie though. He tracked her down and was quite persistent that she meet him downtown. She was wondering how he found out that she was in the area. They were also meeting in one of his warehouses, one more thing out of character. Catalina decided to play it safe and came prepared.

She got to the city several hours before the meeting, and checked into The Four Seasons under one of her aliases. The hotel was a safe choice, because it was not a place she ever stayed before. In Chicago, she preferred The Drake, and thought The Four Seasons was full of noisy families. Today was no exception. She was just hoping that the noise would not penetrate into her room.

She had about six hours to kill. Her plan was to take a nap and then get ready for the meeting. After checking out the room's amenities, she decided to start off with a bubble bath before a long nap. Maybe some room service after. She wasn't sure if she was coming back to spend the night.

———

"Did she say where she was going?" Frank was pacing the room, steaming.

"No, she just said if I needed anything I was to ask you for help because she had some business to attend to and might not be back till tomorrow," Mark was starting to think that he somehow messed up. Again.

"Business? What business?" Frank was still pacing. "She has no business in Chicago. What the hell is she up to?"

"Eddie's in Chicago. Maybe she's gone to see him," Mark was well aware of who Eddie was, since it was Eddie's plane that flew him and Sofia to Sicily and their luggage was not the only cargo.

"Eddie? How the fuck does Eddie know where she is?"

"Hey, no swearing in front of the baby," Mark was now getting fed up with his father's pacing and foul language. "How about you let it play out before jumping to conclusions. She can take care of herself."

"And what conclusion should I come up with when she comes back in a body bag? I don't like this."

"I doubt she'll come back in a bag, she's got a higher body count than you ever did and she's been better trained. Plus, she didn't go unprepared. She was in the basement last night packing some things. Might want to see what's missing before completely losing it. I need to feed Sofia, call me if you need anything," Mark picked up the baby and went off to the kitchen in an attempt to put some distance between himself and Frank in case the old man lost it completely.

"How do you know she was in the basement?" Frank yelled after him.

"I watched the security feed this morning, as I always do," Mark yelled back.

"That's my boy," Frank smiled and went down the basement.

Her knifes and a couple of Berettas 92G Elite were missing. Along with several clips of 9x19mm Parabellums. That was in addition to the Glock 19 and the ceramic blade that she always carried. "OK, so your brother's right this time. I hate when he does that," Frank said out loud. On the way up the stairs he decided that it was time for some serious bathroom cleaning, to keep himself busy for the day. Then he'd take over Sofia's bedtime routine since he wasn't about to sleep tonight.

13

Eddie's warehouse, on West Cermak Road, had riverfront access, for undetected late night boat deliveries. From the street, it looked like a normal business, with a large glass lobby and a cute receptionist. A hallway off to the right led to company's offices, a legitimate small export/import firm specializing in exotic foods. At the end of the hall was a massive steel door, labeled 'storage.' A 24-hour guard manned the door. Beyond it laid the heart of Eddie's operation.

Eddie owned the whole block and that was the reason why Catalina parked several streets over, in a residential area. She then took a cab to the warehouse and presented herself to the receptionist. A minute later she was greeted by a security guard, whom she recognized as one of Eddie's personal bodyguards, and was escorted to the 'storage' area.

Catalina never saw the room until today. It was not what she expected. The massive room was the size of football field, several stories tall. In the corner closest to the massive door, was a makeshift 'IT department' as Catalina dubbed it. All the equipment was attached to metal racks on wheels, the whole setup could be packed up and rolled on to a truck in seconds. The rest of the space was completely empty, save for two enormous comfortable chairs and a coffee table in the middle. She figured they brought that in from the lobby.

The bodyguard asked her to make herself comfortable on one of the chairs and left.

Eddie appeared a minute later. He was impeccably dressed as usual, in a white summer suit. He was carrying a small metal briefcase, which he put on the coffee table between them.

"*Ciao, il mio vecchio amico,*" Catalina greeted Eddie in Italian.

"*Ciao, Catalina. É stata un tempo lungo.* How are you?" Eddie's Italian was rusty and he wanted to make sure he was making himself very clear in this conversation. He knew she came well armed and he wasn't intending to end a friendship in a shootout that she would win anyway.

"Ah, you need to practice more, you'll get rusty." Eddie's switch to English after only a hello was disturbing. Catalina shifted in her seat to have quicker access to her guns. "Other than this little exile, I'm fine. But you already know that, Eddie. Where's the merchandise?" She twisted her finger around pointing at empty space.

"This isn't a sales call. And I removed the toys this morning so you have nothing to aim at my head. Except for what you already brought with you," Eddie said, sitting down in the chair next to her.

"Ha-ha, very funny. Better that way anyway, I don't have room in my trunk. I forgot to take the stroller out."

"You have a stroller in your car?" Eddie raised an eyebrow. "What do you need a stroller for?"

"My niece. I've taken her out to check out the sites a couple of times. Had to get a stroller that fits into the car. The one her Daddy had was too big for my trunk. First time I went out, it was either take the Behemoth, which I can't drive efficiently, or put all the gear into my car. I got the seat in, and then somehow jammed the stupid stroller in. But once I got in to town I couldn't get it out. Took me half an hour. Well, it wasn't going back in that's for sure. So I found one of those overpriced baby boutiques and just said that I needed a stroller to fit into a BMW. They sold me a Bugaboo Bee. Very nice, actually. The boys were furious though, said it was now the most expensive stroller on the block. I told them that it went with their new gay personas."

"Gay? Is that their cover? Nice!" Eddie tried to picture Frank playing gay. "What did you do with the old stroller?"

"I pushed it into a church and left a note that said 'donation.' And the neighbors came up with the gay part, figured two single guys living next to each other and sharing a fence can't be anything but."

"Must be a fun place to live," Eddie chucked.

"Why am I here?" Catalina abruptly got serious.

"OK... I was asked to share some info with you. And deliver a word of advice." Eddie watched as her eyes narrowed slightly and she sat up straight.

"Who's the delivery boy?" asked Catalina.

"Sotto Capo himself. A pleasant fellow," Eddie was being sarcastic, an effort that did not go unnoticed. "They're worried they might lose one of their best."

"What did he give you?" Catalina was eyeing the briefcase.

"Ever heard of ICtech?" Eddie searched Catalina's face for a glimmer of recognition but got nothing. "You should look them up. Your last job was their investment. He developed something they want for their boys in CIA. Only things went fishy after they forked over the money. Do you know what he was into?"

"No," Catalina lied.

"Well, Sotto Capo thinks you do. And they're wondering what you're planning to do with it. Said they don't want it, and the faster you get rid of it, the faster this will all go away."

"And how does he propose I get rid of it? Not that I

have it, what ever that might be." Catalina shrugged her shoulders.

"Suggestions are in the case, I guess. That," he nodded to the case on the table, "came from Capo himself. I didn't open it. I know better. And the faster you remove it from my possession, the better I'll feel."

"Anything else?" Catalina reached for the case and put it on her lap.

"Yeah. Keep your head low and stay put for a while. One more thing, and this one is from me. Tell Frank to back off, people are getting curious why he's asking questions. And…" Eddie paused, not entirely ready to say the last part, "don't trust Mother. Word on the street he's involved up to his eyeballs in this."

Catalina sat there, slowly absorbing what Eddie said. Frank's quiet snooping around was not a surprise; she was his baby daughter after all. Mother, on the other hand…

"I need some privacy," She nodded toward the case on her lap.

"Sure, take all the time you need. There is a burn chamber in the corner, use it when you're done," Eddie pointed toward the wall and started to walk away.

"Eddie," she called after him, "thanks. And don't leave town, I might need a way out."

"Whatever you need, honey. Whatever you need," and with that he walked out.

14

Chicago's Western Suburbs

Sofia was surprisingly quiet that night. She went down without a fuss and fell asleep right away. 'Must've tired out from all the attention I gave her today,' thought Frank. He figured that she might sleep through the night, but he still settled into the chair upholstered in sage velvet in Mark's family room with the baby monitor within earshot. Mark was out for the evening, Frank was planning to spend the night babysitting.

The night turned out unusually cool for this time of the season and he enjoyed the nightly breeze softly blowing in through open windows. Frank settled in deeper into the chair and closed his eyes. His thoughts drifted back to Catalina, his baby. He drifted through memories of her as a baby, a happy friendly child enjoying life, a girl growing too tall for her age, her first dance recitals, basketball game… And the first time she took a life. For him.

It was right after they buried Maria, his wife and Mark and Catalina's mother. Maria died suddenly, of a heart attack. She died alone, in her kitchen. Catalina was in high school, Mark was already in college, and Frank was out of the country on a job. His whole world collapsed when he heard the news. The Family came to the funeral to lend support. Aunts stayed behind for several months to help Frank with the children and the household. Frank blamed himself for Maria's death. If only he was home, if only he had a normal, honest occupation. Thoughts like that were tormenting him at night, he couldn't sleep. He hadn't taken a contract in months, and Mother—who was his handler at the time—was getting concerned. And antsy. Frank was his best.

One night Mother showed up on Frank's doorstep. It was dinnertime, and he wasn't expected. Still, he was invited to join. Mother made small talk with the kids about their schooling and Catalina's college plans. He tried to flirt with aunt Anna Maria, who was staying with them at that time, only to find out that she was a nun. "What a waste of a beautiful woman," mumbled Mother after that revelation. Right after the dessert the kids were sent upstairs and Anna Maria went into the kitchen to busy herself with the dishes.

Catalina hid on the upstairs landing. By this point in her life she was already well aware of Daddy's line of work and knew some of his key associates. She knew that Mother's visit to the house was highly unusual. She wanted to know what that was all about.

She had a partial view of the dining room. Catalina saw Mother pull out an envelope out of his jacket and slide it across the table toward Frank. Frank pushed it away. She heard him saying something about being out, and Mother replying that he wasn't allowed to retire yet. They argued for a bit. Catalina heard Mother telling Frank that he either do this job or join his wife. "Do you want your kids to lose another parent?" was the last thing Catalina heard Mother say before he got up from the table to leave. Catalina bolted to her room and pretended to study.

That night she snuck into Anna Maria's room. She slid into her bed and shook her aunt awake.

"*Mio dio!* Catalina! What's the matter?" Her aunt was a bit startled to see her there.

"Zia, I have to help Daddy. He's in trouble," Catalina replied, holding back tears.

"Is this about that man who came tonight?"

"Yes. He said Daddy's got no choice but to go back to work. I don't think he can do it."

"Catalina, *bambino,* stay out of this," Anna Maria got very stern all of a sudden.

"Zia, I know what he does. I've known it for a while. I have to help him. I can't lose him too. Please, help me," Catalina replied with tears running down her face, and she picked up her aunt's hand and kissed it. Anna Maria watched Catalina's face for a while before responding.

"OK, I help," she said and wiped the tears off the girl's face. "Go to bed, I will tell you tomorrow what to do."

The next afternoon, after school, Anna Maria took Catalina to meet an old friend of the Family. They drove to Chicago and met in the back of a tiny Italian restaurant that seemed to be empty even during the lunch hour. The old man offered the women some fresh ziti when they sat down. They talked between mouthfuls of delicious pasta and hot garlic bread.

"So, you're Franco's daughter. You look like your mother, God rest her soul," the old man crossed himself as soon as he said that. "I hear you want to help your father with the restaurant business, yes?"

"Yes," Catalina replied and took a bite of her ziti. She picked up the lingo a long time ago.

"How come your brother's not here? Restaurants... it is a man's job."

"My brother has no interest in the Family business."

"And you do?"

"I don't want to be left alone in the kitchen. Again." Catalina responded in a cool and collected manner and looked the old man straight in the eyes. They stared at each other for a while, then the old man lowered his gaze back to his plate.

"Do you know the recipe?" he asked, in code, after several forkfuls. This was a test, he wanted to know if she was able to keep up.

"Yes," it was Anna Maria who responded this time. She produced an envelope out of her purse. Catalina looked at her in surprise. "I also had a talented father when I was growing up," she said to Catalina with a smile and handed the envelope across the table. Catalina realized that her aunt must have stolen the envelope from her father. The old man took his time looking through the contents before saying anything.

"This recipe, involves very high temperatures. Do you know how to use the broiler?" He finally asked Catalina. He handed her the papers to look at.

"So this is a recipe..." she said with amusement. She looked through the papers, noting that it was a long range job requiring a sniper rifle. "Yes, I know how to use a broiler. This recipe is from a local joint, I recognize it."

"Good then. Makes it easier. Any idea when Frank was planning on making this dinner?"

"No."

"I saw him leave this morning with a grocery list," volunteered Anna Maria.

"Shopping," said Catalina. She knew that her father left to do some reconnaissance.

"Then you need to do yours today as well," responded the old man. He lifted his hand and snapped his fingers. An exceptionally well built but stocky young man in a black leather coat appeared out of the kitchen and stood a couple of feet away from the table.

"This is Tony. Tony, this is a friend of ours, Catalina Benedetto," he pointed to Catalina and Tony gave a small nod. Catalina noticed that she was introduced as one of the Family. "Catalina, Tony will help you. Go with him. Now!"

"*Grazie!*" Catalina jumped up from her seat. Anna Maria remained seated.

"Save it for when nothing comes out burned. Now get out of here!" he waved her off with his fork. She left the restaurant with Tony in tow.

"And I thought you were a nun, Anna Maria," said the old man in Sicilian once the door behind Catalina closed.

"She's family, Giovanni. She's my niece. I couldn't refuse her," Anna Maria replied in a soft voice.

"It should've been her older brother sitting here, not her."

"Leave Marcus alone, he's just a boy."

"I avenged my father when I was only seven. Marcus is old enough."

"Giovanni, please. Not everyone wants to follow their parents' footsteps," said Anna Maria. She seemed to lose her appetite, she stopped eating.

"Catalina does. She's gonna enjoy this. I saw it her eyes. That is why I sent Tony with her. To make sure she does this correctly," Giovanni said and took the last bite of his pasta.

"No one's supposed to know about this. Keep this quiet," she gently put a hand on his arm and gave it a little squeeze.

"I know who you're worried about. I give you my word, that *facia bruta* won't know anything. I never trusted that guy anyway. He never pays tribute," the old man said leaning on back on the chair. "Espresso?"

"I would love some," replied Anna Maria with a smile.

It took Catalina and Tony only a few hours to scout the location. Tony was surprised as to how little direction he had to give her. She figured out right away how Frank would do it. He was going to position himself on the roof across the street and pick off his mark while it was in the office on one of the top floors. Catalina and Tony scouted a taller building behind Frank's, it gave them the view of both the mark and Frank. The position made for a more difficult shot at a much longer range, but Catalina was determined. She was still hoping that her father would be able to do this on his own. Tony suggested a weapon and Catalina answered that she was familiar with it. Even though the dusk was starting to set, they still went off to an abandoned property Tony knew for target practice. To Tony's amazement, Catalina turned out to be a brilliant sharpshooter. He knew from Giovanni that all Benedettos were taught how to shoot various weapons since childhood, but this girl also had raw talent for this kind of work. He was greatly impressed with her ability.

Catalina skipped school the next day. By the time she hooked up with Tony and made her way to their spot, it started to rain. They got there just an hour before Frank. Catalina witnessed her father prepare for his job. She noted that he was extremely meticulous. 'That is how he stays alive,' she noted to herself. Now they all lay in wait.

A couple of hours later the light in the mark's office went on. Catalina watched the mark, Tony watched Frank. Catalina noticed the mark move into the perfect position by the window. But Frank didn't take the shot. She waited. Nothing.

"Lina, take the shot, now!" ordered Tony suddenly.

She pulled the trigger. Pop, and the rifle recoiled into her shoulder. She didn't seem to notice. She watched as the window across the street shattered and their mark fell on the floor. A tiny smile of satisfaction spread across her lips.

"Done! Let's get out of here," whispered Tony as he picked up the ejected shell casing and shoved it into her coat pocket. Catalina grabbed Tony's binoculars and looked for her father on the rooftop below. He was already gone. A second later, they were gone too.

Across the street, a man lay dead on his office floor. A bloody hole gaped right in the middle of his forehead.

That night Catalina snuck into her father's bedroom and left her shell casing on his nightstand. A couple of nights later, as Catalina was sitting in the dining room and looking through acceptance letters from various universities, Frank walked in and placed a rather fat envelope in front of her. When she inquired as to what that was, Frank replied that she earned it and left. Catalina found a large stash of cash inside. She counted out the tribute to the Family before returning to choosing a college, knowing that now she could go to any school she wanted to. And in an empty Italian restaurant, an old man was making a call to Sicily to tell the Family that another Benedetto just made her bones.

Four years had passed before Frank and Catalina discussed that day. Frank was thinking about retiring and wanted none other than his daughter to take his place. She instantly agreed.

15

Catalina ended up spending the night in the city after all. The hotel was surprisingly quiet that evening, she ordered abundantly from room service, took a long bath and watched several movies before finally passing out. She slept well, as usual. Sleeping was never a problem for her, no matter what she was up against. It must have been a survival technique: lack of sleep would make her fatigued and prone to mistakes. And in her line of work, mistakes were usually deadly. Her conscience was quiet ever since childhood, when she figured out what her father did for a living. While her brother suffered with a moral dilemma of this discovery, she told herself that a body in the trunk meant a new bike for her in the future. Every night she said a prayer, in Italian, for her father's safe return home and a job well done, and fell sound asleep moments later.

She returned to Frank's house well after lunch. Frank was sitting on the porch, trying to soothe cranky Sofia. As soon as Catalina walked up the steps, he mumbled something about her taking the stroller and cranky baby, shoved the infant into her arms and stomped into the house to take a nap. It was time for dinner when he finally emerged.

"What's for dinner?" Frank poked around the various food items on the kitchen counter. Catalina was chopping what looked like salad ingredients.

"Ziti and a salad. You ate everything else and didn't go to the store, apparently!" Catalina was not happy with the contents of the fridge.

"Well, excuse me! Next time you decide to disappear, leave a list!" Frank snapped back. She had not said a word about her whereabouts since she returned.

"I had to pick up a note. From Nonno…" said Catalina, without pausing her salad chopping. Frank froze to the floor.

"How?.. Ah, Eddie. Marcus suggested you went to see him. What's in the note?" Frank was hoping that she would share, but her rhythmic chopping told him otherwise.

"Well, there is a suggestion that you need to stop whatever it is you're doing because it's been attracting some attention. And since I'm already here, I'm supposed to stay put until they tell me otherwise," her voice was cold and direct. To make her point, she stopped chopping and looked her father straight in his eyes. Their intense stare into each other's eyes was like two icebergs colliding, slow and piercing. Only this time hers was much stronger, and after a while Frank had to avert his eyes. She lowered her gaze and resumed her chopping.

"What do you mean 'since you're already here'? Where are you supposed to be?" Frank was giving it one last shot. She stopped chopping.

"Sicily." And with that she tossed her knife into the sink.

Catalina decided in Eddie's warehouse that her father would never see the contents of the briefcase. There was a large envelope containing new identity and credit cards, a smaller envelope made out of fancy paper, and a little black square box. She recognized the box and smiled. Capo never sent her any cash, when he thought she might need money he would send expensive diamond jewelry. This time was no exception, the box contained huge princess cut pink diamond earrings. After distributing the items between her body and her purse, she left the briefcase on her chair with a message SANCTUARY written in red lipstick on the lid. It was a message for Eddie; she knew he would be the only one to understand.

Over dinner Frank decided to amuse himself by telling Catalina about his encounter with the Stroller Brigade and their BBQ invitation. Catalina flatly refused, only to be told that she owed him for her disappearance and that the party might prove to be entertaining.

16

SAD, New York

Hacking into computer systems of an international bank in order to obtain surveillance video was not something they liked to do on a regular basis. It was illegal and, this being Credit Suisse in Zurich, most likely cause an international incident if they were to get caught. Their plan was to get in, copy the surveillance footage of anyone resembling Wilson, and get out before the bank noticed a breach. Campbell brought in a hacker he just 'happened to know' to complete the task. It took longer than expected, but the stolen footage revealed that Wilson had met with a personal banker. Herr Lehmann. The two men spent several hours together in Lehmann's office. It was also discovered that Wilson came into the bank with a large metal suitcase, but left without it. Campbell considered a possibility of a safe-deposit box. However, getting to the contents of this box would be totally impossible.

The London team was able to get their hands on a copy of Wilson's will before departing for the States. It was quite generic, except for the part about some Swiss luggage. The will stated that Mrs. Wilson inherited the contents of a Swiss-made metal suitcase. The location of such suitcase was not given, however. Campbell's team deduced that Wilson could only be talking about the safe-deposit box he opened in Zurich.

After giving it some thought over several cups of tea, Campbell ordered his team to scrub all surveillance footage from cameras surrounding the bank as well. He was wondering if Mrs. Wilson came in to discuss her husband's account. It took days but they finally came up with something worth looking into—footage from a security camera of a tram stop across the street. A figure resembling Mrs. Wilson was seen entering the bank. Once again, surveillance footage from inside the bank was needed. This time, they decided to execute the hack themselves. Agent McCarthy said he could give it a shot. His efforts took a long time, making Campbell very nervous. They ended up having to settle only for a couple of minutes of overhead views of the lobby so as not to get caught by the Swiss.

"OK… so this is the banker," pointed out McCarthy to Campbell. The young man zoomed in on a grainy image of a stout well-dressed man talking to a woman with a blond bob and large tinted glasses, "and that must be Mrs. Wilson."

"How do you know?" asked Campbell. He was the only other person viewing this footage after sending the rest of his small team home. In his opinion, the fewer people participating in illegal activities, the better.

"Well, the banker met with Wilson only once, when the account was created and the only other access was when she showed up. Mrs. Wilson's the sole beneficiary." McCarthy had done his homework.

"Can you see her face?"

"Not really. He's blocking the view most of the time and then there are those glasses."

"Zoom in anyway. I want to see closer." Campbell sensed that something wasn't quite right here. His gut told him that the visitor somehow knew where all the cameras were, and was making great effort not getting caught in full view to any of them.

"OK… Sir, this is the best I can do." The screen was

filled with a large shot of the woman's head. The picture was grainy and all they could see was lower half of her face.

"Large glasses and a bob, it could be Anna Wintour for all we know. Can't you enhance that?" Campbell pointed to the woman's lips and chin. "This, work on this."

"What are we looking for, sir?" The Anna Wintour comment didn't escape McCarthy, he wasn't surprised by Campbell's knowledge of the fashion industry considering the fact that he probably bedded most of the models in New York.

"Find an image of Mrs. Wilson and run facial recognition. See if the two match. I'll be back." And with that Campbell left the young man to fiddle with the equipment.

Upon his return, steaming cup of Earl Gray tea in hand, Campbell was greeted by side-by-side views of Mrs. Wilson. On the left was a grainy and blurry image from the bank and on the right was a photo of Mrs. Wilson on vacation wearing large sunglasses with white frames. Both images were covered in green dots blinking off and on— the facial recognition software was running.

"Where did you get that one?" Campbell pointed to the vacation image in curiosity. He realized, with hidden pleasure, that the young agent had caught on to what he was up to.

"Facebook. She's not using privacy settings so I was able to grab this," McCarthy chuckled a bit. "DMV photo was not going to work, bad angle."

They silently studied both photos, both staring at the screen like art aficionados would stare at a newly-discovered Picasso.

"So, this is Mrs. Wilson," Campbell finally said, pointing to the right. " Looks like a horse."

"And this," he pointed to the left, "is Mrs. Wilson in the bank."

"This is *not* a horse," McCarthy offered in amusement, at the same time as the facial recognition dots stopped blinking and 'negative match' message popped up on the screen. Both men stared at the full lips and rounded chin of what must be a perfectly proportionate face on the left image. The woman in the bank was not the real Mrs. Wilson. McCarthy jumped to his desk and started pounding the keys with the ferocious determination of a hungry predator.

"What are you doing now?" asked Campbell, although he already knew the answer.

"Street surveillance, anything. I want to see where she went after the bank. She's good, but she can't avoid all the cameras," shot back the young agent. He was determined to track this 'Mrs. Wilson' down.

Campbell took a long slow sip of his tea and considered McCarthy's last remark. 'Yes... she's really good,' he thought.

————

Chicago's Western Suburbs

Truffles. Homemade chocolate truffles. She couldn't get them out of her mind since the morning. The process of making truffles was usually relaxing to her, and she felt a little tense. Catalina peeled out of the driveway on a mission to find the ingredients as soon as possible.

The recipe called for semi-sweet, bittersweet chocolate, and crème fraiche. She found the chocolate at Williams-Sonoma in the mall, it wasn't her preferred brand but it was still really good chocolate. All she had to do was pop into a local store on the way home and get the crème fraiche. She figured that in less than half an hour she would be elbow deep in chocolate, completely relaxed. She was wrong.

Catalina stood in front of the dairy aisle in disbelief—there was no crème fraiche. Could they be all out? Maybe it was in a different section, only she couldn't fathom where it could possibly be other than next to sour creams. She finally found a stock boy and asked for help. But he looked at her as if she was an alien and directed her to customer service.

"I was wondering if you could help me find crème fraiche, please?" said Catalina in a nicest possible way to a short rotund woman with an outdated hairstyle behind the customer service desk.

"What, honey? What are you looking for?" the woman replied.

"Crème fraiche," repeated Catalina slowly.

"I don't know what that is, honey," the woman said. Catalina almost choked.

"It's a dairy. It's kind of like a sour cream," she said in disbelief.

"Oh… Let me call the dairy manager then." She paged the dairy manager and had a small hushed discussion over the phone before turning back to Catalina, who was now starting to steam slowly.

"He said that we don't carry that. He doesn't even know what that is. It must be a specialty item, you might want to try a gourmet foods store." Catalina could not believe this, as far as she could remember she could get crème fraiche anywhere. But then again, she was not just anywhere, she was in the Western suburbs of Chicago.

"Thanks," said Catalina through clenched teeth and left the store. Her half an hour was wasted and she was nowhere close to her truffles. She got into her car and punched the concierge service. The only gourmet foods store they found in the vicinity was Whole Foods.

There they were: little containers with hot pink lids. Crème fraiche. It was next to sour creams, as it was supposed to be, and Catalina bought five. Whole Foods was nowhere near Frank's house, she wasn't planning on returning. With her bounty safe and secure in her basket she proceeded to check out all the aisles and grab everything else that might be considered "gourmet" in this part of the world. 'They moved to the freaking boonies…' she thought to herself as she raided the aisles, 'how could you be a dairy manager and not know what crème fraiche is?' She still had a look of disgust on her face when she pulled into Frank's street and gave the Worthingtons, who were digging in their flowerbeds and bickering, a dirty look.

Four hours later, she was finally relaxed and sitting out back with a plate of chocolate truffles and a pitcher of cold Bellini. Frank, who followed the scent of chocolate from upstairs all the way to the fridge, found a stash of crème fraiche in the refrigerator door.

"What the…? What is she going to do with all this stuff?" he asked a nearby jar of pickles. There was also no trace of anything chocolate in the fridge. Frank closed the door and followed the scent outside. He stopped dead in his tracks when he saw Catalina.

She was lounging on a chaise, balancing a large plate of truffles on her lap and holding a champagne flute full of peach Bellini with her left hand. Her right hand was busy throwing ceramic blades into a makeshift target on the wooden fence. The target was a little hot pink lid from a crème fraiche container. Frank took in the scene for a while before slowly, and quietly, backing into the house. There had to be a story in there somewhere, but he wasn't about to ask her while she was swinging knives around.

17

South Loop, Chicago

It was Diamond's turn to host the weekly poker game. He was still 'on the clock' as Eddie's bodyguard and was crashing in one of Eddie's condos reserved for his staff and business partners. Diamond was uncomfortable in having his poker buddies here, but since none of them ever had the luxury of staying in any of these condos, they insisted. Tobias was the most vocal about it. Diamond finally consented, just to shut him up.

The group consisted of Diamond, Tobias, Leon, Dwaine, Lamont and TJ. All were employed by Washington Enterprises, as they liked to call Eddie's businesses, and all were a little green in the gills. Except for Diamond. Diamond, once a promising boxer, got to where he was today by keeping his eyes open and his mouth shut. He was one of Eddies' personal bodyguards and took his job very seriously. Usually he could be found within arms reach of Eddie, but tonight, being a weekend, he was relieved of duty. Still, staying in the condo put him within a mile of Eddie's house. If needed, he could be there in less than five minutes. Diamond was never without his SIG Sauer P220 .45s, even at a poker game with his buddies. He carried them on leather holsters, one under each armpit.

Tobias was not a smart man. One might say that he stumbled onto the business, thanks to his cousin Lamont. Lamont, the smarter of the two, usually did all the thinking for both of them. They were all brawn and no brain, usually working the shipments and running simple errands. Both were short and overly muscular, always wearing flashy clothes and too much jewelry. But Lamont, unlike Tobias, usually kept his mouth shut about anything he might have seen.

Leon was a car mechanic, working in one of Eddie's businesses—a garage specializing in custom performance work that also doubled as a chop shop when needed. Leon was hardworking and treated all the cars he worked on like his children. Every time one of them would return 'injured' he would get visibly upset. He was tall and thin with good face structure, and preferred to spend life in his blue mechanic's coveralls.

Dwaine and TJ were the youngest of the group. Raised in Chicago's projects, they dealt drugs on the side and kept Eddie in touch with the street. They showed a lot of growth potential in the business in a very short time. But unlike Tobias and Lamont, they dressed to blend into regular society, not to stand out, and preferred a good basketball game to pumping iron.

The condo had floor-to-ceiling windows on one side and had the North views of the Chicago skyline off the 27th floor. The décor was cream leather and mahogany wood, and everything was softly lit with a multitude of tiny lights recessed into the ceiling along with several pricey speakers.

The guys helped themselves to beer in the fridge and started to take their seats at a large round table by the windows. Leon commented on the gorgeous view of the city at night, while Tobias griped about not being able to smoke in the condo. Diamond reminded him that there was no smoking allowed in any of Eddie's properties since his business was usually highly flammable. Tobias challenged Diamond about Eddie ever finding out that he smoked here, but it was Leon who responded by saying that The Boss was always watching.

They finally took their seats, adjusted their guns— tucked into the waistbands of their pants—to allow for more comfortable seating, and pulled out stacks of cash. Diamond sat with his back to the window, Leon to his left and Dwaine to his right. Tobias, TJ and Lamont sat across him. It was Tobias's turn to deal.

"Man, just deal the cards, will you? And stop blabbing," Diamond said to Tobias in an agitated tone several hours later.

"What's the rush, man? The fridge is full of beer and you seem to be on a roll here," Tobias nodded toward the large pile of cash next to Diamond's elbow. Everyone mumbled in agreement. Diamond was getting extremely nervous about the topic of tonight's conversation. Usually they talked about women and cars, but tonight the woman discussed was making Diamond sweat with fear. He was hoping that Tobias will stop for his own good.

"So how did you see her in the first place?" Leon was curious how Tobias and Lamont came to possess such info.

"Get this: we had to move everything out of the warehouse that night and set up for this 'meeting' Eddie was having next day. Tyrone told us to beat it after were done, but we stuck around anyway and he ain't notice. He more concerned with that fine piece of ass popping Eddie," replied Lamont.

"And that was a fine piece of white ass let me tell you. Italian," volunteered Tobias, coloring his description with some obscene hand gestures.

"Name Catalina Bennett. Or Benedetto, depending on what country you in. Heard Eddie and her go way back,"

Lamont added.

"Is she connected or something?" inquired Dwaine.

"Not connected, the Connection. Born and bred Mafioso," Tobias flashed his pearly whites, proud to be in possession of such info, and finally started to deal the cards. TJ let out a soft whistle and took a long swig of his beer. Diamond and Leon exchanged glances. By this point Leon noticed that Diamond was sweating profusely.

"Hey, Tobias, I think it's time you shut your mouth. And it's Mr. Washington to you. You haven't earned the right to call The Boss by his first name yet," Diamond snapped at Tobias and fanned his cards out in his hands.

"Am I making you nervous? Boss ain't here to hear me, I can say what ever the fuck I want," Tobias answered in defiance. "Anything else anyone wanna know?" he addressed the rest of the gang.

"OK, I'll bite," Leon leaned back in his chair and looked at Diamond. Then he gave a little nod up toward the ceiling. No one noticed the nod but Diamond.

"She buys customs that Eddie gets. Every time there's a purchase, there's a dead body somewhere. She must be really good because I once heard that she don't get out of bed unless it's a rock," Lamont piped in.

"Yeah, she must be good if she's still kicking. Those people don't stay alive for very long," TJ sounded impressed. Leon started to scratch his forehead with his left hand. Diamond gave him a little nod.

"Nah, she ain't that good. Once I had to go find this guy and make sure he gets on a plane. I aksed what he did and he said he was The Cleaner. He was flying out to meet her," Tobias was on a roll now and wasn't about to stop. He found a captive audience in Dwaine and TJ. Even Diamond was quiet now. Leon kept scratching his forehead.

"The Cleaner? What does he clean?" asked Lamont.

He was not present for that assignment.

"You know, cleaning up the mess this broad made somewhere. I guess," Tobias answered and put his card down. "I'm out."

"Yes you are," said Leon and stopped scratching. He then tapped the middle of his forehead with his left index finger before lowering his hand on to his lap.

They all stopped talking for a bit and concentrated on their cards. A moment later Diamond's phone rang. He checked the number before getting up from the table to answer.

"Yes, sir? Is everything all right, sir?... Absolutely, sir. Consider it done." Diamond pocketed the phone and returned to his seat across from Tobias, TJ and Lamont.

"Who was that? Mr. Washington?" Tobias asked in a whiny mocking tone.

Pop! Pop! Tobias and Lamont's bodies fell backward on the floor from the force of the rounds entering their skulls. When the smoke cleared Dwaine and TJ found themselves facing still smoldering barrels of Diamond's P220s.

"What the fuck, Diamond?" managed Dwaine.

"Hey, I told him to keep his mouth shut. The Boss and his associates are not up for discussion. And I suggest you forget the entire night, before I'm asked to pop you two as well." Diamond answered and holstered his guns. Dwaine and TJ sat very still, afraid to even blink.

"Game over brothas. Time to clean up," Leon threw his cards on the table and got up to go find some garbage bags and duct tape.

It took them a while to clean up the mess and pack up the bodies. They wrapped them up tightly in several garbage bags and dumped them down the garbage shoot. There was no worry that someone would find the bodies in the Dumpster, since the garbage company was on good terms with Eddie and a truck was already dispatched for a pick up. At some point, while all four of them were cutting out the bloodied carpet, Diamond looked up at the ceiling and gave a little salute. Dwaine and TJ followed his gaze and finally noticed a little tiny glass dome in the ceiling, right above the table they were playing cards on. They looked at Leon and pointed toward the dome with a silent question.

"What? Told you, he's always watching," answered Leon and went back to cutting the carpet.

18

Chicago's Western Suburbs

On Saturday, the neighbors' BBQ started around 3 pm. The Bennetts didn't leave their compound until an hour and a half later, all due to Catalina's attempts at stalling. She tried pretending that she had a headache, saying she had nothing to wear, offering to stay home with Sofia so the baby won't get neighbor germs, all to no avail. Frank was insistent. She finally emerged from her room wearing a fabulous black and white maxi dress and red-soled flats. Her only accessory was a pair of Dolce & Gabbana gold chandelier earrings. Frank noted that she looked like she was ready for lunch by the pool in Monaco, not a suburban BBQ. Catalina replied that she indeed got the dress while on vacation in Monaco and that it was great for concealing weapons attached to her thighs. By that last statement Frank figured that she was once again armed, but considering where they were heading he wasn't blaming her. The Stroller Brigade, no doubt, was ready to interrogate.

They made quite an entrance. Everyone stopped talking, drinking, and scolding their unruly kids. Jaws dropped, beer bellies sucked in. It got so quiet that one could hear a bratwurst inside the grill hiss out a steam. The silence lasted for a good minute and then the crowd swarmed around them and attacked.

"Ooohhh, the baby is sooo cute!"

"What a nice stroller! Is that a Bugaboo Bee? How fancy! I wanted one but we need one for multiples..."

"Oh, look, you guys have matching Polos! I think my Bob has one just like it. Bob, don't you have one like that? Did you get them at the outlet mall? Don't you just love to shop there? So many..."

"And what do *you* do? Are you staying here for the summer? And what college did you go to? ...Come and sit with us. Bring the baby! She can play with the others." This was directed at Catalina. For the first time in her life she felt scared.

Frank and Mark were swept toward the grill, the Man Land, light beers thrust into their hands. Catalina threw Frank a look that pleaded 'rescue me!' but he just nodded toward the women. Her fate for the evening was sealed.

Chrissie, the host, finally managed to elbow her way toward Catalina.

"Hi, I'm Chrissie! It's so nice to finally meet you! Make yourself comfortable. Let me take that," she reached for a bottle of Pinot Grigio that Catalina was still holding in her hand. "The food is by the grill, so is the drink cart. I've made Margaritas! Go ahead, get something, we can watch Sofia."

"Sure," replied Catalina, silently praying for the baby to spit up all over the woman, and made her way toward the drink cart. She was in need for something heavy.

Margaritas were weak and the wine selection was bad. Riesling and white zinfandel seemed to be the in things in this area, because the table was full of them. The bottle of Pinot that Catalina brought disappeared inside the kitchen, never to be seen again that evening. She was getting desperate to find something halfway decent, until she came across a bottle of rum. A good one at that too. 'Hmm, must be a gift' she thought and decided on a rum and Coke, heavy on the rum.

Pleased with her concoction, she started slowly back

toward the women. Her eyes, concealed by her enormous designer shades, were taking in the yard and the house. She figured that Chrissie would be more than happy to give her a tour of the home, given proper motivation. Judging by the patio and the party set-up, the woman was a show off.

"Your house looks beautiful, any way I can get a tour?" Catalina purred to Chrissie once she reached the group of women and flashed a smile.

"Oh, absolutely! Would you like one now?" Chrissie jumped out of her seat, ready for her tour guide duties.

"Sure, lead the way." Catalina gave her a sorority girl giggle and followed her inside.

The house was similar to Frank's, minus several features. Chrissie was giving a very detailed tour, pointing out every upgrade and naming all the furniture brands. Catalina wasn't really paying attention, but oohing and aahing just the same. She was most interested in finding a suitable hiding place for her item, presently strapped to her thigh. What caught her eye, finally, was the pedestal sink in the powder room. Chrissie just finished explaining that they recently renovated this bathroom with new high-end fixtures. Which meant that the sink was staying in the house for a while. Catalina thanked Chrissie for the tour, and politely asked if she could try out the facilities. The woman was more than happy to oblige.

Once alone, Catalina carefully looked over the sink. It was Kohler, bright white and quite beautiful. The vertical column was hollow in the back, and it was not mounted flush to the wall. Catalina realized that she could easily slip her hand inside. She peeked inside the medicine cabinet above the sink and found a box of Band-Aids. In less than a minute, the silver flash drive that she picked up in Zurich and which never left her side since, was safely taped with the aid of some large Band-Aids deep inside the column. "Safer than a bank" Catalina thought. She flushed the toilet and ran some water before exiting the bathroom.

Outside, she caught the men attempting a game of bocce on the long stretch of grass by the fence. The metal balls where tossed around with no skill, landing and rolling everywhere. Catalina found her father and brother standing safely off to the side, silently observing. As she joined them, Mark leaned over and quietly commented: "Nooooone's near the *bocce*," the Italian word rolling of his tongue in perfect staccato. Catalina could not help but let out a laugh.

————

Miami, Florida

The job of setting up Catalina's Sanctuary fell on Tyrone, Eddie's right hand man, and his crew. Eddie figured it would be faster, and cheaper, to set one up from scratch than transport one of the existing ones into the US. Catalina had several Sanctuaries scattered all over the world, near places where she could be conducting her business. She never needed one set up in the US. Catalina decided on Miami because it gave her the fastest exit strategy out of the country—by water—and she knew the city well since it was one of her favorite vacation spots.

Eddie designed every one of Catalina's Sanctuaries, including this one. Only this time his plans called for a lot more weapons and medical supplies. Just in case.

Each Sanctuary was designed to shelter and protect Catalina for a continuous two weeks. But she never used one for that long. She usually would just 'pop over' to change identities, reload, and sometimes chill out if she felt the heat of pursuit. Once, after getting injured on a job, she hid in her Sanctuary for three days until one of Eddie's crews airlifted her out. They just grabbed the whole container—with her still inside—using a S64 Skylane cargo-lift chopper, and delivered her to one of Family's properties. It was a ride from hell, and Catalina vowed to herself never to repeat the experience.

The existence of these Sanctuaries was only known to Eddie. Not even Frank knew about them. And, especially, not even Mother.

Tyrone and his men were standing inside one of Eddie's Miami warehouses, looking a bit perplexed as to their new assignment. They had only 24 hours to do this job and deliver it to its destination.

"We have to fit all of that," Tyrone waved his arms over a rather large collection of crates and pointed to an empty shipment container, "into this. At least we don't have to set it up for heating, just AC. Smaller generator too."

"Why do I have a feeling I'll be earning my keep with this one?" said Will, the largest guy on Tyrone's crew. Will was a brilliant car mechanic and was responsible for all the modifications to Eddie's fleet of cars. Those modifications saved the vehicles' passengers on numerous occasions. "OK, where are those plans? Let's get this done before the Miami heat gets to me."

A little over 24 hours later, a shiny black semi would deliver an ordinary-looking shipment container to a private boat storage on Bayside marina and unload it between some old dry-docked boats. The boats' huge hulls would hide the container well. The driver would pay off the manager with a very fat envelope and pull away. A few hours later, the manager would order for a 43-foot Donzi powerboat to be removed from its shelved storage, cleaned, gassed and put into the water. Its gray paint quietly shimmering in the sunlight, the boat would bob up and down with the waves, waiting for its driver to arrive.

19

Chicago's Western Suburbs

It was well past everyone's bedtime, but the party was still running full throttle. It seemed that no one wanted to go home and resume their daily grind. Babies fell asleep in the strollers and parents arms, while older children played in the dark and adults continued to drink. Mark and Sofia left a couple of hours ago, Frank and Catalina were making their goodbyes for an hour now. At some point of the night, Catalina was handed an invitation to a brown bag party that promised to entice the attendant with new sex toys. Finally, they managed to break free and flee back to the comfort of their own home.

"Those people are nuts!" Catalina exclaimed as soon as the door closed behind them. "What possessed you to live here?" She plopped down on the couch in exhaustion.

"Hey, it's the safest hiding place in the world right now. Hiding in plain sight. How was the house tour?" Frank slowly lowered himself into the chair next to her. "Did you find what you were looking for?"

"Looks like she's making huge monthly payments to Pottery Barn. And yes, I did find what I was looking for."

"She works there part time. For the sole purpose of getting discounts on furniture. Whatever you left there, I'm not going in there to retrieve it. Although it'll be a piece of cake, they have no security, and the door from the garage is always unlocked."

"Yeah, but wouldn't I need to break into the garage

first?"

"1908 is the code."

"How do you know that?"

"They all share the same garage code and always leave the inside door open, in case they need to visit."

"Why 1908?"

"The last time the Cubs won the World Series. It's the only four digit number they all know."

"I'm not even justifying this with a response. *Buona Notte!*" Catalina got up and kissed Frank on the cheek. He patted her hand in response, but did not say anything.

He sat in the dark, watching the neighbors finally disperse into their residences, listening to the sounds of Catalina's shower. He waited until his house and the street went completely quiet. Then, he slowly got out of the chair, moved through the house barefoot, slid out the kitchen door and started carefully walking to Mark's house. Another silent moment, and Frank disappeared inside. Several minutes passed before a light went on in one of Mark's upstairs rooms. If anyone were looking, they would have thought that the baby needed something. Only the light wasn't coming from the nursery, but Mark's office.

———

Catalina wasn't asleep. She went through all the motions of getting ready for bed, for Frank's benefit, then rearranged the pillows on her bed to look like a body, grabbed a flashlight from her nightstand, and hid inside the walk-in closet in her room. The space was small, but she could still sit down on the floor comfortably. She used dirty clothes to close the gap under the door so no light would escape and turned on the light. Before continuing, she listened for any sounds coming from downstairs. Nothing. Satisfied, she felt underneath one of the sweater shelves. The envelope was still taped to the shelf, where she left it. With flashlight in her mouth, she slowly peeled back the tape as to not make any noise. Soon she pulled out the envelope. Catalina carefully held it in her hands. The envelope was made out of expensive heavy cotton paper. She remembered the one other time when she held such an envelope. It was shortly after she made her first kill. A congratulations of sorts and a welcome to the Family. She was flattered and scared at the same time, for Capo never wrote. She was told that she'll never receive a letter from him again, and that it was a good thing. But tonight, she was holding another one of these pure white cotton envelopes. She still had no clue what was inside because a letter from Capo was not something one reads in the presence of an arms dealer. She ripped it open.

Inside was a letter and a memory card. She was a bit puzzled by the card, but figured it would be explained. She took a deep breath and unfolded the letter. Their family crest was foil-stamped in gold on top of the page. Capo's name was printed below the crest in royal blue. The letter was handwritten in Italian. She ran her fingers over the writing, her grandfather's flawless penmanship always evoked warm memories of him in her head.

> *Catalina,*
> *The news of your current situation saddened me. I never thought that you would be so reckless. I decided to look into this for you. What I have found out is very troubling. The mark you took out belonged to an American venture-capital firm ICtech. They invest in anything that might benefit the Company. It was one of their employees that ordered the hit, not the father-in-law. Someone we all trusted, someone who betrayed our Family, is behind the elaborate set-up you got caught in. If you were careful like I taught you, you would have realized that all this was as trap. The Company bankrolls ICtech, your mark*

was their asset. It is the Company that is look-
ing for you now. You need to fix this, before you
can come home. I am including the proof of the
betrayal. Please handle this for me. I ordered the
Family not to be involved in any of this, however
Eddie will be well compensated for anything you'll
ask him to do. Deal with this before coming home.
Nonno

Catalina leaned on the door, letting the letter fall out of her hands. She got greedy over a Fabergé egg and messed up. She was now on her own. If she was home, she would run down into the vault and smash the egg into smithereens. But she wasn't home, so she just bit her lip and forced herself to re-read the letter.

A traitor... It wasn't Eddie, since he was being paid to provide support. She wondered how much money Eddie would get from the Family... So it's not Eddie. She twisted the memory card with her fingers and started to look for her camera.

The camera was finally located on the bottom of her Louis Vuitton suitcase. She inserted the card and turned it on. "These better not be the photos of my villa," she mumbled to herself. They weren't. The images startled her. They were surveillance shots of two men meeting in what looked like an urban park. One was young and wore a dark ill-fitting suit. The other wore glasses and a baseball cap, but he looked very familiar. There was a long black stick under the bench. "Is that a cane?" She clicked through the more images. The photographer kept zooming in on the faces of both men with every shot. Closer and closer. The baseball cap man was looking more and more familiar to her. She clicked faster. The last shot was clear and in focus. The man's face filled the entire screen of the camera. She was staring at a very familiar face. Mother.

———

"What is it?" Frank's question was directed at Mark, but Mark just shrugged his shoulders. They were in Mark's office going through the files from Catalina's flash drive. The same drive she removed from Credit Suisse and the same flash drive she hid in the bathroom of Frank's neighbors. Frank pocketed it a couple of hours after she put it there. There were 10 levels of encryption, it took Mark over an hour to break them.

"Ask Catalina, she's the one with a chemistry degree. Oh, wait, you can't ask her because this is hers!" Mark gave a pissed off look to his father. "Wait till she finds out you took this."

"Google it."

"Nope. The files were encrypted for a reason, I put this on the web and all sorts of trouble will head your way. And I'm assuming she's already dealing with some of it."

"You took some chemistry, come on give me something," frustration was showing in Frank's voice. "I know you can at least make a guess."

"OK, fine. Go sit somewhere, don't hover."

Mark clicked though some more files for a while before turning in his chair to face Frank who found a spot on a small leather couch.

"It's a compound."

"Even I can see that," snickered Frank. "What else you got?"

"It's organic. Well, it's based on something that's organic. See all the carbons?" Mark pointed to a diagram of molecular structure. "But it looks like it was heavily modified."

"What does it do? Is this some kind of corporate espionage thing? Because that's easy to take care of."

"I doubt it. I have a feeling it's something CIA would

be interested in. Look at this." Mark turned back to his large screen and opened some additional files. A blueprint filled the screen.

"It looks like this is some kind of a delivery device for the compound. See, it's got a reservoir and a needle." He pointed the parts out to Frank, who was now hovering over his shoulder to take a closer look at the screen. Frank stared at it for a while.

"Shit!" Frank finally said. "No wonder. Hmm, that would explain some things." He went back to the couch and slumped into it.

"What do you think this is?" Mark asked his father.

"Something that would put us out of business." Frank leaned back into the couch and rubbed his temples. "I bet you she figured this thing out. And I bet you she decided that no one will get their hands on this."

"I think she deleted some files. The blueprints are incomplete. You can't notice at first glance, not until you start building this. Let me show you." Mark opened some windows on his screen for Frank to see.

"So no way you can get this to work now? What about the compound?"

"I think it only has one way of delivery. My guess it must be pretty unstable."

"And you can't recreate the missing files? Un-erase them somehow?

"Not that I can see. And I've been over every single byte on this drive. Whoever deleted them knew what they were doing. "

"Smart girl." Frank smiled a little.

"What are you going to do now?"

"Put this back where I found it and keep my mouth shut."

"You think she'll ever tell you about this?"

"Nope. The less we know the better."

Mark closed the files and pulled out the drive from one of the many CPUs sitting on his desk. He tossed it on Frank's lap, who was back sitting on the couch. "Here, go return it before the sun comes up. I'm going to make sure that none of this is left on my systems." His fingers started their dance across the keyboard again. Mark had a surprisingly light touch, Frank could not hear him hitting the keys. He picked up the drive from his lap and got up to leave. At the door, he paused and looked at his son.

"Remember I told you to have your go-bags ready at all times?"

"Yeah," Mark turned and looked at his father with suspicion.

"Are they?"

"Hm, no. I have Sofia, how can I run with her?" Mark's eyes narrowed.

"Tomorrow, do it tomorrow. I'll kick the girls out of the house and help you. If you want to live to see Sofia have children of her own, you should always be ready to move. Didn't the Family teach you that while you were in Sicily?" And with that Frank left.

After he finished purging his computer systems, Mark went to peek at Sofia. The baby was making slurping noises in her sleep and moving her lips. "Must be dreaming of a bottle," thought Mark. He lingered in the room for a while looking at his sleeping child, thinking. Thinking about what his sister did for him last year. Finally, he turned and went into his bedroom. There was a storage ottoman at the foot of his bed. Mark opened the lid and rummaged under a pile of blankets stored inside. He finally located what he was searching for and yanked it out. It was a large backpack. His 'go' bag. He opened it and dumped out the contents on his bed. He decided that by the time the morning would come, at least his bag would be ready.

20

SAD, New York

"Sir, you have to get down here ASAP!" McCarthy yelled into the phone. "I think I got her!" The last statement made Campbell leap out of his chair and race down the hall to his Op. room.

"What? Where?" it was his turn to be out of breath.

"Well, I was still following up on that Zurich lead we've got. Remember how I tracked her into the Baur au Lac hotel? And then the trail got cold because she went in but never came out? Well, I stayed on it. I finally found something." McCarthy was grinning ear to ear.

"Yes?" hissed out impatient Campbell.

"I found a chin."

"What?" Campbell thought that McCarthy finally fried his brains looking at all these screens for too long.

"The same chin we discovered in the bank, sir. Here, let me show you!" He pressed a couple of keys on his keyboard and a face popped up on one of the plasmas. The glasses were different and the bob was replaced by long wavy dark hair, but the lips and the chin looked now familiar. The owner of these lips and chin was seen getting into a Bentley limousine. There was a busboy loading luggage into the trunk.

"She was a guest. Did you find out who she was?" asked Campbell. He was staring at the lips. They were full, painted red, parted just a tiny bit. Not smiling. Seductive. His stomach did a little flip, but he instantly put it to rest.

"Yes, registration was under Lina Ivanov. The front desk clerk that was so helpful said that she was one of those New Russians. Stayed at a very expensive suite, never left, and paid with cash."

"Did you check the airport?" Campbell asked while still staring at the woman's lips.

"Yes, but no one under the name Lina Ivanov checked in on any flights. We traced her into the first class lounge but then lost her again."

"OK," Campbell finally turned away from the screen, "stay on it. Let's check all the flights in the three hour window after she went into the lounge, see what we can get. She won't be able to sit there forever without raising suspicions. Good job!" Campbell patted McCarthy on the back, nodded to the rest of the team and left the room. He was in dire need of a cup of Earl Gray at this moment.

———

Chicago's Western Suburbs

"You have to take Sofia to her swim class," said Frank after shaking Catalina awake. He thrust a steaming cup of cappuccino under her nose to make her wake a little faster. But instead of getting up, she groaned and rolled to the other side of the bed.

"Why me?" she moaned into the pillow.

"Because Marcus is finishing up something for work and I don't do pool," replied Frank and pulled off her covers.

"Why not?" another pillow-muffled moan.

"Old bullet hole-covered men like me do not get into a public pool," said Frank. "You know that my back looks like a sieve, how am I going to explain that to the neighbors?"

"Vietnam. Plus, isn't it all got covered up with hair by now?" she lifted her head to say with a wink and a wicked smile.

"*Aayy!* Now you're really taking her," Frank shot his fist into the air and turned on his heel to walk away. Catalina swung her legs out of bed and stretched. "And you're taking the Behemoth!" he shot back at her.

"Why? Do I have to?" she yelled after him.

"Trust me on this one, you'll live longer," came Frank's response from down the hall.

The class was at an odd time of 10:50 am. It was a "Mommy and Me" swimming class, Mark being the only dad. He played his gay dad cover to the fullest here, but tried to spend as little time socializing as possible. He told Catalina that pool mothers scared him, but asked her to go unarmed. He didn't want any incidents. Catalina was intrigued, and quietly stashed her Glock 19 beneath the swim diapers.

The black Yukon Denali pulled into the pool parking lot a little bit after 10:30. The large vehicle narrowly escaped being hit by an out of control Honda Odyssey as soon as it turned into the lot. The Behemoth found a parking spot under the tree, but didn't reveal its inhabitants for a bit. Through the windshield, one could see a young woman covered by large sunglasses, looking around and still holding the steering wheel. As if she was still deciding whether or not to stay or go. Or, more accurately, flee.

Catalina slowly surveyed the parking lot. She was parked next to a Toyota minivan in an odd shade of green with magnetic decals of flames plastered to the sliding doors. "Let's just hope that whoever's driving this thing did this with a sense of humor," she said out loud. In front of her an odd scene was unfolding in a topless Jeep. A child, completely naked, was swinging from the top roll bar. A fat redheaded woman in something that resembled a blue tie-die short moo-moo—but was actually a swim-suit—was attempting to put a diaper on the swinging child. Another half naked kid was running around the car in circles. Catalina stared in horror for several minutes. Then, convincing herself that it'll be better by the pool, she finally got out of the car.

They definitely did not belong. A tall, tan, striking young woman outfitted in Prada swimwear and effortless-ly caring a chubby baby with angelic curls jarringly stood out amongst the typical pool-going multi-children fami-lies. The previous lesson was long over, but the mothers still lingered, with their wet children running amok and blocking the entrance to the pool for everyone else. Cata-lina gently pushed the kids aside, careful not to be noticed by their mothers. With her hips softly swinging from side to side, she proceeded to the end of the pool and found a chaise under a large mushroom-looking umbrella. She sat Sofia on the chaise, gave her a toy to chew on, and lowered herself on the chaise next to her. She dropped Mark's pool bag in front of Sofia since it was full of toys as well as tow-els and diapers. She wasn't worried about Sofia finding the gun on the bottom of the bag, she would never leave the child unattended.

Catalina stretched herself on the chaise and took a good look around. The pool was impressive, she was pleas-antly surprised. The facility actually had several pools: a large one with zero-depth area in one end and a large lap swim area in the other, a diving pool with slides and boards, and a medium size pool where screaming children would splash after going down a three story serpentine slide. They had a playground under a large canvas shade, sand boxes, grassy areas for a picnic, and concession stands. But what impressed Catalina the most were the lifeguards. There must have been over 20—she couldn't count them all because they were everywhere—all upper classmen in high school, or college students, all attractive, well built, tan, and wearing well designed swimsuits in navy and red. They were positioned every 10 feet, with some standing directly in the water, intently watching all the kids. They had to, Mark once told Catalina that the guards were also unwilling free babysitters when mothers would let loose their little ones in the pool while catching a long snooze face down on the chaise.

Right before the lesson started she found out that she would have to get into the pool with Sofia. Catalina was not happy, she preferred the salt water pools of her Family's Sicilian estates. But nonetheless, she took off her cover-up, grabbed Sofia and stepped into the pool. And, for a moment, everyone got quiet. Her swimsuit left nothing to the imagination, it was made out of four tiny triangles and held together by very thin string. The purpose of the suit was to leave as little tan lines as possible while providing some kind of coverage. She didn't have any other suits, her sunbathing was usually conducted in either Miami or Monte Carlo, where skimpy attire was the norm. She was also used to people gawking at her, it was a regular occurrence during her presence on a beach.

Sofia happened to love the water. The baby squeaked with delight as soon as her chubby toes touched the water and she almost wiggled out of Catalina's grasp, eager to get into the pool. She kept her aunt laughing throughout the entire lesson with splashing and non-stop giggling. Toward the end of the lesson, Catalina realized that the other women were all interacting with each other, but no one said even a simple "Hello" to her. She found the behavior offensive and got out of the pool as quickly as possible when the lesson was over.

Catalina's plan for immediate departure was suddenly halted, when while changing Sofia into some dry clothes, she noticed a small congregation of women talking and turning toward her. She quickly finished with Sofia, threw on her cover-up, grabbed her bag, and started walking toward the exit. She passed close to the gossiping women, enough to pick up their conversation with her finely honed hearing.

"She has to be completely shaved in order to pull that off," she heard one woman say to another. Catalina stopped dead in her tracks. She turned toward them and took off her sunglasses in a dramatic slow motion. The women stopped talking.

"Why, yes I am!" she said to the women and slightly cocked her head to the side. Then, she slowly looked at them from the bottom up. Her blunt assessment made them squirm a bit. "Aren't you? I guess not, that would require a *lot* of shaving cream," she finally said, turned around and left.

In the parking lot she encountered what she could only describe as a hostile takeover. Minivans were arriving at top speeds, doors were opening even before the parking lights were off and kids pouring out from the insides in droves. Each car held, on average, four children. They were followed by a mother with a pissed-off expression on her face and carrying bags of beach gear and a large cooler. Catalina slipped her hand inside her the bag on her shoulder and her fingers wrapped around the Glock 19. She tightened her grip on Sofia and tried to maneuver to their vehicle as fast as possible. For a moment, she considered shooting her way out of the parking lot, but then changed her mind.

"Here's your child, your pool bag, and your car keys!" She plopped Sofia into Mark's lap and tossed the rest on the couch. She didn't notice the duffel bags standing next to the couch, fully packed.

"What, didn't go that well?" Mark looked amused.

"Let's just say that I have a huge desire to shoot someone right now," Catalina replied and stormed out of the room.

"Did Zia Catalina have a bad time at the pool?" Mark asked the baby and rubbed her cheek with his index finger. He suddenly stopped and looked at the baby worriedly. "Did she just say 'shoot someone'?" Sofia giggled in response. "Dad!" he yelled out and bolted after Catalina with Sofia still giggling in his arms.

Frank was enjoying his newspaper and yet another cup of coffee in Mark's living room when he saw Catalina storm out of the door. He raised one eyebrow and went back to his paper. A moment later Mark yelled "Dad!" and was pounding down the stairs. Sofia, still in Mark's arms, was laughing apparently finding whatever was going on rather funny.

"What's up?" Frank asked Mark when he pounded into the room.

"She's off to shoot someone! You have to go stop her!" Mark spat out and pointed to the door. "Go! Go after her!" He ripped Frank's paper out of his hands and waved it toward the door.

"Relax, she's not going to shoot anyone," Frank said with an amused grin on his face and snatched the paper back from Mark. "She's very level-headed, a true profess…"

Frank was interrupted by the sound of screeching tires and a powerful BMW engine revving up. They barely saw a flash of metallic gray through the windows before the car disappeared down the street.

"Professional? Is that what you were trying to say? Dad?" Mark said and looked at his father.

"Well, sometimes you just need to blow off some steam, that's all. Let's just hope that Eddie has a long to-do list, because I guarantee that's where she's heading."

Mark let out a long sigh and turned on his heel toward the kitchen. Frank settled back into his chair and looked out the window. He sat, watching the street and thinking, for a while. Then he pulled his cell phone out of his pant pocket, and scrolled through the numbers until he found what he was looking for. His call was answered right away.

"Eddie, Frank. I think she's heading your way... I have no idea, cabin fever probably... Got something light? She just needs to blow off some steam... *Grazie,*" he ended the call. He sat there for a while longer before getting up and going to the kitchen for another refill.

"God help who ever pissed off Washington Enterprises and is in town right now. Because the Devil is coming your way. And she's quite mad," he said out loud to no one on the way to the coffee pot.

Two days later, after Sofia was put to bed, the two Bennett men sat down to relax in Mark's family room. Beers in hand, they were channel surfing. Suddenly, Mark stopped on a local news channel. The particular segment dealt with a shooting of six gang members inside a house. As usual, there were no witnesses to the crime. The only unusual thing the preliminary police report mentioned was that the killings appeared to be done by a single weapon. Upon hearing that tidbit, Frank raised his beer in a silent salute. When Catalina happened to join them with a glass of wine and a plate of antipasto, Frank looked her up and down and said:

"I take it we're open for business in Chicago now."

"Nah, it was too easy. They're not worth getting out of bed for."

21

Georgetown, Washington, DC

Mother couldn't sleep. Again. The old bones ached everywhere, the hip was throbbing, and he had his usual indigestion after yet another large surf-n-turf dinner. He was an old man and he was forced to accept it. He never thought he would live this long. He always imagined himself dying in his prime in the field of glory. But here he was, old, crippled, bitter. And tonight, drowning his insomnia in a bottle of Powers.

He was sitting in his usual armchair in the living room. Next to the armchair was an old wood table with a crystal lamp and an almost empty bottle of whiskey. It was pouring outside and he listened to the sound of the water pounding on his windows between sips from his glass. The chair was upholstered in brown leather, and was old as Mother. In fact, his whole house was just as old.

It was an old brownstone in Georgetown, with a need for some major TLC. On paper the house was owned by an offshore real estate investment corporation, and he was just a tenant with a very long lease. In reality, he owned the shell corporation that owned the house. But that was all very well hidden. His attorney handled all the bills for the property. Once, a young yuppie and pesky couple tried to muscle the attorney into selling the place. They were 'dying to get into the neighborhood' and they were not taking 'no' for an answer. One day their bodies were found floating in Georgetown Waterfront Park. Their heads have yet to be recovered.

The inside was dark, but without any old smells. He recently changed the AC, but that was only because the old one died. This morning he found a slow leak in the roof, which he dealt with by throwing down some towels and positioning a huge plastic bucket under the leak. He knew he needed a new roof, but wasn't in the mood to get one. He was sure that right now the broken laundry room window was letting in rain, maybe he'll mop it up tomorrow. The needs of this old house just made him feel his own age that much more, and he hated the fact that he was old. What he really wanted was some posh estate somewhere in the Caribbean, with warm sand underfoot, gorgeous blue sky above and a slew of servants at his beck and call. Like Frank. But unlike Frank, Mother's past was well documented with the government and large gestures of wealth would attract unnecessary attention. And, over the years, this little problem made him loathe the Bennetts. Here was a guy that killed for a living, and yet was free to flaunt his money. His daughter was even worse: with her vast art collection, couture clothes, little side jobs paid for in stolen goods. She was even closer to the Family than Frank was. A couple of years ago Mother found out she made her bones covering up for her father's incompetence. Over the years he started to loathe them. Then it slowly grew to hate. Now he finally had a way to take them all down by feeding them to the Company. Never mind the fact that he made his living by brokering their skills for a very handsome handling fee.

And so Mother sat in his old chair, drinking, listening to the rain, and hating his house. Suddenly, his cell phone rang startling him back into reality. He pulled it out of his trouser pocket and looked at the number before answering.

"What do you want now?" Mother barked into the phone. "I gave you everything you wanted."

"It looks like your henchman took my stuff. I want it back!" the voice on the line sounded pissed and was getting higher in pitch with every word. "Tell me where it is or our deal's off!"

"I don't know what you're talking about. I gave you the video. What, your CIA boys can't follow clues?" It was a jab below the belt by Mother, intentionally, on an unsecured line.

"Just give me what I want, you crippled ass, or I'll feed you to the dogs! Don't you think I checked who you are before I contacted you? You've got a file three inches thick with the FBI, one call…"

"Fine…" Mother took a deep breath. "There is an address. I'll send it to you. Tell your boys not to get caught, or you won't see your next birthday."

"Yeah, right. Like you can touch me." The shrill voice hung up.

Mother sat there a while longer, in the dark, recalling how easy it was for him to come up with a plan of using his MI6 connections to suggest to Wilson's father-in-law that eliminating Wilson would solve all his domestic problems and that there is a certain female assassin perfect for the job. He pictured the meetings in the gentlemen's club, pieces of information whispered between sips of cognac—the images made him chuckle a bit. He tossed back the last of his Powers before finally getting up and going upstairs into his office. In a safe, among hundreds of manila envelopes containing details on contracts he handled, was a small piece of paper with an address. Mother typed the address into his phone. He hit send without any hesitation. The address was for Frank's house in the suburbs of Chicago.

22

New York City, New York

It took Jim Campbell over an hour to get home. He took the most indirect route possible. He was no longer a field agent, yet he always took the longest way and changed it daily to avoid or flush out any possible tails. There was nothing to rush home to anyway.

He owned a loft in NoHo, one of the most expensive and desirable neighborhoods in Manhattan. A luxury on a government salary, something he was only able to afford due to his large inheritance from his rich uncle. He bought the loft a long time ago, it was a bit raw and needed work, but he never bothered. When he was out in the field, he was rarely home, and only for a short period of time. Now that he was permanently assigned to a desk, he still hasn't bothered. He lived alone and had very basic needs. Except for his love of film.

His loft took up an entire floor. It was on the top floor of an old building and Jim even had the roof rights. A couple of years ago he spent his vacation building a rooftop patio. He designed it himself: it was large and beautiful with lots of seating areas, a covered dining and cooking area, and surrounded by strategically placed lattice walls. The walls provided privacy, no one from surrounding buildings could see in, but Jim could see everything, and was able to enjoy the fabulous view of the city. He even put in a hot tub, to soak his battle-battered body.

Downstairs was a whole different story. The windows

were covered with newspaper, the floor boards creaked, with the only walls surrounding a tiny bathroom all the way in the back corner. He kept his clothes on a couple of rolling racks, and some laundry baskets shoved against one wall; there was an old desk and an office chair against the other; a huge mattress and a box spring were taking center stage in the middle of the floor. Now that was something he actually spent money on. The pillow-top bed was king size, the only size big enough for his frame. In front of the bed was a 60-inch Sony television with a multitude of components and speakers. He stored movies in office file boxes, labeled by genres first, then in alphabetical order within each genre. The whole set-up spoke volumes about Jim as a man to women that he brought here (and he did bring quite a few), but they didn't seem bothered. In the mornings, he always found himself alone, sometimes being woken up by the creaking of the floorboards as his latest night companion was sneaking out the front door. Even though they all left him their phone numbers, he never called any of them back.

As soon as he walked through the heavy steel door of his loft he tossed his keys, phone and mail on the desk, relieved himself of his weapon, and plopped down on the bed ready to enjoy his large bag of Chinese food and a Netflix. He was looking forward to this all day. Movie ready to go, shoes off, container of chow mein open, remote in one hand and cold beer in another, he was ready for some undisturbed R&R. But tonight that was not meant to be.

His peace and quiet were disturbed by the ringing of his phone. For a moment he considered not getting it, but climbed out of his bed anyway. *'Jason Ellis 1 missed call'* displayed the caller ID. 'This better be good,' Jim thought before calling back. He was getting increasingly tired of this Ellis character bugging him about the status of Darwin.

"I'm off the clock," he almost barked into the phone once the line was picked up.

"I've got an address for you. It's in Illinois. My stuff should be there. I just emailed that to you, send someone over there." The voice on the other line demanded.

"Your stuff? It's *your* stuff now? What am I, your personal retriever? You seem to have resources that we don't know about, you go get it." Jim got instantly pissed with the demands.

"You're son of a..." Ellis didn't get to finish, Campbell hung up on him. He tossed the phone on the bed and started pacing up and down the floor.

He paced for over 10 minutes. Then he stopped abruptly and lunged for his phone. He scrolled through his contacts menu and dialed McCarthy.

"Get to the office, right now. Something's come up," he gave the order as soon as the young agent picked up the line and hung up. For the next several minutes he rushed through his loft, packing up his Chinese food to go and changing into jeans and a black shirt. He shoved his weapon into his waistband, grabbed his wallet, phone, and his food, and stormed out the door. He forgot to lock his door in his haste.

McCarthy was already waiting for Campbell in his office. Despite the late evening hours, the young agent looked fresh as a daisy in a light gray summer suit and a lavender tie. Campbell looked him up and down and snorted.

"Do you even own regular clothes?" he asked McCarthy. The young man was always impeccably dressed.

"I was on a date, sir," answered the young man with

a blush.

"Why didn't you tell me?" Campbell felt a hint of guilt.

"You didn't give me a chance, sir. That's oK, she's my 'close and continuing', met her in college. She's used to me disappearing by now."

"Marry her, women like that are hard to come by."

"Planning on it, sir. So what's up?" McCarthy was eager to change the subject, discussing his monogamous relationship with his playboy of a boss was making him uncomfortable.

"First order of business, get this food reheated. It was supposed to be my dinner. And make some tea. I'm going to check email," said Campbell and shoved the bag with Chinese food into McCarthy. The young man grabbed the bag without a word and left to find a microwave.

There was an email from Ellis labeled 'location'. It contained an address in Illinois, but no name. Campbell did a quick search and found that the location was smack in the middle of a very populated residential area in the Western suburbs of Chicago. The public records revealed that the property was owned by a trust. He tried tracing the trust, but the trail quickly died in the Caribbean. He wasn't really interested in that anyway.

Earlier, while pacing around his loft, he worked out a new target to focus on. He no longer cared whether or not ICtech would ever find Wilson's research. What he now wanted was the assassin. A freelance mechanic, as the Company preferred to call them, like this one would be invaluable to the CIA. And this mechanic was most likely a woman. Even better, female assassins were hard to come by.

McCarthy returned carrying a tray with steaming plates of Chinese food. "He must've gone all the way to the canteen for this," thought Campbell as the heavy tray was carefully put down on his desk. If this was up to him, they would be eating straight out of food containers and most likely dripping grease all over themselves. McCarthy produced a couple of plastic forks and pulled up a chair to join in the feast.

"Don't forget the tea," reminded Campbell and dove into the food.

They ate for a while in silence, until Campbell started to reveal why they were here at such late hour. He also shared with McCarthy his thoughts that the assassin was a much more valuable catch than the lost Wilson's research. The young agent agreed.

"OK, so let's get someone down to Chicago to see if this will yield anything of value. Don't waste resources, most likely it's a wild goose chaise. Get one of the newbies to do it. Someone who's been at a desk for a while but itching to get out," instructed Campbell and scooped up the last of the Chinese food off his plate. "Then, call Ellis and get him in here."

"How?" McCarthy inquired mid-chew.

"Tell him we found something and he needs to see it. Put him in the Op. room, but shut everything down first. I don't want him to see what we're capable of."

"Why the Op. room?"

"It's sound proof and has no windows. He's going to tell me who his source is."

"And how are you planning on doing that? You've asked before and he's not revealing anything," asked a puzzled McCarthy.

"The old fashioned way," replied Campbell nonchalantly then scooped up his dirty dishes and threw them into his wastebasket with a loud thud.

"Ah, and we'll need a sound-proofed room. Gotcha!" McCarthy's face spread into a satisfied grin of understanding. He also couldn't stand Ellis and was eager to kick his ass. McCarthy wiped his mouth with a napkin, crumpled it up, and tossed it into Campbell's wastebasket. Perfect shot.

They settled on John "Johnny" Higger to go down to Chicago. He was with the Company for a couple of years now, but did not get a lot of field assignments. His skill level, however, was adequate for the task of breaking into a suburban house and looking for a flash drive that resembled a cigarette lighter. In the morning they would give him the assignment, tell him to check in every 12 hours and send him off. Next on the agenda was getting Ellis to come in. McCarthy concocted an elaborate story to tell Ellis, and after Campbell's approval, made the call. Since it was already past midnight, Ellis was told to fly in the next day. He eagerly agreed. With the trap in place, the two men bid goodnight to each other and finally left the office. McCarthy went to his girlfriend's to crawl in between the smooth sheets and snuggle next to her warm body. Campbell, not having anyone to come home to, went over to The Bowery Electric. They were promising a good lineup tonight and great music always drew in interesting women. He was quite sure that he would not be returning home alone.

23

Chicago's Western Suburbs

The Chicago summer heat suddenly broke Saturday morning. It looked like it would be a beautiful cool weekend. Everyone rushed to turn off the AC and open the windows. Frank refused to do so in his home, but Catalina was insistent. She kept complaining about smelly and stuffy air until he finally caved in. A cool lazy breeze was now blowing through the house, moving the curtains and rustling a loose paper or two. It made everyone surprisingly calm and in good spirits.

In the early evening, Frank decided to take Sofia on a long slow stroll through the neighborhood. He was hoping that the fresh air would tire her and she would pass right out. Bedtime was getting a bit difficult these days, Sofia figured them all out and learned what buttons to push. His granddaughter reminded him of Catalina when she was that age. And so he strapped her into the stroller, packed a bottle, put on his walking shoes, and strolled out of the driveway.

Catalina decided to use this alone time to clean her guns. The best breeze was in the kitchen, but she closed all the shades and drew the dark curtains on the French doors before spreading her gear all over the round kitchen table. The cool air still managed to blow in through the curtains and shades. She grabbed a cold beer from the fridge before starting her task. Just like cooking, gun cleaning was relaxing to her—it calmed her and cleared her head.

She was looking forward to this. But before starting, she put her ceramic blade next to her on the table. 'Never be caught without a weapon,' she told herself and smiled.

She was almost done with her Glock 19, when she heard the mudroom door opening. She looked up from her task, her hand slipping the blade off the table and on to her lap. She sat, waiting for the visitor to appear. It was Mark. He stopped at the kitchen doorway and leaned on the frame.

"Oh, it's just you." The blade was put back on the table.

"Seriously, sis? You're planning on stabbing me?" Mark lifted an eyebrow. She gave him a look and made a circle with her finger, silently asking him if he swept for bugs recently since he was talking so candidly. He mouthed 'all clean.'

"I didn't know it was you. As you can see, I'm a bit vulnerable right now," she said out loud, sweeping her hand across the table indicating to her task. "What's up?"

"Nothing. Thought I'd just come and visit. Mind if I join you? I won't touch anything."

"Fine. Grab me a refill then, will you?" She waved her empty bottle at him a little.

Mark brought a couple of cold ones to the table, along with an antipasto platter that always seemed to be full and ready in Frank's fridge ever since Catalina showed up in their lives. He took a seat across from her and positioned the platter between himself and the guns. Catalina took a sip of beer and popped a salami into her mouth before getting back to her task. Mark ate the cold cuts washing them down with his beer and watched her without saying a word. His sister was clad in a boldly-patterned halter maxi dress that emphasized rather nicely her straight shoulders and well-toned tanned arms. To Mark, her choice of dress—which he figured was expensive—for such an ugly task was a little strange, but then to Catalina gun cleaning was as mundane and normal as grocery shopping to everyone else. Catalina finished cleaning the Glock 19 and spread all the parts in front of her in what looked to be some kind of order. Mark noticed that there was a small stopwatch among all the tools. She took the stopwatch and slid it across the table toward him.

"Time me."

Mark picked up the stopwatch. "Ready?"

"Yes."

"Go!"

Her hands flew over the gun parts. Pieces clicked together with precision and ease. It was so fast, Mark could not even figure out what she was doing. She put the assembled weapon on the table, her hands on either side. Mark stopped the watch. He turned it so she could see the time. A little frown flashed across her face, she was not happy.

"Still a bit slow on the Glock. And it's not a difficult gun to assemble. Why can't I do this fast enough?" She picked the gun and it disappeared into the folds of her dress. Mark figured that she had a holster strapped to her thigh.

"This is slow? Are you nuts? Daddy can't even do it this fast, and he's fast!" Mark was impressed and amused at the same time.

"I'm not our father," replied Catalina and moved on to one of her Berettas.

They sat in silence again, while she took apart the Beretta and laid out of the pieces. She took her time with it, carefully examining every piece. Mark knew that she could disassemble a gun even faster than she could put it together. It was a skill that, against their mother's wishes, was taught to them early on. It was Catalina's favorite activity as a child. Mark remembered how one evening their father came home to find all his guns in pieces and a very proud Catalina sitting in the middle of her handiwork, smiling ear to ear. Frank was only mad for a minute and the two of them had a ball assembling them back together. Mark was upstairs in his room reading while all the fun was going on. An activity like that was of no interest to him.

Catalina was concentrating on cleaning the barrel when Mark finally spoke.

"What happened?" He startled her.

"What do you mean?" Catalina was confused.

"What did you do? Why did you have to come and hide here, why couldn't you stay at your house? I thought your house was like a fortress."

"Do you want me to leave?" Catalina asked evenly.

"No, I'm glad you're here. But this is business and you never mix business with family. Our family," clarified Mark.

"Mother sent me here. I wanted to go to Sicily instead, but he insisted that I come here. I couldn't figure out why, but now…" her voice trailed off.

"Now what?"

"It's better that you don't know. Stay out of this. This is not your life," Catalina stopped her task and looked Mark straight into the eyes.

"No! Two days ago I had to pack a go bag for myself and Sofia. Dad made me. I'm part of this life now. When I called you that day in January, I became part of this life. So tell me what's going on. You can't do this alone."

"It's better if you don't know. You'll live longer. We would all live longer."

"What, in case your CIA buddies get a hold of me? You might not believe me, but I can take care of myself and my daughter. *So tell me!*" He slammed his beer on the table, anger glowing in his eyes.

"Fine, it's your funeral," said Catalina. She shrugged her shoulders and started cleaning the barrel again. A full minute passed before she finally spoke.

"I was in London, staying at the Ritz. I just finished a job somewhere else and was on my way back to the States. I always take different routes, and change IDs several times. One afternoon, as I was enjoying my high tea, the hotel concierge delivered a message. It was a small side job. With over half a million CCTV cameras in London, the Brits always know when I'm in town, but that really doesn't bother me because we have an understanding. I do their wet work once in a while, like Daddy did CIA's. This side job followed MI6 protocol but it was a personal contract," she stopped what she was doing, leaned back on her chair and moved the antipasto platter closer to herself. She popped a couple of cold cuts into her mouth before continuing.

"I got my hands on the security footage from the hotel lobby and figured out who hired the concierge. Then I did some digging on Google, it wasn't hard. The guy was the target's father-in-law. He left a burn phone for me to use if I would accept the job. The envelope also had a wedding photo of his daughter and my possible target, her husband, and a handwritten note stating that the husband threatened to kill her if she ever decided to divorce him. The family was so connected and wealthy that icing the son-in-law was a lot easier to mop up than a public divorce scandal. With British press the way the are, I can see their reasoning."

"I cased the mark that evening. He went prowling for hookers in a really shady area of London after work. Picked up two before going home. It just looked so easy.

On the way back to the Ritz, I stopped by this art fence I know. He's small game, but sometimes he gets really interesting things. This time he had an Imperial Fabergé egg. Of course, I really wanted it. But, I already bought myself a reward for the last job. The egg would've been unearned. So I decided to do this job and ask for the egg as payment. I called the old man in the morning and he agreed." Catalina paused and went back to her gun cleaning. She cleaned another piece of the Beretta before continuing her story. Mark never interrupted.

"This was really easy. I did it in an abandoned building I knew of. No one could hear him scream there. He turned out to be such a sissy. I took my time with him... Do you want the details?"

"Those you can skip. I take it this is not your first torture," Mark was a bit disgusted with his sister.

"No, but I really don't enjoy it. Usually I serve them a cocktail and just wait for them to start singing. But this one had to be hands on. And it got really interesting."

"How so?" Mark made a move to retrieve the food platter, but got a slap on his hand. If she was talking, she was eating the entire thing on her own.

"He never thought this was about his wife. He thought this was about his work. I didn't even know what he did for a living. First it wasn't making any sense, but then I got curious and started to ask him more direct questions. He started to offer me money to stop. Nope. Then he said that he was a chemist, and he's got this invention and he's got a deal no one knew about and he'd cut me in. That didn't get him anywhere. After an hour he started saying that I can have the invention, just let him live. Gave me all the details and finally mentioned his wife. Well, that got us back on the subject. I asked him about her. He said she was an ugly stupid bitch whom he married for money. All that pain and he still wasn't getting it… So I finally had to tell him why he was in this predicament. Right before I iced him. And then I chopped his dick off. I found a kid off the street deliver it to the old guy… I wonder what he did with it? Probably fed it to his dogs… Men like that always have dogs." Mark choked on his beer after the last remark. Catalina gave him a wink and a smile.

"I went back to my hotel," Catalina continued, "and there was a package for me. My Fabergé egg! It was so beautiful… Out of curiosity, I followed the mark's instructions to his safe deposit box. Pretended to be his wife to get access to it. All this time I thought he was talking about drugs, you know, 'chemist' and all, but he wasn't. I found a flash drive, some money and some other very peculiar things in there. It made me realize that there was really something to this guy. He was definitely someone, and his research was very valuable to some circles. So, I get back to DC, and Mother gets on my case. Somehow he got a whiff of this little job I did and was saying that 'The Company' was not happy. He didn't know about my discovery and I wasn't about to tell him. You see, I recorded my handy work because all the blabbering was so interesting. So I showed Mother the video to get him off my back. But I edited the footage after the trip to the bank, so no one would find out that he told me the details. Mother took the video with him to share with his 'Company men'. Told me he'd use it to calm things down. But then he made me come here." She paused and looked at Mark. "I got here and Eddie was looking for me. He had a message from the Family. Apparently, they knew a lot more about the situation. There is more to it, it seems…" Her voice trailed off. She stopped what she was doing and lifted her head to listen to any sounds. But the house was quiet. Her Beretta was ready to be assembled, but she didn't ask Mark to time her this round. She just snapped it together with lightning speed, loaded and put it off to the side.

"Do you know what ICtech is?" Catalina suddenly asked Mark. He nodded in response.

"I came across them once or twice. This guy you killed, was he one of their 'investments'?" Mark made quote marks with his hands in the air with that last comment. Then he rolled his eyes.

"Yep. They want his invention and it seems they would go to great lengths to get it."

"Well, I bet they put a lot of money into him."

"Without a background check into what kind of a psycho he was? Doesn't look like a wise investment to me." She was now leaning back in her chair, holding a beer with one hand and waving around a rolled-up piece of mortadella.

"So to what lengths would they go to get it? Any ideas?" asked Mark and went after the olives on the platter, the only thing she hadn't consumed yet. He always wondered how could she stay so thin while consuming large amounts of food and alcohol.

"Well, they're having their CIA buddies run an illegal operation within the States." The waving of mortadella stopped and the rolled up goodness disappeared into Catalina's mouth. "Probably called 'Operation I Fucked Up Now Fix it!' ...Mmm, good mortadella..." she partially closed her eyes in enjoyment.

"What are you planning to do about it?" Mark eyed the platter and noted that there was nothing left but a lonely piece of salami, which Catalina was now reaching for, and a bunch of olives. He would have to make himself a sandwich upon returning to his own house.

"Well," she was talking with her mouth full, "I'll see how things play out for a bit longer. If things are quiet, I've got a loose end to tie up and then I'll disappear for a while.

No one's getting Wilson's stuff by the way, I'm going to make sure of that. Some things should never be created."

"And if things are not quiet?" Mark grabbed a handful of olives and shoved them into his mouth. Catalina raised an eyebrow.

"Go out with a bang. Only there will be a higher body count. Ball's in their court."

"Yeah, but I doubt they know who they're playing against. Because you're completely off the grid." Mark's words were a bit mumbled with all the olives, which made Catalina chuckle a bit. He looked a bit comical in his Abercrombie getup of a v-neck tee, jeans and flip-flops, with a mouthful of olives.

"Don't choke!" she reached for the last Beretta, yet to be cleaned. "I got to clean this one, want to take it apart?"

"And mess up your gun? No! I prefer to sleep with both eyes closed, thank you very much," replied Mark and waved her off.

"I'm not going to kill you while you're asleep, relax! Fine, I just thought you might need some practice. And if it misfires at the range tomorrow, I'll dispose of it. We've got plenty downstairs to choose from, you know." She slid the weapon toward him.

"Do you know what is it this Wilson developed?" asked Mark before picking up the Beretta.

"Yeah, I actually have a pretty good idea. I don't know all the details, but I figured out the general principal."

"And?" The Beretta was coming apart. Not as fast as Catalina's approach, but still the hands handling the weapon knew what they were doing.

"All I'm going to say is that it's something that will put me out of business. And I'm not ready to retire yet." Catalina grabbed the last olive off the platter and popped it in her mouth. Mark finished with Beretta and spread out the pieces. "Nice work by the way! And you pretended you didn't know how to do this." She kicked her brother in his leg under the table.

Frank and Sofia were on their way back home when Frank noticed a compact size car parked near the Worthingtons' house. The car had a little green 'e' sticker on the trunk. Rental. Frank slowed down by the car for a second, but then remembered overhearing Melanie Worthington complaining about her husband having car problems and that he might have to get a rental while it was in the shop. Sure enough, the troubled vehicle was not in their driveway tonight. 'I guess they decided to do it this weekend,' thought Frank with a shrug and continued toward his home. A minute later he entered his house and caught Catalina giving Mark pointers on the art of gun maintenance. In Frank's fatherly eyes no other sight could have been sweeter.

24

It was past midnight when father and daughter finally went to bed. Frank stayed up a little longer watching Cheers reruns on TV, and Catalina took a hot bath for another half an hour or so. As she finally slipped between the cool Egyptian cotton sheets, she checked her Beretta under her pillow and stashed her phone next to it. She fell asleep immediately, her hand still resting on her gun. 'Sleeping with one eye open' Frank called it. She called it 'staying alive'. The house finally went dark closer to two a.m.

The ice-cold tentacles of danger started deep in her stomach and slowly proceeded to slither up toward her spine. They only managed to get to her lower spine, when Catalina's eyes flew open. Something was off. She stayed down in bed, fully alert, not moving, listening… Nothing. Quiet. But the danger kept creeping up her spine, its tentacles spreading into her organs, chilling them as they moved upward. Her phone, stashed under her pillow, vibrated. The vibration had a certain rhythm, one of several assigned to the house alarm system. This particular one indicated a breach. Someone was here.

In one fluid motion, Catalina flew out of bed, gun drawn and positioned herself by the door. She listened. Nothing. She squeezed out into the hallway and looked around. In a nanosecond she noticed that there was a faint light moving around downstairs and that Frank was opening his bedroom door to join her. They silently acknowledged each other, both standing with guns drawn, ready to shoot first and ask questions later. Catalina nodded toward the stairs, Frank nodded back and gave her thumbs up. Whoever was downstairs had now become her prey but she was instructed not to kill.

She slowly moved toward the stairs, Frank moving the opposite direction, toward the other staircase that led into the kitchen. Catalina peeked down through the banister. It would've been helpful to check the house CCTV feed on her phone, but the screen would light up the whole hallway and give her away. She had to do this one by touch. The faint light was moving around in the den. 'Figures,' she thought. She studied the light motion for a bit, figuring out her approach. Then, she swung her long legs over the banister and slid down on it. Silently, gun pointed into the den. She landed on the bottom without sound and quickly moved just outside the door.

The intruder was a male. He held a tiny flashlight in his mouth, and he was rummaging through the desk. He seemed to be ignoring all the papers but paying close attention to big fat pens and flash drives. He didn't pocket anything yet; he was looking for something specific. Instantly, Catalina knew what he was looking for. Her eyes narrowed and her hand gripped her gun even tighter than before. But her mind reminded her of Frank flashing a thumb up, meaning 'alive'. She shrugged her shoulders and moved in for capture.

He didn't even feel her behind him. *Bam!* Something smashed into his scalp and he went down in a heap.

25

He thought he was dead. He was laying on something cold and slippery. He slowly opened his eyes, expecting to see the inside of coroner's freezer. But the surroundings looked like something of a basement. A moment later, his senses returning, he smelled the musty odor of cool concrete. He tasted cotton stuffed into his mouth: he was gagged. He tried to move. Couldn't. His extremities were hog-tied behind his back. All he was able to do was to lift his head and look around.

Indeed, he was in the basement. It was a huge and cavernous space, faintly lit. In the middle of the space, there were two rows of military-grade ammunition safes. He got a very uneasy feeling when he lost count of safes after ten. He shook his head, trying to regain his wits and continued to look around. By the faint humming somewhere deeper into the basement, he deduced that this house possessed some very sophisticated utilities. 'Who the hell are these people?' he asked himself. His gaze finally fell on floor. The slippery material he was laying on was none other than an enormous sheet of plastic covering a very large area. '*I was just checking to see if I was standing on plastic,*' the line from his favorite movie, *Lethal Weapon 2,* flashed in his mind. 'Shit!'

———

"You should've let me shoot him. Now what are we going to do with him? It's almost daylight." Catalina was pacing the kitchen floor, nostrils flaring. Periodically, she would stop and glare at Frank, who was leaning on the kitchen counter sipping coffee.

"We need to know why he's here and who sent him," Frank responded.

"We all know why he's here. And I have a pretty good idea who sent him. What I can't figure out is how to get him out of here since you won't let me kill him."

"And you think you can get rid of a body? Where are you going to dump it? The neighbor's pool?"

"That's not something I'll have to worry about. I'll just call the Cleaner. And don't tempt me about the pool."

"The Cleaner's still in business? Isn't he like a hundred years old now?" Frank wondered with a smile.

"Well, unfortunately yours went out of commission a while back. I'm using one of Eddie's men. He's much better actually. Faster too... The Family should just train one of our own for the job... Are we going to do this or not?" Catalina stopped pacing and gave him another stare.

"Fine," Frank gulped the last of his coffee and began to roll up his sleeves.

"Oh, no. We're not doing it your way. How are you going to explain the marks on your hands?"

"Well, there is this marvelous invention called gloves," Frank grabbed a pair of yellow rubber gloves off the sink and waved them in her face.

"Let me do it. It'll be faster," Catalina grabbed the gloves out of his hands, " and cleaner." She tossed the gloves back into the sink.

"And how are you going to do it? Goodnight Cinderella?" there was genuine curiosity in Frank's voice. This would be the first time he would see his daughter at work.

"Something like that. Hey, I wasn't a chem major for nothing. I'll be back." Catalina strutted out of the kitchen and up the stairs. She paused on the top step then turned and bent down to look at Frank. "Daddy, Mark and Sofia need to leave. Now."

Frank gave her a long look of understanding before nodding. "I'll send them to Giovanni's, they'll be safe there. They'll come back when we're done."

———

It was another couple of hours before he heard the basement door opening. From his position on the floor, he saw a pair of very long and bare legs going down the stairs. Female. A pair of trouser-clad male legs followed. The female disappeared into the depth of the basement, the male stayed on the stairs. He heard some strange sounds coming from somewhere deep, metallic sounds. Suddenly, a high-pitched screeching sound appeared and was moving toward him. It was like nails on a chalkboard. And the effect was the same. He shut his eyes and cringed, the sound assaulting his now sensitive ears more and more as it moved closer and closer. He finally willed his eyes to open and realized that the sound came from a metal folding chair being slowly dragged along the concrete floor. The chair stopped in front of him and was unfolded. He saw the male move forward and a moment later he was yanked upright and shoved into the chair. Then, all the overhead lights went on and he went blind.

When he regained his vision, he came face to face with a man in a black mask. The eyes were studying him intently. The gaze was so penetrating and so cold that a shiver ran through him. Then the mask spoke:

"There are two ways of doing it. The old school way and the new school way. Due to some circumstances, we're going to have to do it the new school way. But, look at the bright side, you get to keep all your body parts and it'll hurt less," the mask looked up at someone standing behind him. "Fill 'im up!"

Cool, long fingers slid under his chin, then grabbed his jaw and tilted back his head. Before he could protest, a needle was shot into his neck. He passed out.

He never fully regained his consciousness, nor did he have any control of his body. His vision was foggy, but somehow he managed to see that it was two people questioning him. Judging by the voices, a man and a woman. They asked his name, and whom he worked for. What was he doing in the house. The password to his encrypted phone. Questions about his personal life. Questions about the Company. His current team. He answered them all, the answers just rolling off his tongue, without any restrictions. At some point he was crying like a baby. When they were done, he was injected for a second time. As he was slipping into nothingness once again, he wondered if this was the end of his life.

26

SAD, New York

"Give up your source mother fucker or I'll break your puny little neck!" spat out Campbell, and Jason Ellis' face was shoved harder into the tabletop. His right arm, pulled behind his back, was yanked toward his head. He screamed in pain, but the sound came out muffled. This was not how he thought this meeting with the Darwin team was going to go.

Half an hour ago he joined Special Agents Campbell and McCarthy inside the Darwin operations room. He was so eager to see what that they found, that he failed to notice that the other agents left the room in a hurry as soon as the three of them walked in. He also missed Campbell locking the door behind them. He just kept looking at the wall of screens displaying various data. To Ellis, the data looked like gibberish. And it was total gibberish, Campbell wasn't about to reveal CIA secrets to an outsider. Less than a minute passed before Campbell grabbed Ellis by the arm and pushed him into the chair. Then he started asking him about his source. First Ellis was shocked, no one pushed him around since high school, but then he got mad. He started screaming at Campbell, with his screeching voice climbing in pitch, that how dare he treat him like that. That tactic didn't work. As soon as the words 'you can't touch me!' fell out of his mouth, Campbell grabbed his jacket's lapels and yanked him out of the chair. McCarthy shoved the chair out of the way for Campbell to ram Ellis hard into the wall.

"Your source!" screamed Campbell into Ellis's frightened face before peeling him off the wall and tossing him across the room. McCarthy jumped out of the way and Ellis flew into one of the computer-laden desks. He slid down to the floor. "You're crazy! You're all crazy! I'm not telling you anything!" he spat toward Campbell. Bad idea. Campbell slowly took off his jacket, tossed it on a chair, and pushed up his shirt sleeves before crossing the room to Ellis in two strides. Ellis was hoisted off the floor, grabbed by the right arm, and turned around. The arm was yanked upward behind his back, his head was grabbed by the hair and pulled back, before being slammed into the tabletop. This is how Ellis found himself now, scared out of his mind.

"The name, you son of a bitch!" Campbell pulled Ellis's head and slammed it back down.

"Golshtsh…" mumbled Ellis.

"What? I didn't hear you!" Campbell pulled up his head.

"Goldstein… Gerald Goldstein…" repeated Ellis. Campbell instantly released him. The man slid off the table down to the floor.

"Gerald Goldstein? You dug up Gerald Goldstein for this?" Campbell asked and started to pace back and forth. McCarthy, who spent the entire chit-chat standing by the wall out of the way, pulled up a chair and sat down.

"Who's Gerald Goldstein?" McCarthy asked calmly. He never heard that name before.

"Goldstein was a handler. The Company used his services sometimes a long time ago. But he had only one mechanic worth anything and that guy had died 11 years ago. Goldstein retired after that."

"He didn't. He's got someone really good now. Better than the guy before," said Ellis. He was going to tell them everything he knew. He didn't care anymore. All he wanted was to get out of this room, go home and lick his wounds.

"His first mechanic was a member of a Sicilian mafia. You don't just replace a made man and live to tell about it," said Campbell to Ellis.

"It's all the same Family. And he's really bitter about it… That is why he even talked to me, I had something to give him the Mob couldn't." Ellis sat up on the floor, and rubbed the back of his head.

"What did you offer him?" asked McCarthy. Still sitting down, he rolled his chair toward Ellis, grabbed a water bottle from a table near by and offered it to him.

"Full immunity… Thank you," the thank you was directed to McCarthy. Ellis took the water bottle, opened it with trembling hands and took a sip.

"What did you ask him to do?" Campbell stopped pacing and looked at Ellis.

"Get rid of Wilson so we could take his research. But I didn't tell him to torture the man, for God's sake!"

"But Wilson didn't finish. So there is no product. That's what we called in you here to tell you… among other things," said Campbell and shrugged his shoulders. Ellis choked on his water.

"OK, we're done here." Campbell moved to the door and unlocked it. "McCarthy, have our team get him out of here. This business with Goldstein… this has to go vertical. Get him out and fix this place up. I'll be back… Oh, get Johnny back here, will you?" He grabbed his jacket off the chair and left the room.

"Come on, off the floor," said McCarthy to Ellis and got off his chair. "Operation Darwin is closed. No need to wait for the final report." He grabbed Ellis by the sleeve and started to tug him up.

27

Catalina shoved the plastic tarp further into the garbage bin before snapping the lid closed. She stepped back into the garage and closed the door behind her. But instead of going into the house, she got into her car. Once the solid BMW door closed behind her, she pulled out her phone from her shorts pocket and dialed Antonia. The woman picked up on the first ring.

"*Ciao,* Catalina!" greeted the familiar soft voice.

"Antonia, dear, how are you?" Catalina sang sweetly into the phone.

"Oh fine, nothing new. Your fall collections have arrived. *Loro sono belli!* I already donated last year's pieces. But only the ones you told me to, of course." Along with a mention of Catalina's wardrobe change, Antonia reported that the house was secure. "And how are you?"

"Well, caught a field mouse. Must be the weather, it's getting hot in here. Did Mother call you by any chance?" Catalina told her about the intruder.

"A mouse? Such a disgusting creature. No, Mother didn't call... Maybe you should take a vacation, there are no mice in brand new hotels." Antonia suggested that perhaps it was time for Catalina to move to Sicily, since her villa was now ready.

"I think you've got the right idea. Why don't you pack me up? You have the list. Oh, and have Babinsky pick up his stuff. Do you want me to get you some help with packing?"

"Oh that would be lovely to have extra help around the house right now! Let me know what company you use so I know."

"Don't worry…" replied Catalina then took a deep breath. "Antonia, dear, why don't you take a vacation as well? Perhaps see your family? It's been a while. You can leave as soon as you pack me up. *Capisce?*" She was ordering Antonia to leave for Sicily and not wait for her.

"*Si.* Oh well, I guess I can do that. *Ciao, il mia amico!*" said Antonia, trying to hold back sudden wave of tears.

"*Ciao!*" responded Catalina quietly and hung up. She sat in the car for a while, then got out and went into the house.

————

SAD, New York

"Johnny Higger has not checked in today," was the first thing Campbell heard when he walked into his Ops room. He spent the afternoon in the archives, looking up Gerald Goldstein. He didn't come up with much, Goldstein did have a file but most of it was redacted. Campbell's clearance level was not high enough to see everything. All he got was that the man was contracted for some off-the-books wet work off and on, but that all stopped 11 years ago. That was when Goldstein lost his only operative possessing the skills necessary for Company jobs. Campbell wasn't even sure if Gerald Goldstein was the man's real name. With people like this nothing is real. The most interesting not classified tidbit was that Goldstein had possible connections to the Sicilian mob. The Benedetto Family. Campbell was not familiar with them. Ellis said that Goldstein's past and current operatives came from the same Family—if the new person was just as good as the last one it would be very good for the Company.

"What do you mean, he hasn't checked in? Where is he? Can you get a GPS position?" inquired Campbell. He sounded more irritated than concerned.

"His phone would have to be on to get a GPS lock, sir. But he's off the grid," was the response.

"What was his last position?"

"Checking it now, sir." There was a pause and Campbell saw maps flicker on screens. "Looks like the Hilton Garden Inn, his hotel."

"How old is the information?"

"24 hours."

"Visuals?"

"Nothing, sir."

"Get someone to check out his hotel," ordered Campbell. "Where's McCarthy?"

"Don't know sir!" said someone.

"Find him and tell him it's his job to find out where Higger went. He was his choice, gotta account for your man. I'll be in my office." Campbell left his Op. room and went straight into his office to call his superiors. He was about to seek an official approval to start hunting down this new assassin.

Campbell pulled up the surveillance photo from Baur au Lac in Zurich once he got into his office. The one of a woman with long wavy hair and large sunglasses getting into a Bentley limousine. He sat down into his chair and stared at his screen for a while. He noticed more details, like the fact that she was wearing a white silky blouse that tied into a loose bow at the neck and was carrying a Hermes purse. Her lips—red, parted just a bit—still made his stomach do a little flip. He stared a while longer before picking up his phone and dialing a number in Langley.

28

Washington, DC

"Please tell me again why we had to get on a plane and get our asses here as soon as possible?" asked Leon. "And which house is it again? I don't know any of these flags."

"That one, the one with that black Lexus in the front. That's the housekeeper's car," pointed Diamond. "I guess that's what we get for protecting The Boss' best friend. Hey, at least you won't be here long, I'm staying until The Boss says it's OK to leave." Diamond parked the black Range Rover they were driving behind the Lexus.

The two men walked up the stairs of Catalina's house. Just a couple of hours ago, they were summoned by Eddie, told to throw a change of clothes into a bag and get down to Washington DC to Catalina Bennett's house. They flew Eddie's luxurious Gulfstream 650 and were given the address of the house and keys to one of Eddie's Range Rovers upon their touchdown. As they were putting their bags into the vehicle, Leon overheard one of Eddie's flight crew comment on how they had to immediately go back to Chicago because they might be going to New York that night as well. Leon wondered who the passenger might be this time.

The door was opened even before they rang the bell. A mature, but still beautiful, woman with a round face, short dark hair, full lips and wearing a back pantsuit greeted them with a stern look. She looked them up and down for a full minute before finally speaking.

"IDs please." The men started to reach for their wallets. "No, your *other* ID."

Diamond and Leon looked at each other, then extended their left arms, palm up, to the woman. There was a small tattoo of EWE on the men's left wrists, in a spot that would be usually covered up by a watch. It was a tattoo that only members of Eddie's inner circle had, and it stood for 'Eddie Washington Enterprises.' The woman examined each tattoo closely before letting them into the house.

"I am Antonia, Catalina's housekeeper," the woman introduced herself once they all were inside. She spoke with a slight Italian accent. "We have much to do, please follow me to the kitchen and I will tell you what needs to be done." She turned on her kitten heel and started walking toward the back of the house. The men followed her while trying not to gawk at their surroundings. Diamond always thought that Eddie's residence was spectacular, but this was beyond anything Diamond could ever imagine. The art alone was breathtaking, the furnishings spoke of high quality. Diamond decided that he will not be able to sit down anywhere in this house, he was afraid to ruin something.

"You should've made me change into something cleaner, bro!" whispered Leon to Diamond. "What happens if I accidentally rub against a wall?"

"I will make you clean it, of course," the response came from Antonia. She turned to face Leon before entering the kitchen and looked him up and down. "I suppose I could spare five minutes so you could change. Please go and get your luggage from your car. And be discreet, we have interesting neighbors. There are two guestrooms ready for you upstairs. We will wait for you in the kitchen." And she turned back on her heel and went into the kitchen. Diamond tossed Leon the car keys and followed the woman.

Leon took over ten minutes to clean himself up. He put on clean coveralls, brand new ones, and washed his face and hands with French lavender soap he discovered in his guestroom's marble bath. When he came down into the kitchen, he found that Diamond and Antonia were seated at the kitchen counter waiting for him. He quickly looked around before sitting next to Diamond. The space was so clean and shiny, it hurt his eyes. He'd never seen a kitchen like this, and he realized that he will never again.

"OK, we are all here now. I will tell you what needs to be done. But first, are you hungry? You must be hungry after your flight, no?" Antonia slapped her hands on the counter and got up. "Some panini and espresso?"

"Um, yes ma'am!" Leon responded. The woman frightened him.

"I will cook and you look over the list, it's on the counter." Antonia removed her suit jacket before starting to zip through the kitchen getting her ingredients. The men were shocked to see what she wore under the jacket. She was packing, a Glock under each arm. Instead of a shirt, she wore a Kevlar vest, custom made to fit her precisely. In this getup, and with a large chef's knife in her hand, she frightened Leon even more. Diamond was impressed, however.

"Nice getup!" said Diamond to her.

"*Grazie!* Catalina told me to be careful, this is what I do then," said Antonia with a smile. "Did anyone tell you why you're here? You look confused."

"No, ma'am. Just to get our butts over here. Oh, Leon has to take something to Miami. Do you know why Miami?"

"Miami is the fastest way out for her," she answered without too many details while slicing crispy ciabatta bread into thick slices.

"I need to shut down the house. You will help me," she

continued. "Someone will be coming tomorrow morning to pack up the art, you will make sure they're quiet and fast. I don't know how to get the rest out. The vault... I do not know what to do with vault," Antonia shrugged her shoulders before placing a couple of assembled paninis into the press. The oiled bread sizzled when it hit the hot metal.

"Do you know what those art trucks look like?" asked Leon. "We can get one just like it and I will take it to Miami with what's in the vault. I have a feeling I would have to drive there anyway."

"OK, I like that," replied Antonia and gave Leon a smile. She then plated their food and poured the espresso into tiny white cups on pale blue saucers, before sitting down to eat next to Diamond. The men dove into their paninis.

Meal break over, Antonia checked the security system before taking the men downstairs to see the vault. Never fully trusting anyone but Catalina, Antonia removed all the cash and jewelry right after Catalina told her that she'd be sending someone over to lend a hand. Antonia left a couple of stacks several inches tall of 'working capital' in her bedroom and stashed the coins and the recently acquired Fabergé egg inside a specially designed bust of a Roman god. The bust was a really good copy of an original piece from Capo's house but with an internal compartment for smuggling precious items. She hadn't slowed down since her phone conversation with Catalina, and Antonia had a feeling the next time she'll be able to sleep would be in Catalina's new Sicilian villa.

The trio ascended down into the basement and almost immediately came face to face with the vault. Leon thought it was going to be just a large metal box bolted to the middle of the floor, but the real thing was the size of a room. They stood in front of a large metal door with a retinal scanner next to a wheel that opened the door. Metal walls extended to either side of the door and floor to ceiling. Antonia came up to the scanner and leaned in. Her eyes were scanned, and there was a sound of metal moving within metal. She spun the wheel clock-wise and the door hissed open.

"Gentlemen, please come in," she addressed her two companions and pulled the door open.

The inside was a large room, instantly lit. All four walls were covered with cubbies and slots designed to hold various weaponry. Not every slot was full, less than half, but there still was enough to outfit a small army. In a far right corner was a collection of various briefcases, golf bags and luggage. The middle was occupied by military-grade safes, although they were all open and empty now. Leon let out a small whistle.

"Wow! This is…" he slowly let out.

"Like one of our product storage rooms," Diamond finished Leon's sentence.

"I do not know what she wants to use. Do you know?" Antonia asked the men. "We can use that luggage to pack up the weapons. It is designed to transport guns on commercial flights undetected, although it is getting harder to do now. She started to arm herself on location now. All this is extra, I do not know why she still has it," commented Antonia and waved her hand around the room. "It should all go back to Eddie."

"I think Tyrone might know what she needs. I'll call him," volunteered Diamond and pulled out his phone.

"No signal here, go upstairs," said Antonia and pointed toward the door. Diamond left the vault. She followed him walking up the stairs with her eyes, noting to herself that the man was exceptionally built and attractive.

"It looks like there are guns missing," inquired Leon after examining closely the empty slots. The small scratches left behind indicated that at one time they held something.

"When she does a job, she only uses a weapon once, then gets rid of it right away. When I came here five years ago, this room was almost full," replied Antonia, then waited to see Leon's reaction as he looked around the room. His lips were moving, he was quietly counting the empty slots.

"What's her body count? Heard she doesn't get out of bed for less than a rock."

"You really want to know?" Antonia raised an eyebrow, and folded her arms on her chest.

"Hm, yes, I do. Diamond popped two guys in my presence that were badmouthing her, I think I earned the right," responded Leon.

"Tell you what, you help me pack everything up and I will tell you once I'm on the plane out of here. Capisce? Oh, and she does get out of bed for less than million. But not less than 500,000. But you keep that to yourself."

"Deal! And I will. Don't want to catch a bullet between my eyes."

"OK... What did you find out?" she turned toward the door and startled Diamond who was just about to walk in with her question. Leon himself did not hear or see him go down the stairs, 'this woman must have ears on the back her head' he thought.

"Tyrone told me she only wants her Barrett M82 and all the rounds. Everything else gets locked in here with the intruder alarm on. He said you know what that means," Diamond addressed Antonia. " He also told me to make sure we don't forget her shoes, said that no one wants to be explaining to her why her shoes were left behind. Everything else gets put in here."

"Oh, the shoes. It's always about the shoes. OK, Diamond, you get her gun and we two going to go and pack her shoes now. Come on, Leon! We've got a lot to do now," Antonia grabbed Leon by the sleeve of his coverall and dragged him upstairs. Diamond was left alone to ponder how to get the Barrett into their car without anyone noticing.

The shoes took up an entire side of her walk-in closet. There were several rows of comfortable and quiet work shoes, all new since Catalina never used the same pair twice and always disposed of her entire outfit within hours of completing a job. The rest of her quite large collection shared one unique and unforgettable feature: they all had red soles. The shoes stood on the shelves toes in, the red soles in full view. The effect was stunning: rows and rows of red. She must have owned over 500 pairs. Some of them were the same style, but in different colors or materials. There were tiny labels on the shelves with the name of the shoe and the year it came out. Leon wondered if she actually wore all of them, or if this was yet another obsession, like the art. He picked up a pair labeled Big Lips. It was a black leather pump with the thin pointy stiletto heel made out of metal. 'She should keep this one with the work shoes, you could kill with these,' thought Leon. He carefully put the shoes back.

Antonia tugged on Leon's sleeve to set him in motion again. "There is a large storage closet at the end of the hall that has rolls of bubble wrap and large garbage bags. Would you mind getting it?" she asked him.

"You're going to put all this into garbage bags?" Leon looked stunned.

"What? We will wrap each shoe in bubbles. By the time she'll see them again, they will be all in a closet again. She'll never know, and you're not going to tell. Now go!" Antonia made a shoving gesture toward the door. Leon complied.

It took them hours to wrap up each and every shoe and put them all into large black plastic bags. Dawn was rising when they finally finished. There were too many bags, they had to fill both the Range Rover and the Lexus. The original plan of shipping the shoes overnight and having Antonia leave the country by a commercial airline without suspicion was no longer viable, so Diamond begged Tyrone to let the shoes and Antonia leave with one of the cargo planes he was sending out for a delivery. Tyrone still mumbled something about wasting precious fuel for shoes after they hung up, but went ahead with the plan. The plane was in Richmond, they would have to drive down there once finished.

―――――

Palwaukee Airport, Illinois

Catalina was already getting on board when Will pulled up. He got out of his black Range Rover, grabbed his overnight bag, tossed the keys to a guy from Eddie's airport crew and hurried in behind her. As soon as he was inside the cabin, the door closed and the Gulfstream 650 began taxing toward the runway. The two of them were the only passengers. He didn't see the crew.

"Hi, I'm Will," he said and sat into the cream leather seat across her. There was a highly polished mahogany table between them. He tossed his bag on to the starboard side couch covered in large zebra print.

"I'm Catalina. Thank you for coming with me. You didn't have to," she leaned forward and extended her hand. Will gave her a firm shake. He noted that her hand was cool, dry, with long slender fingers. No nail polish, just an elegant diamond and gold ring on her ring finger which Will recognized as a Cartier Trinity ring.

"You can put your bag into the closet," she pointed toward the nose. The Cartier sparkled in the lights.

"Where's the crew?" Will inquired once he stowed away his bag.

"It's just the pilots this time. The less people the better," she replied. Will wondered if she knew about the demise of Tobias and Lamont in her honor. He decided not to ask. The *fasten your seatbelts'* sign lit up and Will sat down and complied. He noticed that she didn't.

They sat across each other, silently, as the plane started its run down the runway. They studied each other for a bit, then Will turned his head toward the window. Catalina kept looking at him. It was dusk, the sky was clear and one could see the Chicago skyline and the deep blue of the lake as soon as the plane lifted off. But Will's mind was on the woman in front of him. He was trying to comprehend how this tall, slender and beautiful woman clad in skinny jeans, ballet flats, a black tank top, and wearing a ring worth over 30 grand could be one of the best assassins in the world. He looked at her again. She looked fragile, a bit funny still wearing those huge Chanel sunglasses even though they were inside a plane with lights dimmed. And then she slowly took the sunglasses off and he saw her eyes. Her cold, steel blue eyes. Her gaze instantly frightened him and sent chills down his spine. At that moment Will understood. *'The eyes are the window to the soul'* he read once, and if this was true then he was looking at an iceberg.

"Heard that Eddie got a bedroom onboard somewhere," said Catalina, bringing Will out of his thoughts back to the present.

"That little room aft. The couch converts into a bed," answered Will and nodded toward the back of the plane.

"Mind if I take a snooze? It's been a long day," she asked.

"Nope, go right ahead," answered Will. He wasn't going to tell her that the only person who ever slept there was Eddie himself. Figured that if she already knew about the bedroom, Eddie would not mind.

She got up from the seat and started to move down the aisle. Will turned his head and watched her. He noticed a pistol sticking out of her jeans waistband, she didn't even bother to pull down her tank top to cover it up. A moment later she disappeared inside the bedroom and Will turned away. He stretched in his seat then sat there for a while before getting up and going forward into the galley to find something to eat. The plane continued to gather altitude and speed on its way to New York.

29

New York City

On the drive into New York City from the airport, Catalina explained to Will how she came to posses the information about the CIA agent they were now after. There was a break-in at her father's home. It appeared that the CIA thought rummaging through their house would be a piece of cake, because Catalina knocked the guy unconscious within five minutes of him entering the house. She complained how her father didn't let her just shoot the intruder, adding that she's "shoot first, ask questions later" kind of a girl. Will found this all very amusing. They were driving yet another black Range Rover, a vehicle of choice for Washington Enterprises. Catalina programmed the GPS, but Will was at the wheel. He drove like someone who spent his entire life in New York, and Catalina found that quite intriguing. She decided to ask him about it later, when they would be sitting in front of Campbell's house for hours with nothing else to do. She munched on Fig Newtons and drank chocolate protein shakes on the way to their destination. They stopped at a Target after they left the airport for some provisions. Will appeared not to be hungry, he spent the entire flight relieving the plane's galley of its contents.

They arrived in NoHo when the action on Bowery Street was still in full swing. Campbell's place was within walking distance on Bond Street. They found the building and then circled around a couple of times before finally snagging a parking spot across the street. The street was devoid of people. Catalina rummaged through her bag she stowed in the back seat and produced a camera with a telescopic lens, a night vision monocular, and a large amount of papers. The papers were dropped on Will's lap.

"This is Campbell's file that I got thanks to Johnny 'the super agent'. His clearance wasn't high enough to get all the juicy bits, but there was enough to find where he's living and some personal preferences... He's on the top floor of that building," she pointed to a brick warehouse-looking structure across the street.

"It looks like newspaper's covering the windows," commented Will looking at the top floor. Catalina nudged his arm and handed him the night vision monocular she'd been looking through. Will tried it out but had a hard time with the instrument.

"I can't see anything with this. There should be a pair of binoculars in the glove compartment. Do you mind?" Catalina opened the glove compartment and found a pair of Leica binoculars and an envelope with an inch of cash. She raised an eyebrow in silent question. "Grease money. The Boss doesn't like surprises, all his cars have that," explained Will.

"What, no gun?" Catalina asked and handed the Leica to Will.

"You're sitting on it. There is a handgun in the seat. I have no clue what kind though, but it supposed to be an automatic. My job is to figure out where to stash it, it's Tyrone's job to supply the weapon," replied Will while continuing to check out the building through the binoculars. Catalina spread her legs and examined her seat. It looked like any other Rover seat. "The top lifts off. Not an easy access, but it's designed for the driver to use. Cops won't find it either," explained Will after noticing her perplexed look.

"Maybe I should bring you my car to modify. This is impressive."

"No problem. I'm sure The Boss won't mind. But he'll charge you," said Will with a smile and returned to his surveillance. "I don't see any lights on in that joint. Maybe he's asleep."

"Then we'll wait 'till morning." Catalina moved the seat back and reclined it. She tried to stretch her legs, but there wasn't enough room.

It was close to three in the morning when they heard some voices. A man and a woman. Catalina shot up in her seat. Will pointed to the corner of the street and grabbed the camera to snap some shots. A drunk couple was walking in the middle of the street, supporting each other. The woman was swinging her purse in large circles. The man's shirt was untucked, he was trying to hold the woman upright. She was loud, saying something about a band they just heard and how great they were. The man was trying to shoosh her, but to no avail. They made it to Campbell's building and disappeared inside. Soon, the lights in Campbell's loft went on. Will and Catalina looked at each other. Will handed Catalina the binoculars. She declined it and used the monocular instead.

"It's like looking through a rifle scope. It's what I'm used to," she explained. They both directed their eye pieces toward Campbell's windows. There was a small tear in the paper covering one of the windows, but it wasn't big enough for them to see through. The lights went out after a couple of minutes.

"I bet we both know what they're up to in there, no need for a visual," commented Will.

"Let me see that camera, maybe we got something," said Catalina. She used the camera screen to view the photos. "Too dark, can't see his face. All I can figure out is his height and build. I think that's our guy. We'll have to get him tomorrow... Woman's tall and thin... Where did they hook up?"

"Must be around here somewhere. She said something about a band. There is The Bowery Electric, they always have something going on. Maybe that's the place. Should I take a walk over there and check it out? Those two are not going anywhere, but you probably want to stick around in case they're early risers as well. Plus, I don't want to lose this spot."

"Yeah, go. See if you can find out if the guy's a regular. That might come really handy." She turned off the dome light so Will could slip out without drawing any attention to them.

Half an hour passed before Will returned. He was shaking his head a little and smiling. Catalina noted that he was irresistibly handsome when he smiled. Will got into the car, chuckling.

"What's so funny?" inquired Catalina.

"You're not gonna believe this. Those two did come from The Bowery Electric. Muscle on the door got really friendly for a price, said our guy is a regular. Comes in every night between midnight and two. Has a Grey Goose on the rocks, stays no more than an hour and almost always leaves with a woman. A different woman every time," explained Will and shook his head.

"Did your new friend tell you how he likes his women?"

"Yeah. Young model types. Gullible. He tells them some bullshit story that they eat all up and gets them into his bed... Why's the interest?" Will raised an eyebrow and looked into her eyes. Her eyes shimmered with the same bone-chilling ice he saw on the plane, but her mouth had a mischievous grin.

"Well, sleeping in the car's kind of uncomfortable, I wouldn't mind a warm bed," said Catalina and winked. While Will was away, she decided to sleep with Agent Campbell. Sometimes she liked playing with fire.

"You're not going to kill him in his sleep are you?" asked Will suspiciously. He wouldn't put it past her.

"Nah. I'll just play with him a little. Clone his phone while I'm at it, it might come in handy," answered Catalina. "Hey, let's take a little ride, there are a couple of things I'm going to need in the morning."

"OK," Will shrugged his shoulders and started the car. "Where to?"

"Brooklyn."

30

Brooklyn Heights, New York

Ari Abramowitz was woken up by the loud sound of a car idling in front of his building. He slowly got out of bed, as not to wake his wife, and walked over to the window to take a peek. A black Range Rover was sitting in front of the building, waiting for someone. Then he heard the door of the apartment below him slam shut. The apartment belonged to his elusive tenant, Lina Benn. 'She's back!' he thought as he watched her exit the building and get into the car. The car took off and disappeared down the street. Ari wondered if he should wake his wife to tell her the news. He decided against it, he wasn't sure if the girl would come back again in the morning.

Catalina rented a small apartment from the Abramowitzes in Brooklyn Heights right out of college, eleven years ago, under the alias of Lina Benn. It was her only place in the States, until she got the house in DC. Ari and Ruth were a pleasant old Jewish couple with no children of their own. They treated their tenants with respect and kept the building in great shape. One day Ari was working on her sink and Catalina noticed a crude vertical scar on the inside of his left arm. She has seen scars like that before on older people in Israel. She realized that Ari was a Holocaust survivor.

The apartment was small, but at 400 square feet was considered a palace by New York standards. It was on a third floor of a four-story building. It had a main room, a small bedroom just big enough for a bed and a dressing table, a tiny kitchen and even tinier bathroom. The kitchen window led to a fire escape and the bedroom closet was quite large, two features Catalina liked best. Her furniture was minimal, but extremely comfortable. She kept some of her clothes and a go bag in the bedroom. She paid rent for a full year in advance, and her only utility, electric, was withdrawn automatically from a bank account. The Abramowitzes had no complaints about her, she was clean, quiet, never complained, never brought anyone home, and most of the time was never there. She was the prefect tenant, and they were the perfect landlords. Until one afternoon.

Catalina had been renting for over three years now, when Ruth came home from grocery shopping and announced to Ari that Lina Benn just received a delivery of a large heavy box from a hunting store. Ruth was wondering what would a girl need from a hunting store. Ari asked her how did she know that it was heavy. Ruth replied that it took two guys to carry and they barely managed getting it up to the third floor. She spent the rest of the afternoon looking out their windows that faced the front of the building. She saw Lina leave and then arrive by cab several hours later with a couple of black duffel bags. The bags also looked heavy. In the evening, when Ruth noticed that Lina left the apartment again, she nagged Ari into sneaking into Lina's apartment and seeing what the delivery was. He reluctantly agreed, just to stop her from nagging.

He was in Lina Benn's apartment only once before, to repair a leaky sink. He noted then how clean and organized the place was. It was not the case when he snuck into the apartment that evening. Clothes were everywhere, it looked like her closet exploded. Ari followed the mayhem into the bedroom. It was the same situation there, with clothes all over the bed. He noted a large stack of shoe boxes next to the dresser, they were all taupe in color, with labels facing out. He didn't recognize the brand, but he noticed the price of one of the pairs. It was close to a thousand dollars. She paid a thousand dollars for one pair of shoes!

He turned his attention to the closet and discovered why all the clothes were strewn everywhere. A half of the closet was occupied by a gun safe. That must have been the delivery from a hunting store Ruth was talking about. Ari took a step back. He looked around the apartment again, but with different perspective now. He noticed that most clothes were high-end designers a girl her age would not be able to afford yet; he noticed metal suitcases in the living room; the fact that she had no regular phone, but there were several cell phones on her dresser. There was a small gold cross hanging above her bed and a statue of the Virgin Mary on her tiny nightstand. He peeked into her medicine cabinet and saw lots of cases for contact lenses. He opened the window to the fire escape and noted that the window was well lubricated and moved smoothly and with no sound. He did not do that. He closed the window and cautiously exited the apartment. He didn't tell Ruth about what he found, instead he told her that the box must've been furniture, she had a new chair. He spent that night sitting by the window waiting for his tenant to come back home. But she didn't return until the following afternoon.

Ari fought the Nazis and survived the concentration camps. He was not afraid of some girl with a suspicious job. He just didn't want it to be drugs. He decided to confront her after dinner, when Ruth would leave to play pinochle.

"Who are you?" asked Ari as soon as his tenant opened her door. She looked at him for a while, then invited him in. They stood in the middle of the room, sizing each other up, before either of them spoke. Ari noted that she had changed since he last saw her up close: she was much thinner—lost her baby fat—which made her breasts larger, and her hair was much longer. But the biggest change was in her eyes. Her gaze would always burrow right through a person, but now her eyes were ice cold, untrusting and unforgiving. "I want to know who you are," he said again.

"Why?" she asked looking deep into him.

"Is it drugs? You can't live here if it's drugs," replied Ari and looked around a bit. The place looked cleaner, he interrupted her organizing.

"It's not drugs."

"Then what do you do? Who are you?"

"I'm a freelancer. I followed my father into the family business," she responded and cocked her head to the side. Even though Ari was a small man, he straightened his back and stuck out his chest. She looked him up and down then motioned for him to sit down on the couch before plopping into the chair across.

"Are you Catholic?" he asked. Catalina found the question odd.

"Well, I'm Italian, so yes."

Ari sat on the couch for a bit. Italian, family business... Mafia? "What is your real name?"

"You know my name."

"No, I don't think it is your real name. I have seen too much to know that it is not your real name. It doesn't fit you. Not any more."

"Tell me about your tattoo on your arm, the one you removed. Did you escape, is that why you cut it out?" She nodded toward his left arm. Ari looked stunned by the question. He had a long sleeve shirt on, how did she know about the scar? "I saw it when you fixed my sink that one time. Ruth has it too, but it's faded by now and she covers it up with make-up," she continued, as if she read his mind.

And so Ari told her his life story. He didn't get into all the details, it was still too painful. She made tea at some point and offered him some pastries. He noticed that there was life in her cold eyes after all, he saw them flash with rage several times during his story. She moved to sit on the couch next to him, and when he was finished she squeezed his hand.

She looked him in the eyes again, as if searching for something.

"My real name is Catalina Benedetto. I kill people for a living. When I was 17, I defended my father's honor and then I followed him into the business. We're both part of a Sicilian Cosa Nostra, but don't just work for them. I never worked inside this country. Does that answer all your questions?" She released his hand.

"Yes. I just wanted to know," replied Ari. He was surprised at her sudden disclosure but did not find the truth shocking. At that moment he also realized that she already knew he would take her secrets to the grave. "You can stay here, we won't bother you." Ari stood up to leave. She walked him to the door. At the door he turned to face her, a question on his lips. He scratched the scar on his arm, afraid to ask. Catalina answered anyway.

"Once, there was an old Nazi Colonel hiding in South America. He got what he deserved."

"Thank you," said Ari and left the apartment.

Two days later, Ari came over again, this time with a couple of keys. One was for a basement storage space.

Another one was for the back door to the alley. He told her that she could use the storage space for her gear and that the alley access would allow her to be a lot more discreet. She took the keys without a word and nodded in thanks.

So now, after being absent for almost a year and a half, she was back again. Ari was wondering who was in the car with her, in the past she was always alone. About a month ago she renewed her lease, by mail, for another year and paid the entire year's worth of rent in advance as usual. To Ari, every lease renewal was a sign that she was still alive. Not that he approved of her line of work, but every week he asked God to forgive her.

————

On the way to Brooklyn, Catalina explained that they would need two cars to tail the CIA agent in the morning. She reasoned that most likely he would be taking a non-direct route to his office, making sure no one would tail him. That surprised Will, who would want to tail a CIA agent on his own soil? "People like us," and "that's how they're trained to live" was Catalina's response. Her plan was to pass him off to each other in an attempt not to get caught. She said she's got spare set of plates in her place in Brooklyn, and they can unload their luggage there as well, it was a place she intended to return to in the afternoon for a nap.

The plates were New Jersey. She said they were clean and would do for a day. They drove around the neighborhood a bit, before finding a car that suited their needs. It was a Ford Focus, a couple of years old. It was black, needed a wash, and had scratches on both bumpers. "That's New York drivers for you," commented Catalina. Will was to take the Ford and Catalina would drive the Range Rover. It was decided that—if anything happens—it would be a lot easier for him, being a car mechanic, to ditch the Focus and get a new ride rather than for Catalina. They circled the block one more time, then split up, agreeing to meet up on Campbell's street.

She got lucky. The same spot they were in during the night was still available. Will managed to grab one further down and across the street. Besides plates, Catalina grabbed her communications gear from Brooklyn, they were both now wired so they could talk to each other on the move. They didn't have to wait too long: the woman emerged first, still wearing the clothes from last night, hair all in disarray. She came out of the building and turned right, then grabbed a cab on the corner of the street. The man emerged an hour later.

He was clean-shaven, wearing a gray suit, white shirt unbuttoned at the collar and a navy striped tie that he didn't bother to tie. He stopped in front of the building door, looked both ways, stood there for a bit, then started to cross the street. Catalina ducked inside her car. He stepped on the sidewalk in front of the Rover, and turned to take a brief look at the car. Then he started walking toward Lafayette Street.

"Shit! He's going opposite way of traffic! I'll have to do this on foot! See if you can grab his face with the camera, I want to take a closer look," said Catalina and got out of the car as quietly as she could. She waited for a couple of people to walk down the street, then fell in behind them. Her prey was tall, it was easy to pick him out above average people's heads. She slouched, her own height also made her an easy target.

"Got his face. I just sent you the photo. You want me to stay or try to turn around?" asked Will.

"Stay. I want to see what he's up to." Catalina felt the vibe of her phone in her jean pocket. She pulled it out and pretended to make a call. Suddenly, her target turned around and she quickly ducked into a doorway. She took a second there to look at the photo Will sent her. They were on the right track. The man she was following was in fact Agent Jim Campbell. Suddenly, she recognized his face as the man who almost botched up her African job five years ago.

Her mark reached Lafayette Street and turned left. She followed him down to East Houston Street. He took his time, stopping to look at store windows, buying a paper from a box by the curb, every time looking around to see if anyone would stand out. Catalina was one step ahead of him at this cat and mouse game: she would duck or hide just a moment before. She was trained even better than he was, he never made her. He reached East Houston, crossed it and turned left again.

"The little shit's going in circles. Get out, I bet you he's going to grab a cab any moment. You can pick him up on Bowery," she instructed Will. Sure enough, Campbell suddenly stepped off the sidewalk and flagged a cab passing by. Before jumping in, he quickly looked around, but Catalina already ducked behind a crowd of people. Again, he didn't notice her. She watched the cab turn right on Bowery, told Will the cab's plates, and went back to her car.

"Tail him for a bit to get direction. If he's going toward Downtown, then drop him and come back. I know where the CIA offices are Downtown, no need to waste energy on that one," she told Will when she reached the car. "Dump the car before you return, we won't need it."

Will was back within half an hour. He joined Catalina back in the Range Rover. She was sitting in the passenger's seat looking over the printouts of Campbell's dossier. Will told her that he dumped the car after wiping off his prints from the inside. He left the plates, they won't lead to anyone anyway.

"What's up?" He nodded toward the dossier spread all over her lap.

"I know him. I didn't connect all the dots first, plus in his file photo he's so much younger, but after I saw the photo you sent me it all clicked. I better not get caught, he's got a bone to pick with me."

"Why?" Will was curious. He noted that Catalina had a strange look on her face: satisfaction mixed with amusement. He got the feeling she was really enjoying the fact that Agent Campbell was the mouse in her somewhat twisted game.

"Did you read the part how he's lost his kidney after being injured in a firefight?"

"Yeah... So?" Will's eyes narrowed a bit when he looked at her. But he couldn't read her.

"I gave him that injury. He was in my way." She answered matter-of-factly and started gathering her papers. "He aged a lot in five years. Must be the desk job."

"Or the bullets. Was that in Africa?"

"Yeah, CIA had one agenda, my client had another. I'm better." With that comment she shoved the pages into the glove compartment and the conversation was over.

"So, what's next now?" asked Will to change subjects. He was certain that she had something else up her sleeve.

"Ever broke into someone's place before?" she asked.

"Yeah, why?"

"Because we're going to break into his."

"Payback for your father's place?"

"Something like that. Come on," said Catalina with a wink. She reached back, grabbed a black nylon Prada crossbody bag from back seat, something else she picked in her Brooklyn apartment, and got out of the car. Will silently followed.

One of Campbell's neighbors happened to be a fashion photographer. Catalina recognized the name on the entrance directory which she checked out earlier on the way back to the car. They hung out by the front door until a male tenant opened the door to leave. They giggled and slipped inside saying something about a photo shoot. The man didn't give them a second look, models came into this building all the time.

They rode the old freight elevator with huge heavy wood doors, the only one in the building, to the top floor. They walked out into what could potentially be a very nice foyer: a nice size square space with a window facing the street and a large steel door facing the elevator. The space was empty, except for some old newspapers still in their plastic sleeves piled into a corner by the window. Catalina handed Will a pair of rubber gloves she pulled out of her Prada bag. He noted that she only got out one pair.

"Don't you need a pair?" he asked while trying to get the gloves on.

"I don't leave prints. I have none to leave," she answered while carefully examining the big steel door they were about to unlock. "I don't see any booby traps but let's take it slow anyway." She got out an electric lockpicking gun from her bag and bent down to examine the lock.

"Wait, what do you mean you have no prints to leave?"

"See?" she stuck the tips of her fingers under Will's nose. They were unnaturally smooth. "No prints. I had them removed."

"How?"

"Acid."

"Did it hurt?"

"Oh yeah…" And with that comment she inserted the

gun and the torsion wrench into the lock and after a couple of seconds cracked it open. "Very strange... Checks for tails on the street, yet doesn't use security measures for his own home."

"I gotta get one of those," Will commented. He slowly pushed the door ajar with his gloved hand while Catalina was putting away her tools.

They stood in the door jam, taking in the sight. Campbell's place was not what Catalina expected. Will cringed his face in obvious disapproval. In his opinion, a person should always take care of one's abode, Will's own impeccably clean condo was clad in warm mahogany, whiskey leather and chrome. Catalina's facial expression matched Will's. They stood there for a bit taking in the sight of a large almost empty space with a huge mattress in the middle surrounded by high-end media equipment. The bed was unmade and the place was messy.

"So... This is how the other half lives... Don't touch anything, I just need to get the layout and find all points of exit... This is gross," she said and cautiously stepped inside. The board under her foot creaked. They slowly walked inside and spread out, following along opposite walls. The floor kept creaking under almost every step.

"You sure you want to get into that bed? I doubt he washed the sheets recently. Or ever." Will was standing by the bed. Catalina came over to take a look. The sheets indeed looked like they haven't been washed in a while. There was an empty bottle of wine by the bed and a couple of glasses. She looked around and saw a desk by the windows. Catalina walked over to check it out. Will moved into the kitchen to check out the contents of the fridge.

"Counter looks clean, maybe you can use that instead of the bed. Then just knock him out and leave right after," he commented to Catalina after giving the kitchen a quick look on the way to the refrigerator. She snorted in response.

There was yesterday's mail on the desk. She carefully looked through it. A couple of bills and what looked like a bank statement. She mentally noted the bank in case she felt like snooping around Agent Campbell's financial matters. There was a fine layer of dust on the desk, she noted some smudges that might have been made by a fingers grabbing something off the desk. 'Maybe that's where he tosses he keys and phone... Where does he keep his gun then?' Catalina thought. She looked around the place. There was no safe around. 'Probably sleeps with it, like I do,' she decided.

"Hey, you've got to see this! Looks like he's got the upstairs too!" Will called out to her from a metal staircase in the corner by the kitchen and disappeared up the stairs. Catalina followed.

She let out a quiet whistle when she stepped outside on Campbell's roof terrace. This space was like a whole different world of the one below. Will stood with his jaw open in awe. Catalina took a long and slow look around. Breathtaking. She noted the rich wood, the lattice panels providing privacy, the multitude of seating areas with thick wide cushions covered in cobalt blue fabric with white piping, the covered cooking area full of stainless steel, and the covered hot tub. She walked over to take a closer look at the tub.

Catalina lifted up the cover a little to peak inside. Unlike the bed downstairs, the tub was clean and full of sparkling water with tons of air jets lining the walls. She lowered back the cover and looked around.

"Here, we'll spend the night here," she informed Will.

"I don't think he brings just anyone here," responded Will. He walked over to Catalina after poking around in the outdoor kitchen.

"How do you know?"

"Well, see all the little torches and the strings of lights everywhere? There is a huge control panel in the kitchen that operates all of that. I bet you there are more twinkling lights here than the Rockefeller Center Christmas tree. All that light… if it was on last night we would've seen it from the street. But we didn't. And it was a perfect night to be outside. He must be selective."

"He'll just have to make an exception," she replied with a shrug. "Let's get out of here, I need a nap."

31

Brooklyn Heights

"Ari, that car is back!" yelled Ruth from her perch by the window. The short but plump white-haired woman had been camped out there since morning, when Ari couldn't hold it in any longer and told her that their very special tenant made an appearance last night. "I knew she would come back!"

"Don't let her see you snooping! Get away from that window!" yelled Ari back. But Ruth was already in the kitchen, banging the stove door and checking on steaming pots and pans filled with delicious food. She pulled out bowls and containers and started ladling things out.

"She must be hungry, you go and take that to her!" Ruth instructed Ari. "I made all her favorites!"

"Aha! I knew it! I knew the brisket was not for me!" Ari exclaimed and shook his index finder into the air. He looked with longing as juicy pieces of brisket and steaming glossy vegetables disappeared inside a large white serving bowl. Huge matzo balls were then placed into a large jar and piping hot soup poured over them. Ruth even wrapped up some thick slices of bread from a Jewish bakery.

"Ruth, she's a *shiksa!* But you still cook her Kosher food, oy!" Ari said while trying to steal a carrot from the white bowl, only to get a slap on the wrist from Ruth.

"It's ready! Just take this down to her, and don't eat it on the way!" ordered Ruth. She had everything stacked on a large wooden tray, ready for Ari to carry this downstairs. He wondered if he's going to make it down without dropping the heavy tray.

"At least open the door!" he shot back and picked up the tray.

His tenant finally opened the door after third knock. She had her left hand on the doorknob and her right behind her back. Upon seeing Ari, she smiled and opened the door wide. Ari walked inside and almost bumped into a large tall black man. The man took the tray from Ari without a word and put in on the small dining table.

"I told you there'll be food," said Catalina to the black giant. "Ari, this is my associate. His name is Will, but you're going to forget it once we'll leave."

"Already forgotten," replied Ari. He looked her up and down, something he did every time she came back. This time she looked the same. Her right hand was now by her side, holding a handgun that she was hiding behind her back when she answered the door. She put it on the table, next to the food. "Are you in trouble?" he asked her.

"Nothing I can't handle. Thank you for the food, Ari. I will bring the dishes back once we're done." It was a dismissal, she didn't want to discuss anything right now. Ari nodded and left.

"Hope you don't have aversion to Kosher, because this is what this is," she informed Will while taking the lids off the containers. "Ruth always makes me food when I come back here. Dishes are in the cupboard above the sink, utensils in the drawer next to the dishwasher."

"It smells delicious, I'm starving!" replied Will and went to rummage through the cupboards.

They ate in silence. And they finished it all. Will even wiped the bottom of the white bowl with his bread to get the last of the yummy bits. Catalina leaned back and patted her stomach.

"Ahh, I'm so full! Would you mind putting the plates into the dishwasher while I take the tray back up? Then it's nap time until about 8 p.m."

"No problem. I've got a call to make before that though. What car did you say you wanted?" Will was referring back to the conversation they had on the ride over here. Catalina asked if Will could get her a flashy sports car for the night. Will replied that he knew someone with a chop shop that could help in that department.

"Surprise me. I can drive anything at this point," she said with a smile. Eyes stayed ice cold. Will was getting used to it by now: smiles and humor, but it was all surface deep. He only saw a flicker of warmth when Ari walked in. He watched her gather up the serve dishes and put them back on the tray. Before taking the tray upstairs she picked up her phone and shoved into the back pocket of her jeans. She left her gun sitting on the table.

"I have a favor to ask you," was the first thing out of her mouth when Ari opened his door. Ruth was hovering behind him. Catalina stepped inside and walked over to the kitchen to put the tray on the counter. "Everything was delicious, as always, thank you Ruth, you always take care of me," was the other thing she said.

"What kind of favor?" asked Ari.

"I have a brother and a baby niece. He's not involved in the business," she said as if reading Ari's mind. "If one day he shows up at your doorstep, then things went bad and I'm gone. Please take care of him. I never changed the locks on the storage space you gave me, there are things in there that will help him. I'll show you what he looks like," she pulled her phone out of her back pocket flipped through some screens and then handed it to Ari. Ruth came over to take a look as well. They took a good look at a photo of a handsome man with dark hair holding a pudgy giggling baby. Ruth pressed her hand to her heart.

"Your niece is beautiful. Where is the mother?" asked Ruth.

"No mother. Actually, he could use a woman in his life. Perhaps a nice Jewish girl?" said Catalina to Ruth and winked. She knew if Mark landed in here, he wasn't getting out. And it suited her just fine.

"We will take care of them, I give you my word," said Ari and looked into Catalina's eyes. She nodded her head and took back her phone.

"Thank you!" She bent down to first embrace Ari, then Ruth. After rather a long embrace with Ruth, she straightened and turned to leave. Ari and Ruth both stared at the door once it closed behind her for a while, before Ruth turned on her heel and went into the kitchen to busy herself with the dishes. Ari went to sit in his favorite chair and think.

"You can sleep on the couch if you want. There are extra blankets and pillows in the cabinet below the TV," said Catalina to Will as soon as she got back to the apartment. "I'm off to take a nap."

"Car's going to be ready at 10," informed Will. "It's clean, but they need it back in the morning. I think you're going to like it."

"Do I get a clue on what it is? So I can dress appropriately?"

"It's various shades of black, and it's really fast. Does that help?"

"Yes it does. I'm off to bed now. See you in a few hours," said Catalina and went into her bedroom. Will heard a mattress creak a bit a minute later.

Unlike Catalina, who slept the sleep of the dead, Will could not fall asleep. At all. Not that the couch was uncomfortable, on the contrary it was really soft and opened up to a queen sleeper, and the sheets and pillows Will got out were freshly pressed and smelled of lavender. He even tried the chamomile tea that he found in one of kitchen cupboards. But his mind just would not stop. He kept thinking about Catalina. He was trying to figure her out but couldn't. While she was upstairs, Will managed to call Tyrone and found out that Diamond and Leon were put to work wrapping up expensive footwear in Catalina's fancy home in DC. Yet this apartment was anything but luxurious. It was very clean and organized, the only luxuries he found were in the bedroom when he sneaked a quick peek. The closet was stuffed with designer clothes, she had several real hair wigs. He wondered where the weapons were, he didn't see any anywhere. While getting out the linens, he discovered several movies in foreign languages with no subtitles. That made Will conclude that she spoke more than just English and Italian. He figured she must also be fluent in French, Spanish and German. The profile of Catalina he was slowly assembling in his mind was painting a quite disturbing picture: a smart beautiful woman that enjoyed killing people and was brilliant at it. And those cold eyes of hers, Will shivered every time he thought of them. They were beautiful, yes, but so cold… He wondered if they will stay cold tonight, while she's seducing Agent Campbell. 'She's probably going to fake the whole thing anyway, make him feel like he's God's gift to women,' thought Will. He smirked, then took a deep breath and closed his eyes. His mind finally calmed down and he was able to fall asleep.

———

SAD, New York

It was late afternoon. Agent Campbell spent his entire morning with 'the man upstairs' as he referred to his superiors. McCarthy spent that time sitting in Campbell's office reheating the electric teapot. He figured that his boss would need a hot cup of tea as soon as the meeting was over. Another hour, another teapot gone cold before Campbell burst through the door and threw his jacket against the wall.

"Tea!"

"Yes! Sir! Making it right now! Sir!" McCarthy jumped up in front of the teapot. Less than a minute later, a steaming cup of Earl Gray was put into Campbell's outstretched and waiting hand. He took a long sip, followed by a deep breath.

"Op. room! Now! Get everyone in there!" snapped Campbell and stormed out of his office with his teapot in the direction of the op. room. McCarthy followed after him, while frantically texting the team to report in immediately.

"Gentlemen, Operation Darwin is no longer active. We have a new objective," Agent Campbell addressed to his small staff. "McCarthy, screens please!" he ordered.

The two large plasma TVs on their walls lit up with images of Gerald Goldstein and the mystery woman from Zurich.

"This is your new objective! You have to find out what Goldstein was up to for the past 11 years and if she," he pointed to the woman's image, " has any connection to him."

"Agent Campbell, sir? What are our exact orders?" asked Peter Gruber, one of the members of the team. Peter was young, short, thin, and pale. And always nervous.

Campbell still could not figure out how this guy made it into CIA. Or why would a guy with a degree from MIT keep asking mundane questions.

"This!" Campbell leapt to the TV displaying the woman from Zurich. "This! We're after this woman!" he banged on the screen with his open palm. "She's a mechanic, a really good one because she seemed to have eluded us for quite a while. We want to get her! Is that clear now?" he barked at Gruber. The young man shrunk into his seat. "Any more questions?" Campbell looked around the room, nostrils flaring. Silence.

"I can take the lead on this one, sir!" volunteered McCarthy.

"Good!" replied Campbell and started walking toward the door. "Walk with me," Campbell asked McCarthy and opened the door to let him come out into the hall first. The door hissed closed behind them.

Campbell was moving so swiftly down the hall that McCarthy almost had to break into a jog in order to keep up with his boss's long stride. He noticed that they were not walking toward Campbell's office.

"That Gruber guy, what's his name?" asked Campbell suddenly.

"Peter," replied McCarthy.

"Replace him. No intuition whatsoever." It was not a request.

"No problem, sir!" answered McCarthy. However, finding another person for Campbell's team would be a challenge, he was hard to work for and was not allowed to have women on his team anymore since he had a tendency to bed them all.

"Are you leaving the building, sir?" inquired McCarthy after a minute.

"Yep. I'm going home to do some laundry. I noticed

last night that my sheets smell." Campbell grimaced.

"Maybe you should purchase a clean set instead, sir. I prefer Calvin Klein myself."

"What does your girlfriend prefer?"

"Same thing, sir. She bought them."

Chapter 32

Washington, DC

It was close to dinnertime when they finally finished with the house and took off for Richmond. They took both cars. Antonia was exhausted but was trying not to show it. It was quite complicated to close up a house that someone lived in for five years overnight. Babinsky, concerned and scared, showed up first thing in the morning with three trucks and six guys to take all the art along with the Chihuly chandelier from the dining room. The bare electrical wires were left dangling above the table, a stark contrast to the beautiful furniture. Antonia asked the men to help her scrub every surface so no fingerprints would be left behind. The vault was locked and set to self-destruct, should anyone other than Catalina open it. Before setting the sequence, Antonia explained to the men that the vault's walls were loaded with explosives. Upon hearing this, Leon started to itch to get out of the house as soon as possible. He did not envy Diamond who would have to return—once Antonia was in the air—to monitor the security in case anyone unwanted showed up. He was to contain himself to the surveillance room and the kitchen, and not to leave any prints.

Three hours later Antonia was finally getting onboard Washington Enterprises C130 Hercules cargo plane, bags of shoes in tow, the Roman god bust in her arms. Antonia wondered how exactly Eddie obtained such a plane: it looked as if it was used previously by the military. This was not going to be a direct flight to Sicily, they were making a couple of stops on the way. But the crew was informed that this unexpected passenger had direct ties to The Boss so they made her as comfortable as possible. Diamond and Leon stepped onboard for a moment to say good-bye. Diamond promised to take care of the house and eat everything in the refrigerators, Antonia was upset about leaving behind her lasagnas; Leon shyly shook her hand. She pulled him into an embrace and whispered something into his ear. His face flashed with surprise that did not go unnoticed by Diamond. He decided to ask him about it once the plane taxied away.

The men stood by the cars, as the heavy cargo plane gained speed down the runway and finally took off. Leon was heading to Miami to deliver the Barrett. Diamond was heading back to DC. They said their customary goodbyes, Diamond suggesting Leon take a rest on the road, neither man slept since they landed the day before. Before Leon got in the Range Rover, Diamond asked:

"What did she whisper to you? Was she hot for you or something?"

"When we were looking at the vault, I asked her what Catalina's number was," answered Leon and started the engine.

"Number? As in people she whacked?"

"Yep."

"Did she tell you?"

"Yep."

"Are you going to share?"

"Nope."

"Come on, man! Don't you think I earned the right to know?" Diamond looked like he was about to beg.

"You did, but I won't. We should not know this." Leon started to close the car door, but Diamond grabbed it. They stared at each other for a moment, then Diamond released the door. It closed with a dull thud and Leon drove off. Diamond stood there for a bit, looking at the rapidly disappearing the taillights of the Rover, and shaking his head. Then he got into the Lexus.

————

Brooklyn Heights

Catalina left the bedroom door open as she started getting ready for her 'big night' as she called it. Will was reclining in the chair by the small dining table and had a view straight into the bedroom. They just finished yet another feast brought down by Ari, this time of roasted chicken and herbed potatoes, and he could not move. He watched Catalina rummage through her closet. She finally popped out into the living room and held up two dresses for Will to choose from. One was an Emilio Pucci gold and turquoise sequined number with open back and not much of a skirt. Another was made of a navy jersey, knee length with a deep cowl neck. There was no back. Will chose the navy one. It wasn't much on the hanger, but he sensed that the dress would be a knockout once on. Catalina went back into the bedroom, tossed the Pucci on her bed but gently hung up the navy jersey. She then dove back into the closet, and Will heard shoeboxes moving around.

"What about a nude shoe?" she called out to Will.

"Show me!" he requested. Will preferred women who were impeccably put together and always offered his opinion on wardrobe matters when asked, even though sometimes his honesty was not appreciated. Catalina stuck out her arm holding a pair of patent leather nude peep-toe pumps. "Oh, that's really nice. I think that would be great! You don't want to look like you're out on the prowl, even though you are out on the prowl," said Will in approval.

With dress and shoes picked out, Catalina sat down in front of her dressing table and started getting ready. She was in her underwear but left the bedroom door open—Will's presence did not bother her. The process of getting made up was a lot more involved than Will anticipated. She pulled up hair and hid it under what Will could only describe as a nylon sock. Will realized that she was planning on wearing a wig. The wig she chose was a short red bob. At some point Catalina noticed Will looking and motioned him to come into the bedroom with her index finger. Will came over and perched himself on her bed. Her dressing table was covered with various makeup and hair items. Catalina checked out the wig before starting to put it on.

"I don't want to leave any of my own hair behind tonight," she explained to Will.

"Won't he notice that it's a wig?"

"No, because I know how to put it on correctly. When I first moved in here, I would spend a lot of time hanging out in drag clubs on Friday nights. Young career girls in New York are supposed to go out on Friday nights. I didn't want to make friends and I didn't want to be hit on, so I would go to drag clubs. No one bothered me there. After a while the queens befriended me and would invite me backstage. So I asked them to teach me how to put on a wig properly. They're real hair, hand-made and cost a small fortune." She finished putting the wig on and was now running her fingers through it to make it look a bit messy.

"What if he yanks on your hair in the throws of passion?" asked Will with a smile and carefully touched the hair with his right index finger.

"Oh, it's very secure. This isn't my first time doing this,

this sucker will stay on until I decide to remove it." She replied before popping in a pair of light brown contact lenses into her eyes.

"What about being in that hot tub?"

"It'll be fine. I'm not about to submerge," she replied with a smile. She dusted her face with powder and then started to dig through her eye shadows. Will sat back down on his perch to watch as she expertly applied, blended, and lined using various brushes and liners. To a man who never watched a woman put on her makeup this was quite a show. Will noticed that all her makeup and brushes were Chanel. A touch of mascara on her long lashes, a swipe of soft nude gloss across her full lips and she was finished.

"Voila!" she turned to Will for an inspection. The result was stunning. Will figured that Agent Campbell would not be able to resist. "Let me just throw the dress on and we can go and get the car." It was a sign of dismissal. Will left his perch and went into the living room to change as well.

Ruth and Ari watched them leave with their luggage from their window. Catalina looked stunning in her back-less dress, nude pumps and a red wig. Her black companion was wearing a plum shirt and fitted dark jeans. Before they got into their car, both looked up at Ari and Ruth and waved goodbye. Then they drove off, picking up speed toward the end of the street.

"She's up to no good in that dress and that hair," said Ruth and closed the curtains. "Do you think she'll come back?" she asked Ari.

"Only God knows that, Ruth. But we will keep her place for her, just in case," replied Ari and put his arms around his wife. She embraced him back. They stood like that, embracing each other, each praying for Catalina's return, for a while. Then Ari let Ruth go and turned to leave the apartment under the pretext that he needed to get the dirty dishes from downstairs. Ruth noticed Ari trying to discretely wipe his eyes with the back of his hand on the way to the door.

33

Clutch. Shift into second with a loud clang. The engine revs up. They drove all the way to the Bronx to get this car. Catalina giggled with delight when Will's friend tossed her the keys to the black pearl Audi R8 5.2 liter V10. She secretly hoped her ride tonight would not be a Ferrari, she could drive those in Sicily any time since Nonno happened to be a collector. She ran her hands over the car's sleek lines before getting in. Manual 6-speed transmission, and a 525 horsepower engine. She started the ignition and the beast came to life. Full tank of gas, she smiled—Will anticipated her needs. She was planning on taking a nice little ride down to The Bowery Electric. Thanks to Nonno's relentless driving instructions throughout her teenage years she drove like a racecar driver. Even in heels.

Clutch. Third, clang. A beautiful roar came from the back in response. The car handled beautifully at higher speeds. She loved every moment. Out of the corner of her right eye she noticed Will getting a bit tense, he probably thought that she was getting reckless. But she wasn't. She was fully aware of her surroundings, and driving in a congested city traffic at high speed was not her first time. She effortlessly weaved around the slower drivers, all they saw was a sleek black shape whizzing by and a flash of blue LED lights in the back. She dropped into second just so Will could catch a breath.

New York City at night was breathtaking. Catalina loved summer New York at night. Tonight, the temperature dropped a bit and slight breeze brought in some fresh air. New York, unlike Chicago, does not have alleys and the garbage is disposed of curbside, where it sits and rots in the summer heat, giving the city a certain permanent smell of a sewer. But at night the smell is subdued, and lower temperatures and a breeze made it almost undetectable. Add the sparkle of colorful lights reaching into the blackened sky and—*poof*—magic! She would look around every time she stopped at a light.

Clutch. Back into third, clang. There was something old-fashioned about the clanging, she hadn't decided yet if she liked it or not. Catalina saw a window in traffic and a clear stretch ahead. She hit the gas. Will clenched his jaw. The car flew forward. Will turned to look at Catalina, whose full mouth was smiling with excitement while her eyes kept a cold gaze on the road. Her right hand dropped to the gear shift. Will groaned.

She turned and winked at him. And popped into fourth. She pushed over a hundred for a bit then dropped back down to second gear. For the rest of way to the club she stayed at legal speeds, which now felt like crawling.

It was a little after 11 pm, when a sleek black pearl Audi R8 with carbon fiber sideblades slowly rolled past a long line of people and came to a quiet stop right in front of the door to The Bowery Electric. Someone let out a long whistle. The car sat there for a full minute, its 5.2 liter engine softly purring, before the passenger door opened to reveal a red leather and carbon fiber clad interior. A young, tall and extremely handsome black male wearing a plum silk shirt and dark denim got out of the car and shut the door behind him with a heavy dull thud that only expensive cars could produce. He walked over to one of the bouncers at the door. The two men shared a greeting, they appeared to know each other. The visitor whispered something into the bouncer's ear and they shook hands. With the R8 being the center of attention at that time, no one noticed the handsome stranger slipping a wad of bills into the bouncer's palm. The bouncer nodded and the visitor turned to the Audi, bent down and waved to whomever was still inside. The engine shut down and the driver's door swung open.

A long, lean and beautifully proportioned left leg extended out of the R8 before being joined by its mate. Several seconds passed before the rest of the body emerged. It was a woman, whose appearance hushed the crowd. The men's jaws dropped in awe, women's lips tightened in envy. The woman was elegantly dressed in a navy knee-length dress, nude pumps, wearing minimal jewelry, and carrying a small gold leather clutch. She closed the car's door and sashayed to the front door. Her companion offered her his arm, which she took before tossing the keys of the Audi to the bouncer.

"Keep her warm, will ya?" she said with a wink. The two then disappeared inside. The people closest to the door were treated to a view of her bare back and a flash of red covering the soles of her shoes.

"What did you tell him?" asked Catalina once they elbowed their way to the bar through a large crowd of dancing people and ordered their drinks. Will was drinking gin and tonic and she asked for a glass of champagne.

"I told him you were eager to meet our Casanova from last night. And to lose all of tonight's security footage. He probably won't resist driving the car around the block once or twice as well," replied Will. He had to lean close to her in order to be heard over the noise. She smelt of citrus and sunshine, something Will did not expect.

"OK, go mingle. Keep your phone on vibrate, I'll keep

you posted," Catalina waved him off and turned a bit to have a better view of the front door. Will took his drink and disappeared into the crowd.

She didn't have to wait long. Her target was earlier than predicted. She just asked for her second glass of champagne when, out of the corner of her eye, she caught him moving toward the bar. He was wearing a white shirt with sleeves rolled up and gray slacks. Both items of clothing were fitted, showing off his muscular build. His chiseled features were darkened by stubble, he tended to grow a bit more than an average five o'clock shadow, and his black hair was tussled as if he took a nap right before. The whole look together was quite a package, she could see why women threw themselves at him. When she noticed that his brown eyes were scanning the room, she got out her phone and pretended to be texting furiously. He finally made his way to the bartender and asked for his usual: Grey Goose on the rocks. He leaned on the bar and looked around the place. Surveying. He took his time looking around before turning back to the bar and picking up his drink. He took a sip and looked to his right. And then he turned left.

He saw her right away, even though she was partially blocked by a couple of giggling coeds. But then he'd been tipped off by the bouncer that a 'very fine woman' was eager to meet him. She was described as a tall redhead with a knock-out dress and a gold purse. At this moment, she didn't look that eager to meet anyone. He could only see the top half of her face and her hands texting. She was frowning. Suddenly she stopped texting, shoved her phone into her gold purse and picked her champagne glass. She raised her glass in a small toast before downing it all. She needed a refill. He picked up his drink and started to make his way toward her.

He approached from behind. She was sitting straight up, her backless dress exposing the muscular structure of her back. He already could see that she was tall and well built. He pegged her for a dancer, or a model. He could see miles of legs tucked under the bar. Her red hair was cut short into an angled bob with bangs and had that 'straight out of bed' sexy feel. He slid next to her and signaled to the bartenders. One quickly appeared.

"The lady needs a refill," he ordered. She turned to face him. He turned his head in her direction and froze.

She was beautiful. She had a well-proportioned face with slightly defined cheekbones and perfectly arched eyebrows. Her eyes were light brown, with a cool hue. But it was the lower part of her face that made him freeze. Those full lips and that rounded chin looked somehow familiar, like he's seen them before. His stomach did a little flip of warning, but he paid no attention. She bit her lip slightly and then picked up her new glass placed in front of her. He snapped out of it just in time.

"Thanks!" she said to him and raised her glass. "I needed that."

"I figured that much. Tough night?" he asked before taking a sip of his own drink.

"I got stood up if you can believe that. But… it's his loss," she smiled. He didn't believe her for a second.

"I'm Jim by the way. Jim Campbell," he introduced himself.

"I'm Lina. Nice to meet you, Jim!" she took another sip. "And what do you do, Jim?"

"I work for the CIA," he said and smiled. She let out a tiny snorting sound, in the manner of 'yeah, right'.

"Well, in that case, I kill people. Now, what do you really do?" She wasn't buying it, but was playing along. Her face showed amusement.

"How far would I get if I'll tell you that I'm just an IT consultant?"

"A lot farther than telling me you're a secret agent," she winked and turned her body toward him. Her crossed legs were now slightly brushing against his thigh.

"And you don't actually kill people, I take it." He was done with his drink but was still holding his glass.

"Nope. I'm a trust fund baby," she said with a little giggle. She looked around and wrinkled her nose. "Too noisy tonight and the music is not that great. Not what I expected from this place."

"This is your first time?" He liked his nightly conquests not returning to this club.

"And last." She looked straight at him and uncrossed her legs. "Want to get out of here?"

"Let's go." He put down his glass and handed her the gold purse off the bar. She took it with a nod and gracefully slid off the chair.

She walked in front of him. It was just a few steps but enough for him to take in the whole view. Her knee-length dress was hugging all the right curves and exposing her whole back past the waist, yet it was done with extreme taste and craftsmanship. He recognized the shoe brand, the shiny red soles were unmistakable. He noted the lack of jewelry, except for an extremely sparkling diamond band that she had on her right ring finger. He first noticed the ring when she picked up her champagne glass. She sashayed to the door and he followed her out. He picked up a familiar bouncer disappearing into the street as soon as they exited. She paused on the sidewalk and turned to face him.

"Where do you want to go?" she asked. Jim heard a powerful engine come to life somewhere down the street.

"My place is just around the corner actually," he replied.

"Well, I hope you have a place to park because I've got a car here," and as soon as those words left her mouth a glittering black Audi R8 pulled up to the front. She turned and started walking toward the driver's side. Jim raised an eyebrow and went over to the passenger side. But before getting in, he looked over the car, taking it in. It was pearl black with carbon fiber sideblades and five-arm double-spoke wheels wearing performance tires with back tires being larger than the front. The rear engine block was illuminated by a soft blue glow emanating from tiny LED lights around the rear windshield. He took a deep breath and got into the car.

She was already inside, enveloped by the red leather seat, with her right hand gently caressing the gearshift. Her dress was hiked up to her upper thighs, to give her legs the freedom to operate the pedals.

"So, how do I get to your place?" she asked holding the gearshift in neutral, waiting to shift. He gave her directions on what would be a minute long ride and buckled his seat belt. She shifted gears like a pro and peeled out.

They made it to his front door in less than a minute, but then had to circle around to find a spot. She found one half a block away from Jim's building. The spot didn't look big enough for the R8, but she masterfully squeezed in anyway. They got out of the car, Jim letting out a sigh for not spending more time with it, and walked over to his place.

"Well, this is a real bachelor pad, if I ever saw one!" exclaimed Catalina once they walked inside. She looked around. Again. There was a faint smell of clean laundry, something that was not present in the morning. She noticed that there was a different set of sheets on the bed.

"Would you like something to drink?" asked Jim from the kitchen. He pulled out a bottle of Veuve Clicquot from the fridge. She smiled and nodded.

"Have you got a bathroom around here, or is it a hole on a floor?" she asked. She was perfectly aware of where the bathroom was, but wasn't about to tip her hand.

"Ha ha, very funny. I do have modern conveniences, you know. It's that way," said Jim and pointed toward the far end of the loft. She disappeared into the bathroom while he busied himself with the cork.

She didn't need to go. What she needed was some privacy to text Will and tell him where the car was so he could pick it up and deliver it back to his friend. 'Ciao!' she quietly said goodbye to the car she fell in love with. Catalina then checked on her wig in the tiny mirror, flushed the toilet and ran the water before stepping out. She found Jim half way up the stairs.

"Come on, I want to show you something. Plus, I don't have a place to sit." He waved her to join him. She followed him up the stairs.

The rooftop was dark. He asked her to wait for him to turn on the lights and disappeared into the dark. She heard a panel open somewhere and, suddenly, the whole place lit up. Will was right, this place was magical with the lights on. There were tiny lights going up the lattice walls, ground lights, spot lights, sconces… Everything and anything one could imagine was in this place. She wondered if this was professionally done, because if Jim designed this himself he was in the wrong business. She was in awe.

"More up your alley now, trust fund baby?" he came to her holding two filled champagne glasses.

"This is stunning. This really seals the deal, huh?" she replied and took a glass from him.

"Perhaps, but this is just for me," he said. And then he raised his hand to her face and gently tucked a loose strand of her hair behind her ear. His fingers lingered behind her ear, and then slowly slid down her neck before falling away. "Nice diamonds," he remarked. His gesture revealed that she had on more jewelry than just the diamond ring. She was also wearing huge princess-cut pink diamond earrings, Jim figured each stone was about three carats.

"Thanks," she said and took a sip from her glass. "So, what did I do to deserve this honor?" she asked and slowly started walking toward the middle seating area. "Can't be my money, you don't know me."

"You drive a nice car, what can I say," he said with a smile and followed her. She dropped her purse on the ottoman before reclining on the couch. He sat next to her. She leaned back and put her feet on to his lap.

"Well, this is really something, that's for sure." She took another sip from her glass and tipped her head back to look up at the sky. Jim put his glass down on a side table before lowering his hand onto her left leg to slowly caress it. Her skin reacted to his touch with a flicker of goose bumps. She lowered her head and looked at him. "Does that hot tub work?"

"Yeah. Want me to turn it on? It'll take a bit of time to heat up." She slid her legs off his lap as an answer. He got up and went over to the tub.

She watched him take the cover off and fiddle with the control panel. She watched his body move under his clothes, wondering what would he look like naked. Would he be covered in scars? She liked men with scars, liked running her fingers along them, kissing them... He turned to her.

"Give it a couple of minutes," he said. She motioned with her index finger for him to return to her. He complied.

She straddled him once he sat back down. He took a deep breath. She silenced him by placing her finger on his lips, and bit her lower lip. There was movement in his pants. She smiled and proceeded to slowly undo his shirt. The water started to bubble behind them. She opened up his shirt and fanned her fingers across his chest. Yes, there were scars. He had a long scar across the top of his abdomen and a smaller one closer to his right shoulder.

"Secret agent, huh?" she said slowly running her index finger along the large scar. He took her hand in his.

"Car accident," he said and kissed her fingers. She pulled away her hand and leaned down to kiss the scar on his shoulder. 'I gave you these scars loverboy' she thought, 'and if I like you I'll let you live through the night.' She started moving up his neck with her kisses, until he suddenly grabbed her by the back of her head and pulled her mouth into his. His kiss was deep, possessing and a bit rough. She liked it. The water behind them was bubbling really loud now. She pulled away and got up.

"Is it ready now?" she asked and nodded toward the tub. The jets were bubbling vigorously and the lights inside the tub were slowly changing colors. 'Chromatherapy, nice' she commented to herself. She kicked off her shoes, one by one.

"Yeah, it's ready," he answered but didn't move from the couch. She stood in front of him and slowly raised her hands behind her neck to undo the buttons holding the dress together. Then she let go and the soft jersey slowly cascaded off her body and pooled on the floor around her feet.

"Then what are we waiting for?" she asked before stepping out of her dress and getting into the tub. She turned to see if he was following her in before lowering herself up to the chest into the warm bubbling water. He got undressed and joined her.

34

Sicily, Italy

During her long flight to Italy aboard Eddie's cargo plane, Antonia had a bad feeling about Miami. She understood why Catalina was planning to end this affair there, but she still had a bad feeling. And Antonia always trusted her gut.

She worked for Catalina for five years now. During that time she picked up a trick or two and made contacts of her own. It was hard not to, Catalina never denied her access to her address book and Antonia had a lot of free time on her hands when her employer was away. Antonia's connections revolved around keeping Catalina alive and safe. She had good relationships with private hospitals in Switzerland and Cuba. Both places could be reached by air, if needed.

By the time her plane finally reached Italy, Antonia alerted her contact in Cuba that her boss might require medical services. She transferred a significant amount of money as advance payment and, with a knot in her stomach, requested that they prepare to handle major gunshot injuries and severe loss of blood. She ended her call right as the wheels of the plane touched down on the runway with the grace of an elephant. The plane finally came to a stop and she rushed to get out. She was stopped by the pilot, who came out of the cockpit to say goodbye.

"*Ciao*, Antonia. Sorry it took so long," he said to her and extended his hand.

"I have a request," said Antonia as she took his hand into hers.

"Anything."

"A message for Mr. Washington, please."

"Yes?" the pilot looked at her a little uneasy. The crew had opened the large cargo door in the back of the plane by now and the pilot could see a rather large welcome party for Antonia. He was surprised by this, he thought this woman was just a housekeeper. But judging by the armada of cars and the size of men standing on the tarmac waiting for her, Antonia must have been very important.

"Please tell your Boss that he has to guarantee that my boss survives, no matter the costs. Tell him that if she dies out there, he might as well join her. *Capisce?*"

"Um, tell him just like that?"

"*Si.* He'll know that I speak for la Famiglia," replied Antonia and gently patted his hand. The pilot looked at the welcoming party outside. They were busy loading Antonia's luggage and lots of black garbage bags into the trunks of their cars.

"OK then. I'll pass it on verbatim."

"*Grazie!*" she released his hand and walked out of the plane. He watched her walk toward her party. He saw the men silently nod in welcome, one opening the door of a black S-class Mercedes for her. She handed the Roman bust she held on to during the entire flight to one of the men. Antonia paused before getting into the car and turned back to the plane.

"*Ciao!*" she yelled back and blew a kiss to the pilot. Then she slipped into the car and a moment later the armada sped off the tarmac. The pilot went back into the cockpit to make a phone call. It would be hours before they would be able to refuel and turn back home, he couldn't wait that long to talk to his Boss.

―――――

New York City

She liked him. He was perfect. It was as if they were made for each other, instantly knowing each other's likes and dislikes, possessing the same rhythm. Some people would call it 'soulmates' but she knew this relationship was not meant to be.

They started in the tub on his fairytale rooftop and ended in his bed. There was no foreplay, no games – just two people that knew exactly what they wanted. He was now sound asleep, Catalina slipped him a sedative once they got downstairs. She did not want to take any chances. If he was anything like her, and she had a feeling he was, he could have an orgasm then turn around and kill some-one within a second of each other.

She was sitting at the foot of the bed, fully dressed, looking at him sleep. Her shoes and her gold clutch were in her lap, she was holding her phone, waiting for Will to let her know that he was downstairs. It only took her a couple of minutes—once she made sure that he was out for the night—to zigzag through his place to first clone his phone into another one she brought with her, then get her clothes from upstairs and grab the garbage from under the sink. She noticed earlier that he tossed the used condoms in the kitchen garbage, she wanted to take her DNA with her. She wasn't worried about the glass she used, she just slipped the glass into the hot tub, the jets bubbling away what evidence she might have left there. And now she sat on the foot of the bed, looking at him sleep. Wondering if she'd miss his touch.

It's been close to a year since she last enjoyed the company of a man. That's how long it's been since her last hook-up with Marcello, the Family capodecina and her off and on boyfriend. Marcello and his soldiers moved to Naples a year ago, she hasn't made it up there to see him. She never missed him, he satisfied her but didn't excite her. But Agent Campbell excited her tonight. She realized that she will actually feel something when she would finally have to kill him. Her phone's screen lit up: Will was downstairs. She got up, grabbed her things, and left trying to avoid all the squeaking floorboards. She put on her shoes after she got into the elevator.

Will pulled away as soon as she got into the car. He was wearing a black tee and his hands were a bit greasy. She figured he hung out with his buddies and probably stripped a car or two when took the R8 back. They drove silently for five minutes before Will finally asked:

"So… is there a body floating in his hot tub?"

"No, no body. I left him snoring downstairs. He changed the sheets before going out," she replied. "Is the jet ready?"

"We'll take off as soon as we get on board."

"OK then, let's get out of here." She lowered the visor and opened the little flap to expose the mirror. She then popped out her colored contacts and tossed them out of the car through the window. Next she carefully peeled off the wig and then took out all the pins that held her hair together. The wig got shoved into the garbage bag from Campbell's kitchen, something she would ask Eddie's ground crew to put into their incinerator. She knew that Eddie had all his garbage burned, he was very careful. She then reclined her seat a bit and closed her eyes. Will turned on some music and concentrated on driving. They didn't speak until they pulled into the private airstrip. Dawn was just starting to break, coloring the horizon deep orange and turning the clouds purple. Eddie's Gulfstream 650 was sitting on the tarmac with engines already running.

35

Chicago

Eddie's pillow was vibrating. He groaned and pulled his wife closer. The vibrations stopped only to resume a second later. He groaned again and finally, reluctantly, released his wife and sat up. He dug for his phone under his pillow and answered on the last vibe.

"Yeah?" his usual baritone voice was even deeper post sleep.

"I'm sorry to wake you, but you asked me to call you when they're on the way back, and they're on the way back." It was Tyrone.

"OK, I'm going to meet them. Anything else?" Eddie was rubbing his eyes. His wife stirred.

"The CIA guy is still kicking, she didn't do him," said Tyrone after a small pause.

"What?" boomed Eddie in full voice and threw off his covers.

"Will said she just… slept with him… and cloned his phone. They're going through his phone now," answered Tyrone. He knew that right now Eddie was pacing his bedroom and his stomping around would wake his wife. Which could be a good thing since Seline was the only one that could explain Catalina's actions to Eddie.

"What the fuck is she doing? I'm pretty sure she was ordered to clean this up as soon as possible!" Tyrone was right, Eddie was now pacing his vast bedroom. His wife woke up and sat up in bed. They slept in the nude, and now

Seline was watching her giant-of-a-man husband stomp around the bedroom completely naked. "Will thinks that she and the agent might have a history together. She mentioned that she ran into him five years ago."

"Shit! That must be that African mess. She still steaming about it, even though they got paid for all the extra bodies and she made out with that nice house of hers. But that might have put her on Company's radar... Shit!" His stomping got harder, which prompted his wife to leave the bed and come over to his side. She gently put her hand on his shoulder. Eddie turned to face her. His nostrils were flaring, eyes burning. He looked at her face. "Get me their ETA and get over here!" he finally ordered Tyrone and hung up.

"Anything you'd like to share?" Seline asked softly. She then led Eddie to sit down on the bed. She climbed on the bed, knelt behind him on the golden silk sheets and started rubbing his shoulders.

"Why didn't she just pop the bastard?" Eddie asked. Her soft thumbs were moving up and down the back of his neck with gentle pressure.

"Maybe it wasn't the right time. She has a reason for doing things a certain way, you know that. Don't interfere, just do what she asks you to do," replied Seline softly and continued to massage his shoulders. Eddie just sat on the bed not moving, in a trance.

"I want you and the kids to visit my mother for a while," he said after some time. "Take the new plane, I have a feeling she's going to put more miles on the 650... I'm putting you on the plane in two hours. "

Seline's hands slipped off his shoulders. He turned to face her. Her beautiful dark face had a worrying look. Her hands were embracing her rounded belly. Seline was pregnant with their third child.

"Maybe we should look for a permanent place this time? You send us there every time you think it might get a bit dicey in here. Why don't we just stay there?" she said. She'd been wanting to move back to the Cayman Islands for a while now. Eddie put his hand on her belly and felt a little kick. It was as if the baby was giving him a nudge.

"Fine. Find us a villa, you know what I like." Seline nodded. She was well in tune with Eddie's preference for exotic dark woods contrasted with shades of white in various high-end fabrics and supple leather. "I'll send the boys down there to put down roots. Tyrone can run Chicago until we get settled in," continued Eddie before planting a big kiss on his wife's lips and leaping off the bed. He went into their large master bath to take a shower. Seline put on for her silk and lace robe and left the bedroom in search of their housekeeper and the kids' nanny to tell them they're leaving for the Caymans. Again. The women were so used to it, they could get everything ready in under 30 minutes.

Eddie stood in his Carrara marble shower, his large hands leaning on the wall, letting the multiple Kohler jets pulsate hot water all over his body. He was thinking about Seline. How he had to thank Catalina for bringing her into his life.

It was about eight years ago. Eddie's empire was fast expanding, thanks to Catalina's introduction to her Family. He was starting to steal market share from his competitors. Knowing who was backing him, some would negotiate with him and share the clients, and some would just move out of the way. Except for one, Lorenzo Cruz, the slimy Spaniard who controlled a large part of the African weapons market and who decided to take Eddie out. Things got so bad, that the Family ordered Catalina to deal with the problem. She did, swiftly and effectively with a large body count. There was no one left from Cruz's organization to bother Eddie again. 72 hours after, however, she showed up at the doorstep of Eddie's mother's new Cayman Islands residence with a young woman in tow. Seline. Her only explanation was that Lorenzo kept her captive. Seline was in bad shape, it took months for Mrs. Washington to nurse her back to health. Eddie took one look at Seline and knew she was perfect for him—smart, educated, with a very attractive petite frame, and a bright smile. He liked that she kept her curly hair cut short and favored classic tailored clothes. He didn't have to pretend with her, she knew who he was and the true nature of his business. They discussed everything, except for the three days she spent with Catalina. What ever went on during that time had a profound effect on both women. They stayed in touch by exchanging emails in French. They talked about shoes and decorating, Eddie figured it might have been a code, but he had hard time figuring it out. Seline bore Eddie two children, a son and a daughter, and was now carrying a third. Eddie was her first priority: she loved him and took care of him, knew when to speak up and when to disappear, treated his men well, gave sound business advice when asked, and created the perfect household. Eddie also knew that she always stayed on top of his business dealings. In case something was to happen to him, she could take over without skipping a beat.

The water kept pounding his body as he kept thinking about his wife. About how Seline knew that Catalina's New York actions, or 'inactions' as he would call them, were somehow part of her master plan. Catalina always had a plan, she didn't get out of bed without a plan. He just hoped that this time she didn't miscalculate. Eddie turned off the water and got out. Wrapping himself in a plush terrycloth robe, he went looking for his wife to see if she needed any help. As he passed by the large living room window, he noticed that a storm was brewing over the lake.

36

Gulfstream 650

"Whiskey Alfa One hold your approach. Whiskey Alfa Two Foxtrot has not cleared the runway. Over."

"Tower, this is Whiskey Alfa One, roger that. We'll go around. Over."

"We're climbing again," Catalina said and got out of her seat. She looked toward the cockpit. "Why are we climbing?"

"I don't know," replied Will who also stood up. He noticed that her right hand disappeared behind her back, no doubt to get a hold on her Glock. She had gotten noticeably tense since they figured out that her cover was about to be blown by the Company. Catalina looked out the windows, checking their position against landmarks.

"Find the emergency chutes. I'm going to find out what this is all about," she ordered Will and drew her Glock.

"Chill, will you? Eddie's not going to sell you out, especially when you're onboard his most expensive toy," responded Will only to get stared down by the look of death. She stealthy moved toward the cockpit. Will noticed as well that the plane was making a turn. He drew his own gun before pulling off the couch cushions to reveal emergency parachutes. Catalina reached the cockpit door and turned to Will. He nodded, grabbed the shoots and assumed a firing position.

The pilot almost jumped out of his seat when he felt something hard and cold press against his right cheek.

"Why are we climbing?" a female voice asked. His extremely dangerous passenger was in standing behind him pressing a gun into his face.

"Jesus Christ! We've got another plane on the runway, we have to let them take off," he answered before pushing her gun off his face. He noticed that his co-pilot quietly started to prepare to fly solo should the need suddenly arise.

"Eddie doesn't have another plane." The gun was now pressing at the back of his skull.

"He got it a week ago. Do you want me to call them so you can ask who they are before you blow my brains out?"

"Yeah, get them."

"Whiskey Alfa Two Foxtrot, this is Whiskey Alfa One. Please identify yourself and list your cargo. Over." The pilot turned on the speaker so Catalina could hear the exchange.

"This is Whiskey Alfa Two Foxtrot. Are you out of your mind?" Exploded the voice overhead.

"Just do it, will you, Musicman, I've got a gun to my head," answered the pilot. The co-pilot turned his way slightly and gave him a little nod. The nod earned him Catalina's second Glock, which she was holding in her left hand, being pressed to his own head.

"Roger that, Eagle. This is Washington Air Two Family, on the way to Cayman Islands carrying Mrs. Washington with the children and household staff. Over."

"Where's Eddie?" asked Catalina into the speaker.

"Waiting for you to land." The guns were withdrawn. When the pilots got the courage to turn around, Catalina was gone and the cockpit door was closed. Eagle took a deep sigh of relief and turned off the radio speaker.

"Whiskey Alfa One, you're clear to land. Over," said the tower a second later.

"Roger that Tower," answered Eagle. "What the fuck was that?" he asked his co-pilot.

"Maybe we should announce our every maneuver to the passengers next time," answered the co-pilot with sarcasm even though his voice was shaking.

"No shit!"

They were ordered to taxi directly into the hangar upon landing. The pilots waited for a while in the cockpit before exiting. They didn't want to run into their passenger and her guns again. When they finally left the cockpit, they noticed two emergency parachutes sitting on the couch. They looked at each other, both thinking the same thing.

"I'm asking for raise," said Eagle before exiting the plane.

"I'm blown. I've got only a couple of hours head start," was the first thing Catalina said to Eddie when she got into his armored black Mercedes S65 AMG. The driver, along with Will and Tyrone, stayed outside with all the luggage. This was only a conversation.

"I figured that much... Well, Johnny's on ice which gives you a small advantage," replied Eddie. "Why didn't you just kill that son of a bitch while you were doing him?" he suddenly boomed.

"It's not his time. There is someone that has to go first. If I took care of Campbell, then that someone would slip away. I have orders," she calmly responded. She was used to Eddie's outbursts.

"Aha... Seline thought that much..."

"Speaking of Seline... I take this is a permanent move?" Catalina was always one step ahead.

"Yes. Time for all of us to leave to calmer pastures," he replied. Then Eddie took her hand into his: "When this is over, you're going to come to the Caymans and have a nice holiday visit with my wife. This is one loose end you're not about to tie anytime soon." He gently squeezed her hand.

Catalina's response came as a shock to Eddie. She hugged him. He hugged her back and they sat like that for a bit. When they finally released each other, their expressions were all business.

"Show me the plans to my Miami Sanctuary. Did you get my Barrett down there?"

"Yes," Eddie said and got a spiral-bound brochure out of the briefcase by his feet. He handed the brochure to Catalina, who flipped through it with interest. The brochure contained detailed plans of her Sanctuary, as well as lists of all firepower and medical supplies. The last section contained step-by-step procedures of self-administered first aid for various types of wounds. "I've got my Skylane chopper ready in case you need a lift."

"You're not lifting me in that box with that thing again! If I can't make it on my own, then find me another way out. Use your go-fast boats. Use your Cartel connections if you have to. Do not airlift me!" The last warning was delivered through tightly clenched teeth.

"Fine… Some of Tyrone's crew stayed behind in Miami, I'll drop them in the water." Eddie reached for his briefcase again and got out a satellite phone. "Here, it's preprogrammed. 1 is me, 2 is Tyrone, 3 his Miami crew and 4 is Diamond. Burner numbers as always. Diamond's waiting for your instructions in DC. Did you figure out what you're going to do with that house?"

"Yeah," she said and took the phone. "Thanks for everything. I'm going to go now, need to stay one step ahead. Can I use your plane again?"

"No, but I've got someone that can fly you and your car around. Pilot's an old coot, but loyal and knows how to get to DC without a flight plan. I take it that's where you're going first? If you want him, he can be ready in a couple of hours. He can fly out right from here."

"Fine, I'll take it. Better than the Skyline. I need a couple of hours to grab my gear. Thanks!" She kissed him on the cheek.

"Ciao!" he said and smiled.

"Ciao!" she replied and got out of the car. She could see the sky through the plane hanger's wide open doors. The storm clouds had passed and it was bright and sunny.

37

New York City

Special Agent Campbell was woken up by a heavy pounding on the front door. He slowly climbed out of bed and stumbled to his desk in search of his gun. His head was throbbing for some reason. He felt like he could sleep another 12 hours or so. He found his gun and made his way to the door. The body wasn't cooperating, it took him a while to work the locks. He didn't even bother withdrawing his gun, realizing that his reflexes were too slow to mount any kind of a defense. He swung the door open and came face to face with McCarthy.

"What the fuck are you doing here?" asked Campbell and rubbed his temples while still holding his weapon. The throbbing of his head was not going away.

"I've been trying to reach you for hours, sir. Did you not hear your phone?" answered McCarthy and invited himself in. Campbell slammed the door behind him, which turned out not to be such a good idea since the loud bang of the door made his head explode in sharp pain. His ears began to ring.

"Fuck!" Campbell swore and gripped his head. "Phone's off. I was a bit busy last night," he replied to McCarthy and stumbled toward the kitchen. He needed pain killers and caffeine. Somehow, through all the throbbing and ringing in his head he managed to hear McCarthy cough a little. "What?"

"Hum, sir… would you mind putting some pants on?

I'm starting to get a complex." Campbell looked down at himself and realized that he was still completely naked.

"Shit! Yeah, sure." He rushed toward the rack of clothes and grabbed a pair of jeans. As he was stuffing himself into them, he looked around for his clothes from last night. 'They still must be on the roof,' he thought and noted that despite the throbbing headache and general crappy feeling, he still had a clear memory of last night's activities. Well, the activities on the roof, after that things got fuzzy. He looked at his bed, the woman was gone.

"Why are you here? Did the Pope die or something?" he asked McCarthy and went back looking for medicine. No luck.

"I have good news and bad news."

"Okeey... give me the bad news."

"Higger's dead, sir." That tidbit made Campbell stop his search for pain killers.

"Shit! Did you get a confirmation on that?"

"They still have to see the body, but it's in the morgue already." Campbell noticed that McCarthy was not a bit shaken by the fact that he sent an agent to his death recently.

"Hmm, tell them to pull dental and prints for verification. Shit!" Still no pills. He kept on searching. "What's the good news?"

"We found him!" said McCarthy triumphantly.

"Him? Who's him?" Campbell started at his young agent. Was he missing something? "You just said that Higger's dead."

"We found who Goldstein's working with nowadays. I can't tell you, you have to see it. I've been trying to get to you to come in all last night but you were MIA," replied the young man with a huge smile and disappeared into Campbell's bathroom. He emerged a second later and tossed an almost empty bottle of mouthwash at Campbell. It landed in the sink, Campbell made no attempt in catching it. "Come on, just rinse and throw a shirt on. I've got a car waiting, you really have to see this."

"Don't order me around... fine. You're buying breakfast by the way, and it better not be muffins," Campbell ground out and then poured the last of the blue liquid into his mouth and gargled. He tossed the empty bottle into his kitchen garbage not noticing that the can had been emptied out. McCarthy handed him a shirt and guided him gently to the door.

SAD, New York

He was feeling much better. His head stopped throbbing. On the way to the office, McCarthy picked up a couple of cups of very strong coffee. Once they made it to Campbell's office he sent another probie agent out to pick up Campbell a huge heap of scrambled eggs, sausages, a stack of buttered pancakes and what must have been a pound of bacon. He refused to discuss anything until his boss started to look human again. McCarthy never asked, but he was wondering if Campbell was drugged last night. He figured that his boss was with a woman, as usual, and that she had to be absolutely stunning for him to completely drop his guard like that. McCarthy talked Campbell into brushing his hair, arguing that a senior agent should look professional at all times no matter how one might feel, only to discreetly collect the stray hairs left in the comb so he could run a drug test later. He was quite interested in finding out what substance could knock down the Mighty Agent Campbell.

Full of greasy comfort food and caffeine, with teeth cleaned and hair brushed, Special Agent Campbell was finally allowed to go to his op. room for McCarthy's "big reveal" as he called it. Once inside, he realized that McCarthy's show-and-tell was going to take a while by the amount of documents and crumpled up papers scattered all over the room along with empty boxes of pizza and cartons of Chinese food. The men had not bothered to clean up. The stench of the stale food was overwhelming, and Campbell was starting to feel the throbbing in his head coming back. He buried his nose in the steam emanating from the hot cup of Earl Gray tea, put into his hand by McCarthy, and sat down. The pleasant aroma of bergamot orange seemed to hold the throbbing at bay.

"OK, ready," he said to McCarthy. The young man rushed to sit down in front of his computer and someone dimmed the lights.

"OK, so..." started McCarthy. "I started with Goldstein's mob connection. According to our Italian desk, the Benedetto Family is rather small and quiet compared to other Sicilian mobs. However, no one has ever tried to take them over and they never participated in any of the territorial wars. The Benedetto Family," several old and grainy shots of various mobsters filled the plasmas, "have a very unique product. They breed killers. Every member of the Family can kill with precision. That includes the women. They seem to weed out the most talented ones at a young age and then extensively train them in various methods of assassination."

"So this is like Sparta from hell," commented Campbell and motioned to continue.

"Something like that," replied McCarthy. "They leave no evidence and have never been caught by the authorities. The people on screen are the only ones that Interpol was able to get close to, but they have been inactive for decades. It is assumed that most of them are dead. The most interesting part is that every generation they produce one super assassin. That person, once fully trained, is more lethal than anyone that would come out of Mosad. In fact, that person is sometimes contracted by Mosad. The Benedettos are loyal only to their own Family. Contract killing is their main business." McCarthy took a sip of water before continuing.

"I then decided to see if any of the Family members came to the States. I found only a small number of people. According to our friends at the Bureau, all are part of the Chicago mob… Except for this guy." A black and white grainy photo of a rather handsome man appeared on the left plasma. "This is Franco Benedetto, or Frank Bennett as he was known here, who had not been on the grid until 15 years ago. There was a huge convergence of high-ranking Sicilian Mafiosi in Chicago at one time that got FBI very curious. They found out that all these people were in town for the funeral of the wife of this guy. The Benedetto Family Capo even came and that man is rarely seen out of his own house." Another grainy photo filled the right screen. The man looked like an older version of Frank Bennett. "FBI believes that they might be father and son, however they have not been able to confirm it." There was definitely a strong resemblance between the two men. And there was something else, only Campbell's still dulled senses were not able to pick up.

"Where's the Goldstein connection?" asked Campbell.

"Frank Bennett and Gerald Goldstein were army buddies. They served together. Only Frank was going by a different name but we ran face recognition and it's the same man. It is speculated that he joined the service to hone his marksmanship skills. Once again, the best are trained on our own dime." A photo of a group of soldiers was now filling the screen with two faces circled. "The man on the right is Goldstein and the other one is Frank. I believe that

Frank Bennett is Goldstein's mechanic."

"Frank Bennett is dead. Died in a car crash," said Campbell as a matter of fact. "We knew that Goldstein had only one asset and that he was connected with the mob," he went on to explain. "No one asked any questions since his work was superb. But 11 years ago, Goldstein informed us that his best mechanic died in a horrific car crash."

"Frank had two children. A son and a daughter," continued McCarthy. "The son, Mark, is the oldest. We checked out the son first, but he appeared to be a model citizen."

"Appeared? Where is he now?"

"He disappeared off the grid completely last winter. We're not able to pick up his trail."

"So you think it's the son? We're looking for a woman." Campbell was getting impatient.

"I think that Frank Bennett is still alive. That the accident was just a way to change his client base, so to speak. Remember that Goldstein no longer works for us."

"Nah, he's too old for shit like that." Campbell stared at the screen displaying the two Benedettos. There was something about those faces. It's like he's seen them before. But his gut was too busy processing the large breakfast so it didn't respond. "You said there was a daughter…"

"Yeah, name's Catalina, but she's the youngest and it's always the sons that follow into the business in the Benedetto Family."

"Says who? The Italian desk? What do we have on the daughter?"

"Only that she died in the same car crash as the father shortly after graduating Boston College summa cum laude with a degree in chemistry. What a waste…" replied McCarthy. His enthusiasm was starting to dwindle since his boss was not buying into the 'Frank's back' theory.

"Got any photos of her? The funeral maybe? It seems to be a well photographed event," asked Campbell. McCarthy scrolled through a long list of files on his screen and a picture of a tall and bony teenage girl with long dark hair appeared on the wall plasma. She looked to be around seventeen-eighteen years old. There was no resemblance to Frank Bennett except for the eyes and the facial expression. The eyes were the same shape and appeared to be the same light color. Campbell wondered what she looked like now. His gut, busy digesting, was still silent.

"Can you age that fifteen years and then see if it compares to our Zurich woman?" he asked.

"Yeah, hold on," said someone else in the room. Campbell heard McCarthy asking for the Zurich shot to be put up on the right plasma. The left screen went blank, someone was working on aging the photo. Campbell watched as the right side screen started flashing green dots and lines all over the woman's face, they were running the facial recognition software. All of a sudden there was a beep.

"We got it! It's the same woman!" exclaimed McCarthy.

"Put it up!" demanded Campbell. A computer-generated photo of, now age 32, Catalina Bennett went up on the left plasma. Campbell's teacup slipped out of his hand. "Oh my fucking God!" The room went silent.

38

It was her, up on his screen, the woman from last night. Suddenly, his gut fully alert now and screaming at him, he was going to be sick. He jumped out of his chair and somehow managed to grab a trash can from under a desk before puking his guts out. Everyone just silently stared. McCarthy, knowing that Campbell was most likely drugged the night before, had an inkling of what this was all about. But he wasn't about to ask. Campbell stopped throwing up and slumped into his chair. His jeans and shoes were wet from the spilled tea. He covered his face with his hands.

"Sir? Are you all right sir?" someone asked. Campbell didn't bother to look who. He just sat there for a while covering his face, his mind screaming colorful profanities at himself.

"No!" he answered finally. He uncovered his face and looked around the room at his team. "Well… if anyone here is a CSI fan or dying to be one, now's your chance. Because we're going to have to tear my place apart to see if anything useful was left behind."

"Your place?" asked another man, confused. Campbell looked at McCarthy who was strangely silent at this moment. Campbell realized that he figured it out. He took a deep breath before answering.

"Yeah… Because this woman," he pointed on the screen, "was in my bed last night."

Chicago's Western Suburbs

Catalina backed into the garage and flew into the house with her New York luggage. No one was home. Which worked out great for her, she just wanted to grab her gear and take off. She ran up to her bedroom and dumped the contents of the Louis Vuitton duffel on the bed. She briefly examined her nude Louboutin pumps for scuffmarks from when she unceremoniously kicked them off on the rooftop. They would need to be repaired but she wasn't going to bother with it right now.

She rummaged through her closet grabbing anything that remotely resembled her work clothes. She realized that she had no suitable pants. When on a job, she favored comfortable cargo pants with nice size pockets for her knives and ammo. She had none, only skinny jeans and leggings. Running around Miami heat with heavy machinery wearing skinny jeans was not her idea of comfort. Which meant that she would have to get some on the way. She filled her duffel with tank tops, shorts, two very flowing but short dresses that one could hide anything under, a black cashmere wrap and undergarments. She settled on her gray running shoes as 'work' footwear—they were well worn and comfortable and would also be good for the boat. At the last minute she tossed in a pair of red-soled wedges, she just couldn't do without her Louboutins. She exchanged her watch for a fancy men's diving TAG Heuer, that always was part of her work attire. Next, she pulled out the bottom dresser drawer and flipped it over. An envelope containing the new identity from Capo was taped to the bottom. She peeled off the envelope and stuffed into the bottom of her duffel bag.

With clothes packed she ran downstairs to raid Frank's armory. She knew she was fully stocked in her Miami Sanctuary but she wasn't about to travel unprotected. She took two more Glocks, all of the ceramic blades and ten extra clips. Five were loaded with hollow rounds. At the last minute she grabbed a smoke gas canister.

Bags loaded in the car and knifes strapped to various parts of her body, she took a moment to leave a note in the kitchen for her father. In Italian.

Daddy,
Send Marcus and Sofia to the Abramowitzes,
I set it all up already.
I love you!
                    Ciao!

She had one more thing to do before taking off. She had to break into Chrissie's house and get the flash drive. She could see the house from the garage, it appeared that no one was home as well. She thought about her approach and then remembered about all the garages having the same access code.

1-9-0-8. The garage door opened and she slipped inside. Catalina slowly opened the mudroom door and listened for any signs of life before entering. The house was empty, and a complete mess. She walked inside and proceeded to the powder room, carefully avoiding toys and sport gear scattered all over the floor. The flash drive was right where she left it. She ripped it off and quietly slipped back outside.

39

New York City

Nothing. They found absolutely nothing. The team converged on Campbell's loft ready to lift prints and search for evidence Campbell was sure had to be left behind. But they found nothing. The bathroom was wiped clean and the kitchen garbage was removed. The champagne glasses they used last night were found floating in the hot tub, whatever possible evidence they might have contained now washed away.

"There isn't a print left. All we got are yours," announced McCarthy.

"No prints? What do you mean there are no prints? There have to be prints! I know I was drugged, but it's not like she spent the rest of the night scrubbing all the surfaces. My dust is still all here," grumbled Campbell in response.

"Maybe she doesn't have any? She's a pro, remember?" countered McCarthy. He was secretly enjoying this. "Didn't you notice that maybe she had extremely smooth fingers?"

"No, I didn't! I wasn't paying attention to her fingers!" barked Campbell and then remembered how she slowly traced his scars with her index finger. Yes, they were exceptionally smooth, but he doubted it was from the lack of fingerprints.

"I think this is a lost cause, sir," said another agent. He was holding the champagne glass in his rubber-gloved hand.

"I can see that! Fine… wrap it up and get the hell out of here. I need to lay down." The men complied.

They packed up their gear and left him to brood sitting on his bed. Once inside their black government-issue Chevy Suburban, they all decided that this incident never happened. They would cover up for their boss because they all knew that he would do the same for them. He had a weakness and Catalina Bennett somehow found it and prayed on it. McCarthy was silently wondering how she knew about Campbell's personal life. He was going to check some things out once he got back to the office.

40

ICtech Offices, Arlington, Virginia

The office was small but it had a window facing the school grounds across the street instead of the parking lot on the other side of the building. The space was decorated with a mahogany desk, black leather chairs and lots of stainless steel. The desktop was kept exceptionally clean: only a computer, a phone and a zebrawood container containing only black ballpoint pens. Everything else was kept in drawers below, and in contrast to the surface of the desk, in complete disarray. There was a stainless steel tubular coat rack by the door, something that was not a standard office furniture issue. He brought that in himself to add personality to his space. His suit coat, far less superior in quality and price than the coat rack, was always hung with great care on that rack. He was planning to add an expensive espresso machine once his bonus would arrive.

But, unfortunately, the bonus was tied to profits that were expected from the sale of Wilson's product and research to the intelligence community. Jason Ellis was sitting at his desk, staring into space and drumming his short fingers with chewed off nails on the armrest of his Herman Miller chair. He was just informed that he had only a week before he had to produce Dr. Wilson's research and the product to his superiors or be fired. He was drumming his fingers and thinking of how to get out of this mess he created. Picking Wilson to invest in was his idea.

His greed overtook his usually shrewd judgment and he never took the time to investigate just what kind of a man Wilson really was. Ellis saw his associates taking a gamble and getting filthy rich off their investments and he wanted to be just like that. He really thought that Wilson was his way to the top.

His fingers continued to drum as he slowly turned his chair toward the window with his legs and started tapping his feet as well. For a man of above average height, Ellis had rather small feet. He had dirty blond hair with a receding hairline and constantly moving green eyes. He was staring out the window, drumming his fingers and tapping his feet, his eyes focused on something outside and for once were still. Suddenly, he wondered if the Echelon package that was set up for Operation Darwin was still running. He stopped his drumming and tapping and sat up in his chair. If the package was still running, he might still have a chance. He figured that even the most cautious criminal would slip when cornered. There were no hits on Echelon regarding Wilson or his research so far, but maybe if it was changed a bit... He reached for the phone and dialed a number in Sugar Grove of West Virginia. There was a satellite intercept station in Sugar Grove and he had a connection there. He didn't say hello when the phone was answered, just got right down to business.

"Hey, are you still running a package for Operation Darwin?" he asked and waited for the answer. "Can you add to it?"

"Yes, what to you want to add?" asked a female voice on the other end.

"Add Gerald Goldstein and... Mother," said Ellis.

"Mother? Do you know how many times that word is used hourly? Do you really want to track that one?"

"Yes, I know. Make it so it's only picking it up if it's

used with the other parameters. Oh, and Mother is a man."

"Fine. Anything else?"

"Make sure that if you get a hit I know about it first. In fact, don't even report it."

"OK... Listen, I'm free this weekend I could come and visit..." There was a note of desperation in the woman's voice.

"Not until this is over. But once I'm swimming in dough, we'll celebrate in style!" replied Ellis and hung up the phone. 'Not in your lifetime!' he said to himself.

He would give it a couple more days, maybe he'll get lucky and Echelon will intercept something that will lead him to the missing research. If not, he'll empty out the account he's been quietly siphoning money into from Wilson's funds, steal as many top secret files as he could get his hands on, and leave the country. If the books were audited, everything would point to Wilson as the embezzler. And Wilson was dead. Dead men could not talk.

41

From Chicago to Washington, DC

"I can only get you close, I can't fly all the way to DC without being noticed," her pilot's rough voice barked into the headset.

"Just get me within an hour drive," she replied.

"That won't be a problem," he answered and banked the plane left.

She was sitting in the cockpit of an old cargo plane, with her BMW securely locked to the floor behind her. The pilot, an old gizzard who chain-smoked cigars and sounded like he was about to die, used to fly Eddie's first arms loads, before Eddie got his own planes. The plane looked as old as the pilot and Catalina wasn't even sure that her BMW would fit into it, or if they'll be able to get off the ground. But the car fit, barely, she couldn't open the door all the way and had to shimmy her way out. And the plane was able to take off with all the grace of a fat goose.

Catalina kept sneaking peaks at the pilot out of the corner of her eye, making sure not to get caught. This person was fascinating to her. He was an old gizzard, all right. Eddie told her that he suspected the guy honed his superb flying skills flying for Air America when young. He had shaggy silver hair, a deeply tanned face with thousands of wrinkles and a very impressive thick handlebar mustache. There was a permanent Cuban cigar hanging from his mouth. He was thin, of medium height, and bowlegged. He wore a threadbare tee that at some point might have been white and old gray jeans. His exposed arms were fully covered in ink. Skulls, flames, naked women, snakes... he had it all. Catalina just could not stop looking, he was so different from her usual associates. She decided that her father would like this guy, they both seemed to be from the same generation. She smiled at that thought and then closed her eyes and slowed her breathing.

"OK, I think I found a good spot to drop you off. It'll be a little rough, but it's close to a decent road that you can use. I'll give you GPS coordinates so you can find your way back." Catalina noticed that they significantly dropped in altitude. "I know you've got some business to do, but don't take too long, I want to be in the air before the sun gets up."

"No problem," she opened one eye to answer, then closed it again. He turned his head to look at her. 'Lethal' he thought, and puffed on his cigar. They never exchanged names, to him she was just domestic cargo with cash payment upon safe and undetected delivery to Miami. He took another puff, checked his instruments and adjusted his course.

42

Georgetown, Washington, DC

There was someone else in the room. Even at his old age, Mother still could sense danger. Only this time it was too late.

"Time to get up, old man!" said a very familiar voice as he was dragged out of his armchair where he passed out after drinking. "On your knees!" He was shoved in the back with something hard. With shock, he recognized the voice.

"Catalina? What are you doing?"

"Surprised? You shouldn't be, you piece of shit! You sold me out!" She hit him hard in the back of his knees with something and he buckled to the floor. Hard, his old knees made a dull sound hitting the floorboards.

"What are you doing? Can we talk about this? I can explain," Mother was now genuinely frightened. He was breaking out in cold sweat. A cold, hard object pressed into the back of his head.

"No. You're finished." She leaned close and hissed into his ear: "you're going to die like the traitor you are!" Catalina cocked the silenced Beretta she was pressing into the back of his head.

"Listen, I..." *Clap!* Blood and brain tissue splattered the wall across, and Mother's body slowly collapsed onto the cold floor. She didn't even let him finish.

She let him lay there for a minute then flipped him over on his back with her foot. His eyes were still open.

She aimed at his heart and fired. One in the head, one the chest: she was sending a message. To Campbell.

Catalina stood over Mother's body, her breathing getting heavier. Suddenly, she exploded: "You're miserable piece of shit, I trusted you! Daddy trusted you! He made you!" she screamed at the corpse. She turned around in rage, grabbed the crystal lamp off the side table and launched it into the wall covered with his brain matter. It shattered into a million pieces. Then she stormed off upstairs to raid his office.

The raid was accomplished quickly. Catalina filled several black plastic bags with manila envelopes from Mother's safe after she cracked the combination without difficulty. She stomped downstairs with the bags and left them in the hall before popping back into the living room where Mother's body splayed on the floor. She was careful not to step on any broken glass. She looked around the ceiling and found an air vent on the wall opposite the blood spattered wall. It was perfect for what she had in mind. Catalina unscrewed the vent with her knife and placed a tiny remote camera into the cavity before closing it back up. Now she would be able to know when Mother's body was discovered. Once finished with the camera, Catalina left the room without even looking at the body. She grabbed the bags from the hall and exited the house the same way she got in, through a broken laundry room window.

"One down, two to go," she said as she started her BMW. She pulled out of her spot without turning on the headlights. The bags with the safe contents would be taken to a funeral parlor Catalina was friendly with. For a nice fee, they let her use their ovens without asking any questions. She had a key to the back door and could come and go when she pleased.

Once finished in the funeral parlor, Catalina called Diamond with final instructions for her house. As soon her BMW rolled into the plane, it lumbered off the field and laid in a course for Miami.

43

Miami

It was just before lunch when Catalina docked her Donzi at the Epic Hotel marina. She was starving, sweating, and a bit tired. She let the dock help take her luggage out of the boat and then walked toward the front entrance, wondering if they would let her check in early even if she was going to be very particular about the room she wanted.

The front entrance of the Epic was quite impressive. It was all blue glass, steel and spot lights. There was a huge white sculpture of what looked like chain links on a pad of water in the middle of circular drive. The drive was filled with exotic cars – the hotel catered to the jetsetting elite. The lobby was decked out in warm dark woods, soft taupe leathers and exotic stones. A huge flower arrangement resembling a swan and made out of white orchids stood in the middle greeting the guests. Catalina always liked the hotel, too bad she was planning to do some damage to one of the rooms.

They were able to check her in early, and she got exactly what she wanted: a room high above and facing downtown. The front desk clerk was a bit surprised why she specifically asked for the downtown view, most wanted the rooms looking out onto Biscayne Bay. Once inside her room, she showered and changed before heading downstairs to the Area 31 restaurant to eat and to think.

Catalina arrived in Miami early that morning. She was dropped off in a small airport just outside Miami and then drove in. She grabbed a cappuccino and a croissant on the way to her Sanctuary. There was no one around when she pulled into the marina and located her cargo container. She parked the BMW nearby and found a tarp to cover it up. Then, after looking around, she unlocked the padlock on her Sanctuary, slipped inside, and started the generators. Catalina turned on the AC and powered up the computers. She would get her luggage from the car after she had a look around.

Everyone that led a double life or had something to hide—a spy, an undercover cop, an assassin—had a secret stash somewhere. Frank used small apartments in shady neighborhoods as his safe houses. Catalina used storage lockers in bus and train depots when she started, until one day she saw a mobile hospital unit. It was a large trailer pulled by a semi and could be brought anywhere. It gave her an idea of creating a mobile safe house, but it was Eddie who came up with converting metal shipment containers into livable units. He offered Catalina to build, stock, and maintain the unit – all for a nice, slightly discounted on account of their friendship, fee. When Catalina saw the first finished unit, the word 'Sanctuary' came to mind.

The space was cramped but the layout was quite efficient. Eddie was a master in utilizing every inch of space. The end of the container was sectioned off and housed a generator, AC, water and electrical systems. All the walls were covered in soundproofing material so no one could hear anything on the outside. There was an extra layer by the utility space, to prevent Catalina going deaf from all the machine noise. A small toilet and sink were in the back, something that could be found in an RV, enclosed in a closet-like cabinet. The cabinet added weight to the container, but Eddie still insisted on doing it arguing that no one would want to stare at a toilet for days on end. Catalina agreed. After all, this was not a prison.

There was a bed on the left side surrounded by cabinets housing all sorts of medical equipment. Right above the bed, a defibrillator and several hooks for IVs were mounted. The defibrillator was surrounded by wall-mounted containers with rubber gloves and QuickClot pouches. Eddie even hung up trauma shears and several flashlights as well. At the head of the bed was an oxygen tank with a mask all ready to go. Catalina wondered if Eddie got an ambulance and just raided its equipment. More cupboards and drawers were across the bed, each labeled with their contents like 'surgical supplies' or 'bullet removal'. A large rectangular mirror was mounted on the wall and Catalina realized that it was on an extendable arm so she could pull it toward the bed. She figured that Eddie didn't give her a mirror for vanity, it was there so she could patch up areas out of her field of vision. One of the cupboards was a small refrigerator, Catalina found it fully stocked with various IVs. A large drawer next to it was labeled 'saline IVs and warmer'.

"Definitely raided an ambulance," commented Catalina. She checked the bed next. There were waste bins built into the bottom, she found that quite disturbing, but the mattress was soft and Eddie fitted it with a Hermès cashmere blanket. She gave the back of the Sanctuary another look around and finally noted that it looked like a mini-hospital. She never had that much medical equipment before. She remembered hearing from the Family that Eddie now had an ER doctor on payroll, maybe he was trying to get his money's worth.

The computers dinged behind her. They were up and running. Next to the fridge and toward the middle ran a long metal desk. Three monitors were mounted above, with CPU units below the desk. Eddie believed that everything should be bolted down in case the Sanctuary needed to be air-lifted. He didn't want anything to accidentally fly into Catalina's head. Even the wireless keyboard was mounted and the mouse went into a little pocket on the wall. There also was a laptop hanging in a pouch next to one of the monitors. Each Sanctuary always had a clean laptop in case she needed a disposable computer. Catalina looked under the desk and found the chair. She pulled it out and unfolded the backrest.

She checked her security feed first. Tiny security cameras were built right into the container's outer walls and painted to match. She had 360° views of the marina outside. Everything was quiet. She could see her Donzi 43ZR bobbing in the water, the sight of the go-fast made her smile.

Next she checked her systems. She had encrypted WiFi, and was even tapped into the police band. Catalina wondered how small her roof-mounted satellite was this time. She displayed the police band on her left monitor and logged into her communication programs in the center. She pulled up the feed from the camera she left at Mother's house. The right monitor was stand-alone unit with a touch screen and its own back-up power generator. This computer had only one program and once launched it would run without powering down. The screen was deep red and slowly pulsating—it was Catalina's *'Aiuto'* program. *Aiuto* means 'help' in Italian, all Catalina had to do was hit the screen and the program would alert whoever was assigned as her extraction crew that she needed rescue. In all her other Sanctuaries the *Aiuto* units were linked to a Family member, this one was linked to Tyrone's crew in Miami. She only used the extraction once, and was hoping not to repeat the experience.

Finally, she turned her attention to the armory oppo-site the wall of computers. She took her time checking every clip and every chamber of all ten handguns hanging on the white metal panels, inspecting the three different sniper rifles and four sub-machine guns Eddie provided, and looking over the 20lbs of C4 whose detonators were stored separately from the explosives. She had hundreds of rounds of ammunition, half of them having exploding tips. The armory panels slid open to reveal two Kevlar vests: one was standard providing the most protection, another was a custom designed to mold to her curves and hide beneath the clothes. She chose the custom one, even though she knew that it didn't provide much coverage in the shoulders and midriff. When she closed the panels she noticed her Barrett standing propped up by the wall. She inspected it as well.

Catalina decided to see if her brother was online before bringing in her luggage from the car. He was.

<Daddy's furious, are you out of your mind?>

<No, I just needed a vacation.>

<Well, he wanted to come too.
He wanted a family vacation.>

<Too late. He should save his miles.
Oh, and I gave Mommy that present that
Nonno sent. But don't tell Daddy.>

<Was there a vermin problem in the house?>

<You could say that :-) >

<I knew it!>

<BTW, how do I get picked
up by an Echelon package?>

<Easy. I can write you something for that.
Get a spare laptop to run it on.
Do you know what their parameters are?>

<I do, I'll send them in a minute,
they're in the car.>

<Where are you?>

<Somewhere with an easy way out.
Gotta go. Ciao!>

And she signed off.

She got her bags out of the BMW and locked herself in the Sanctuary. It was getting very hot outside and she changed into a pair of very small shorts and a white tank. First order of business was to send the Echelon package parameters to Mark. Johnny Higger was very helpful: he was able to tell her who the other man was in the photos with Mother, and provide her with Campbell's dossier as well as what keywords Echelon was looking for on Dr. Wilson. She inserted the silver flash drive that she previously kept in her bra into one of the CPUs and scanned the files. She did not have to break the encryption since she had the passwords, she found them written on a piece of paper in the Credit Suisse safe deposit box. She picked out pieces of information she was going to give Mark for his program. The whole process took just over five minutes.

Catalina unpacked her bags. The clothes she wanted to keep here were stashed into the little closet between the bed and the armory. The weapons she brought were added to the others. The bag she took from her Brooklyn apartment was left alone. It was her tool kit—containing everything she could possibly need on a job. She plopped on the bed with the spiral-bound brochure that Eddie gave her—the Sanctuary's manual. She still couldn't find where the food was. After studying the plans for a while she finally found it. There was a sliding panel on the side of the closet facing the bed. She opened it and found water bottles, protein bars, nuts and dried fruit. Not a salami or an olive in sight.

"Is this a joke?" she asked out loud. She was getting hungry and decided that it was time to move into the hotel. Her computer beeped, there was a message from Mark, he was finished with his program for her. She thanked him and downloaded it to another flash drive.

Then, she stood in the middle of her Sanctuary and closed her eyes. Catalina took a deep breath in and held it for a while before slowly releasing it. When she opened her eyes, she was all cool and collected concentration. It was as if a program kicked in her brain, telling the rest of her what to do. Her body moved with precision and purpose. She was no longer discovering her space—when she wanted something she knew exactly where it was. Two medium size suitcases on wheels appeared from under the bed, were laid open on the floor, and began to be methodically filled. One suitcase held black nylon pouches of different sizes so she could organize and pack her clothes. She never unpacked in hotels, she kept everything in the pouches and only opened the one she needed.

The suitcases had false bottoms lined in special material to protect the weapons they held from prying eyes of x-ray machines. She paused in front of the armory wall before selecting her weapons. It wasn't a question of how many guns to carry, but how many bullets she could pump out. She finally decided on several Berettas and, of course, the Glocks. She would carry two of the Berettas along with the Glocks and stash the rest in various places in the boat. She packed half of all her ammunition and two sub-machine guns. She even took a couple of pounds of C4 and chargers. She would wear her ceramic blades, they were her secret weapon should she find herself in an unlikely situation of being disarmed. She never wore an ankle holster—she found it uncomfortable and cumbersome when running because the holster tended to move around and the gun inside it would bounce up and down. Catalina managed to pack all her weapons and clothes into one suitcase, reserving the other for something very special.

That special item happened to be a remote weapon system for her Barrett. The item looked like a box that sat on the heavy-duty tripod. The gun would mount on top. It came with a remote whose controls resembled a video game controller. The system weighed about 40 pounds. The Barrett weighed around 30. These two items would not be easy to get in and out of the Donzi but she would have to manage. The Barrett was in a long black bag that was made to look like it was holding fishing gear. Woman fishing… she knew it might be a bit of a stretch but still it was a lot more convincing than the reality. Her phone beeped. It was Diamond, reporting that there was no unusual activity around the house. She checked on her camera in Mother's living room, no one found him yet. A quick check of Campbell's cloned phone also revealed nothing of interest, other than there seemed to be a frantic search for the missing agent Higger. It looked like someone on Campbell's team managed to figure out that there were classified documents downloaded using Higger's laptop. But she still might have to prod Campbell along, he wasn't moving fast enough. Catalina didn't intend to sit in Miami forever waiting for the Company to track her down. Even if she did like Miami.

It took her a while to load her gear into the Donzi. It was already hot and humid and she was sweating. She stowed both suitcases and the "fishing gear" in the cabin below, then went back to lock her Sanctuary. This time she didn't use the padlock but a vein recognition biometric lock which was programmed to the veins of her right hand since she didn't have any fingerprints.

She took a quick look to see if anyone was around before powering up the boat. It had been a while since she drove it, so she decided to take it for a spin before heading to the hotel. She powered up and slowly cast off into the direction of the Bay. Catalina was going to be in a no-wake zone for a little bit before being able to gun it at full speed. Once in the open waters, she cruised for a while before pushing her Mercury Racing 1075 horsepower engines to the max. On a humid day like today she maxed out around 115 mph. Not bad, she was very pleased with the results. She loved driving the Donzi, the superboat was slicing through water like a hot knife through butter. She finally slowed down and did a large lazy circle before coming to a stop. She cut the engines and slipped below deck.

The cabin was done in white leather and shiny chrome. There were built-in lounges on either side and a bed in the bow. She unpacked and, back in the cockpit, proceeded to stash the guns into every possible nook and cranny she could find. The sub-machine guns and ammo were put into a waterproof backpack and placed just behind the acrylic cabin door. Catalina checked everything one more time and then powered up for her run to the Epic hotel.

She tipped quite generously the Epic's marina crew, guaranteeing her Donzi the best care and privacy. No need to snoop around a boat whose female driver was dispensing hefty tips left and right.

44

A clean straight line. It was perfect. She stood back to admire her handiwork for a moment before making final adjustments to the remote system and the Barrett M82 mounted on top of it. She liked the Barrett simply because it made quite a large hole, had a really long range, and guaranteed to defeat its target even behind cover. It was big and heavy but it always made a statement.

Earlier, from inside her hotel room, she checked out the building across the river. She noted several empty office floors promising possibilities. Right after lunch, she made her way over with all her gear. She was able to sneak in without any collateral damage.

Catalina admired her handiwork with a grin of satisfaction. She picked up the remote—a thick rectangular plastic box with a large screen and buttons on both sides—and used it to move the gun up and down, left and right and in a tight circle. She moved the gun back into its original position and turned on the laser sight mounted on the barrel. Green, for best visibility in the bright Miami light. Catalina did a final alignment check before rigging the whole set-up to self-destruct at a push of a button from the remote unit. Her last step was to cut a small hole in the window so the bullet could exit without any obstacles in the way.

Back in her hotel room, Catalina maneuvered a white chair and a little round table in front of the window until they were perfectly positioned in the line of sight of her weapon across the street. She placed the laptop on the table, opened it up, plugged in Wilson's silver flash drive, and started Mark's program. The program was searching the web with keywords Catalina gathered from Wilson's flash drive about his research. The program would key in a word, wait for results, go to one of top hits and then move on to the next keyword as if someone was actively searching for information on Wilson. Mark figured that it would take some time for Echelon to pick up Catalina's 'searches,' which would give her several hours before anyone could possibly show up in Miami. Just enough time for a dip in the hotel pool and a drink in the cabana.

ICtech Offices, Arlington

"Jason, it's Jenny. We've got a hit." Her voice was a bit excited and eager to please him.

"What? When? Where? Can you get a location?" Ellis dropped back into his office chair. He was almost out the door for the evening when the phone rang. For a moment he considered letting it ring, but then changed his mind. He was glad he did.

"Well, it was just a couple of words on the web at first, like someone was Googling, but then…"

"Just tell me if you got a location, I really don't care how you did it!" He interrupted her in a tone she was not accustomed to.

"OK…," she took a deep breath, "Miami. It's coming from Miami. The address is for the Epic Hotel on Biscayne Bay." She wasn't excited anymore. Jenny was wondering if she now made the right choice by calling Ellis first instead of reporting this to the CIA.

"Did you get a room number?" he asked while pulling

up flights to Miami on his computer. He wondered how fast he could get down there.

"No... I could figure out the floor possibly," Jenny replied slowly and with caution.

"Then what's the hold-up?"

"I'm still working on it. I don't have that yet," lied Jenny. Not only did she have the floor, but the location of the room as well. She was starting to get that uneasy feeling in her stomach telling her that perhaps she was doing something wrong.

"Just email it to me when you get it, will you, Jenny? Dear?" Ellis paused his flight search to turn on the charm. "You know, when this is over, I'll take you to Paris. Would you like to go to Paris, Jenny?"

"Paris?" she got excited again. "All right, I'll email you as soon as I have it."

"Thanks!" he quickly responded, "hey, can you do me a favor? Don't report this to the CIA, will you? You're the best, kiddo!" He didn't wait for her to respond before hanging up. There were no non-stop flights available anymore and anything else cost close to a thousand. But Ellis was cheap, so he would wait till the morning to catch a much more affordable flight.

Jenny—the quiet and mousy analyst who worked in the West Virginia satellite intercept station—just sat there, in her little cubicle, still holding the phone receiver. Jason Ellis, the man that she had a crush on, just asked her to go to Paris with him but it all felt so wrong. He also asked her not to report Echelon's findings concerning the Operation Darwin package, an act that would cost her her job. She was getting a bad feeling about this. She finally realized that Ellis just used her to gain access to the information he was not cleared for. She decided to compile a report on the package and send it to CIA before emailing Ellis with the floor and room number. It took her hours before she was finished. It was late. Jenny e-mailed the report to McCarthy, a secondary contact listed for the Operation Darwin package. She was hoping that a less experienced agent, like McCarthy, would not notice the hours-long delay between the time Echelon got a hit and the filing of the report. She called him to confirm the receipt before leaving for the night. Her call went straight to voicemail.

―――――

Epic Hotel, Miami

The pool was located on a rooftop of the lower part of the hotel. There were actually two pools: one a long narrow shape, and another a wide triangle with a concave curve on its wide side. The pools' blue tiled walls were raised from the deck, with water softly spilling over them. Chaise lounges with white plush towels surrounded the pools, shaded by wide umbrellas the same shade of brilliant turquoise as the pools' water. There was also a long row of private cabanas decked out in oiled teak paneling and soft white curtains that gently flowed in the breeze. The pool area provided unobstructed views of Biscayne Bay. Catalina was able to secure one of the cabanas and she spent the rest of the day lounging by the pool, wearing just a tiny white bikini bottom.

Mark was very clever, he also created an app for her phone that would alert her when the 'search' got picked up by Echelon. It was taking longer than she expected. Mother's house was still quiet as well. This idling, this sitting and waiting around, was torture to her. She hated waiting. She always tried to plan her jobs so there was very short waiting time. Perhaps she was getting a bit restless these days, but she was no longer taking jobs that required her to be holed up somewhere for hours on end wearing adult diapers and waiting for her mark to appear. She was actually hoping to finish this all tonight, so she could sail to Cuba under the protective cover of the night. She took another look at her phone and then tossed it back in her bag. The cabana boy brought her one more virgin Piña Colada, her favorite tropical drink. She never consumed alcohol while working. Catalina leaned back on the cabana sofa and watched the cruise ships across the bay while sipping the white frothy concoction decorated with a tiny pink umbrella and a pineapple slice. For a brief moment, she wondered what it would be like to take a cruise—she heard that those ships served food non-stop. Her phone beeped: Echelon finally got it. She put down her drink, tossed a hundred on the table and left the pool.

Back in her room, Catalina stopped Mark's program and then used her other laptop to check in on Mother. His body lay untouched on the living room floor. She wondered if he started to smell yet. She left the laptop on the bed, ordered dinner, and went to take a long shower. Catalina was starting to get a bit restless, all this waiting was not her style.

As the last bite of lobster melted in her mouth, she closed her eyes. Mmm, another reason why she loved Miami—food. Delicious, amazing food. Catalina swallowed, opened her eyes, and looked at her plate. Empty. She slowly ran her index finger around the rim, collecting the last bits of her surf-n-turf dinner, and proceeded to lick it off. She ate her dinner sitting crossed-legged on the king-size bed wearing only underwear and a gray tank. The plate was balanced on her napkin-covered lap. A rerun of *NCIS* was flickering on TV.

Her finger was still in her mouth when, with the corner of her right eye, she picked up some movement on her computer screen. She turned her head toward the screen and cocked it to the right, waiting for the movement to come back. A predator waiting for its prey to flinch. A full minute passed before blue and red flashing lights reflected on the walls. Cops. Someone finally found Mother. She pulled the finger out of her mouth, pushed away the plate, uncrossed her legs and stretched out on her stomach in front of the computer. She watched the cops enter the room and search around with flashlights before turning the lights on. She grabbed the TV remote and muted the show then tossed the remote back on the bed where it slowly sunk deep into the luxurious down duvet.

It was not long before Mother's living room was swarming with cops and detectives. Catalina had no sound, but still was able to figure out that the body was discovered by a delivery boy who had keys to the house which now became evidence. She saw some men leave and then come back: they must have found the safe which she left open and completely empty. The coroner showed up and was now attempting to stuff Mother's corpse into a black bag. Catalina found this part quite entertaining—the coroner was having difficulties since rigor mortis already set in and Mother was a large heavy guy. It took four people to lift him onto a gurney. Watching all this commotion, she almost missed a man in a suit step away to the side and dial a phone. Almost. She picked him out just in time to zoom in and see him cup his hand over his mouth during his conversation while looking around to make sure no one noticed him.

"Bingo! Time to sleep on the boat," she said out loud. Catalina snapped the laptop closed, leaped off the bed and threw on a pair of shorts. She grabbed her toiletries from the bathroom and shoved them into her bag along with the laptop. After giving the room a quick once over, she emptied the contents of the minifridge into her bag and left. The heavy door closed silently behind her, a 'Do Not Disturb' sign swaying from side to side for a while before stopping.

45

New York City

Goldstein was dead. A friendly DC detective called it in, knowing Campbell had an eye on Goldstein. Shot in the head at close range like a traitor. There was another bullet in his heart, but it was purely for show. One in the head, one in the heart, mafia-style kill. Signorina Benedetto, his secret nickname for Catalina Bennett, was sending a message. As in the *'I'm cleaning house and you're next'* type of a message.

Special Agent Jim Campbell was standing on his unlit rooftop deck, looking at the night lights of the city. He tasked McCarthy with finding out as much information about Goldstein's death as possible. It was not an easy task, cops usually hated dealing with spooks and never willingly shared anything. He was looking at the twinkling city lights, waiting for McCarthy to call with updates.

Campbell spent the last night in a hotel, emotionally unable to be in his own loft. He disposed of the sheets and the champagne glasses, and scrubbed the hot tub with bleach. Yet, still, he felt her presence everywhere. He was in a cat and mouse business and he was always the cat. But not with her. He was sure that she planed out their encounter down to the smallest detail. She preyed on him, yet she didn't kill him. Why? Was she planning to do it later? He felt like a walking target and he hated it. But what he hated the most was the way she permanently settled into his mind: the way her skin felt, the way she smelled, the way she tasted… Every time he closed his eyes he would relive their night together. McCarthy was convinced that this was just a side effect of the drug she slipped him, but Campbell had an uneasy feeling that there was much more to it, his mind wondering what would happen if they met under different circumstances. If he could catch her and turn her, perhaps he could have it all.

———

Biscayne Bay, Miami

"How long does it take to put the pieces together?" Catalina asked a seagull perched on the hull of her Donzi. She took the boat out for a nighttime run, and was now sitting in the open water talking to a seagull. By this point she was expecting a swarm of CIA agents converge on Miami looking for her and the flash drive.

"Is he slow or something? I left a corpse behind and a nice trail to follow on Echelon, what's the matter with those people?" The seagull yawned and stretched its wings. "Maybe I should call him and nudge him." The seagull was staring at his webbed feet. "You think I should call him?.. Maybe, I'll call him."

———

Agent Campbell's phone rang. 'McCarthy' he thought and picked up without looking at the caller ID.

"Campbell," he answered.

"Miss me?" the all too familiar voice asked. He dropped the phone.

46

She gave him a moment to compose himself and called him back. This time he looked at the ID. It said *Jim Campbell.* "What the fuck?" he wondered before hitting *accept.*

"My, my... I knew I had a certain affect on men, but no one ever dropped the phone when I called," she said. He heard amusement in her voice.

"The caller ID listed me as the caller. Care to explain that one?" He started to look around for a place to sit.

"Did you think I would leave your place empty handed?" she asked. He could tell she was smiling. He was amusing her, he didn't like it. "I'm a professional, I don't just walk into a spook's apartment without a plan."

"You cloned my phone," he realized, "shit!" He plopped down on the couch in frustration, the same couch they made out on.

"Well, you needed a new model anyway." She was having fun. "You didn't answer my question, did you miss me?" He didn't respond right away. She waited.

"Are you asking me as a woman or as a cold-blooded killer?" He wondered if that remark would make her flinch. It didn't.

"As a woman," she answered.

"Then, yes, I miss you. You have a tendency to stick around," he replied. He leaned back into the couch and ran a hand through his hair. If he closed his eyes he could picture her sitting next to him.

"So do you. Too bad we're on the wrong sides of the game."

"We could be on the same side. You can work with us." Silence.

"I'm made. I do not work for the government," she replied slowly after a pause. And so coldly, chills ran down his spine. "Plus, I don't like being handled."

"Is that why you killed Goldstein? He was your handler, right?" He too could play the cat and mouse game.

"Is that what he was calling himself these days?" she asked, amusement back in her voice. "We called him Mother. He was a traitor and he died like one." She wasn't about to disclose that it was an ordered hit.

"What do you want?" Campbell asked suddenly.

"Well, well, getting down to business… What, not in the mood for some play?" she asked and then continued without giving him time to respond. "I'm calling to invite you to Miami, actually. And bring that Jason Ellis with you, I have something he wants. Rather badly, from what I hear."

"Miami? Where?" he sat up.

"Oh, gee, do I have to tell you everything? And I thought that Echelon could pin someone down within an inch."

"Echelon? What the fuck are you pulling here?" he jumped off the couch. "Look, do you want a target painted on your chest? Because I can arrange that!" He was starting to lose control.

"I decided to end this engagement. You're cramping my lifestyle. And if you're running this Op the same way you ran that African affair, then you're the one with the target."

"The African affair… What African affair… What are you talking about?" he was confused. Then he remembered her interest in his abdominal scar. The scar that he got during an operation in Africa. An operation that abruptly ended with the assassination of a high-profile CIA asset in his care. "Shit... that was you?" he looked around for something to punch.

"Miami," she ordered. "See you!" she hung up.

He just stood there, still holding the phone to his ear. Then he slowly lowered it. He nervously scratched his scar. It was her, the mechanic that took out not only the asset but Campbell's entire team. He was the only survivor. Lucky? He didn't think so. She must have run out of bullets because she vanished while he lay on the pavement bleeding. The CIA always thought that it was a team, not a single person shooter. Suddenly he turned around and threw his phone against the brick wall of the adjacent building. The phone shattered into tiny pieces.

The lack of a landline forced Campbell to return to the office in order to track down McCarthy. He finally located the young agent in the warm embrace of his girlfriend and ordered the man to join him in the office. McCarthy, in turn, woke up the rest of the team. If he had to crawl out of his girlfriend's bed in the name of God and Country then they all had to do it. McCarthy's first task once he got in, however, was to get Campbell a new phone and make a pot of Earl Gray tea.

Echelon, she mentioned Echelon. Yet, he heard nothing on the package. Campbell was turning his operations room inside out looking for confirmation that Echelon got a hit. He was the primary contact, yet he could not find anything. No emails, no fax, no voicemails. He was now going through everyone else's email accounts reviewing everything in their inbox from the last 24 hours. Finally he found what he was looking for in McCarthy's account. Strange. But Campbell didn't have time to deal with this discrepancy at the moment, he had to get his team down to Miami. The Epic Hotel was the location pinned down by Echelon. Morning was starting to rise, they couldn't waste any more time.

"Find Ellis! Tell him to get on the first plane to Miami," ordered Campbell to McCarthy. The young agent dialed Ellis's cell phone. No response. He tried his office, same results.

"I can't get him, sir!"

"OK, see if you can find him." Campbell asked another team member. If this little weasel was able to get to Goldstein, what else was he capable of? Campbell absently looked at the printout of the Echelon report he was holding in his hand. 'This was sent to McCarthy,' he thought, 'why? Did Ellis see this first?'

"Check the airports for Ellis!" he ordered to the room. The team jumped to obey.

"Sir, he's on a flight to Miami," someone responded shortly.

"When?"

"They took off an hour ago."

"Shit! He's got an hour on us! Let's move!"

47

Epic Hotel, Miami

Catalina was enjoying her breakfast in the hotel lobby when she noticed a bony young man in tight jeans and a shirt enter the hotel lobby and proceed straight to the bank of elevators. He moved cautiously and insecure, wearing a red Washington Nationals baseball cap pulled very low over his eyes. Ellis. Catalina put down her croissant on the glass-topped table, slid low into the cream colored leather chair, and watched the man disappear into an elevator. She slowly got up and looked around. He appeared to be alone. Bait?

Ellis got off the elevator on the 23rd floor and slowly moved down the hall. He stopped in front of the hotel room, the number provided by Jenny, unsure of what to do next. There was a "Do Not Disturb" sign on the door. Should he knock? He realized that he showed up here without a plan, which was not good. He looked up and down the hall and spotted a maid's cart. Ellis walked over. The maid was inside a suite, cleaning. He looked over the cart and, as luck would have it, noticed a key card on top of a clipboard. He grabbed the card and walked away.

He softly knocked on the door before slipping the key card in and pushing the door open. He didn't know why he knocked. Ellis tossed the key card down the hall and entered.

The room was empty. He started to look around, checking the closet and the bathroom first—both appearing empty of personal items. Used towels lay on the bathroom floor, a tray with dirty dishes sat on the bed. The white bedding was crumpled, like someone had been sitting or laying on it. He was about to start searching through the dresser when he saw it.

A laptop. It sat open on a small round table by the window. Something shiny and silver was plugged into the side. Ellis moved in. The laptop was on, in sleep mode. The shiny object was a rather large flash drive plugged into a USB port on the side. He sat down in the chair in front and hit the space bar to spring the laptop to life. His hands were shaking, but he didn't notice. The screen woke up and Ellis moved the curser to the little white boxy icon indicating the flash drive. He double clicked and a window popped open. Files. Hundreds of files. He moved a curser to the first one with a shaky finger. The first file was simply named 'Formula.'

Catalina had moved into a seat closer to the main door. Her long hair was now pulled back into a ponytail. She was wearing a black v-necked tee, her Kevlar vest, and cargo pants with pockets full of QuickClot pouches. A Glock 19 was tucked into the waistband of her pants, covered by the shirt. Her waterproof bag was on her shoulder. She was concentrating on the screen of the controller for her remote system. Through the feed provided by the scope on her Barrett M82 Catalina could see Ellis moving around the room. She smiled when Ellis sat down in front of the laptop and started fiddling with it. She flipped a switch from 'safe' to 'arm', corrected her aim a bit using the arrow keys, then sat back and continued to watch the screen. Waiting for the perfect moment. Suddenly, the corner of her left eye picked up large men entering briskly through the hotel door. Her brain instinctively counted the men—five—and registered the fact that they were packing. She recognized one of them as Jim Campbell. The CIA had arrived. Finally.

Ellis couldn't believe his eyes. Wilson had finished his research! The compound, the delivery system, everything was finished and stored on this flash drive. His breath quickened and suddenly he saw green. 'Money, yes!' he thought before realizing that the green that filled his vision was not the color of money but a light. He shook his head to jolt himself into the present and saw a little green light dot dancing around on his chest. Suddenly, the dot stopped.

Catalina zoomed in as close as possible and saw him lift his head and look straight on, his eyes widening in horror, as her thumb pressed the black round 'fire' button. *Boom!* On her screen she watched Ellis, and the laptop, splatter into a thousand pieces all over the room as the .50 BMG caliber pierced through them and the room's door, finally lodging in the wall across the hall. Not much was left of Ellis, just a bloody mess of tissue mixed with computer parts. The shot was heard all the way in the lobby. Everyone froze for a second, trying to comprehend what happened. She looked up from her screen just in time to see the five CIA men fan out and draw their guns as the crowd suddenly erupted in screams and scattered across the lobby.

Catalina bolted from her seat just as Campbell turned around and saw her. For a moment their eyes locked on each other, and Campbell got to see the real color of her eyes. Cold steel blue. Catalina winked at him, then spun around and sprinted out the door. It took him a moment to digest what he just saw, before reacting and following her after her.

It was a long way to her boat and he was right on her tail. Catalina needed to buy some time. She cut to the right, used a line of cars for cover, then jumped over a low cement wall and ducked behind it. Catalina was still holding the remote so she quickly panned the Barrett to the location of the hotel's entrance. A large Hummer limousine, parked next to the entrance, made for a nice target and was now in her sights. She could hear her pursuers shouting, they were already outside. Her thumb pushed 'fire' and the gun responded. The round sliced through the air, hit the Hummer in the back, and the vehicle exploded. The shockwave hurled the CIA team off their feet and into the ground. The explosion set off car alarms in the area, and people started to scream in fear. She bolted from her hiding space toward the marina.

Campbell was lying face down on the ground, McCarthy was nearby. They were charred but alive and in one piece. Campbell got up in time to see Catalina running toward the marina. He followed her, McCarthy right behind him. Neither man realized that the explosion took out one of their guys who was too close to the Hummer. They were down to four people now.

Catalina was almost at her boat. She signaled the dock help and a couple of them rushed to the Donzi to untie her as soon as she was in. Earlier, she tipped the help a handful of hundreds to put the Donzi stern in and asked to have it ready at a moment's notice. Catalina jumped inside the boat just as someone was untying her, tossed her bag on the floor, remote on the seat and started the engine with one hand while drawing her Glock with another. She turned around and saw four men running toward the marina. Campbell was the closest. Catalina shot a warning shot at his feet. They ducked for cover and she took this moment to hit the Barrett's self-destruct function on the remote. *Boom!* Across the Miami river, a large fireball exploded from a window on a high floor of a building, the new explosion causing even more panic in the area. Her pursuers were shouting again, but she didn't care what. She twisted the steering wheel and hit the throttle, the boat reacting with a large spray of water as it jumped forward. *Pop!* Someone shot at her, missing and hitting the windshield. She turned, Glock ready and saw one of Campbell's team in a firing position. She fired at him twice. He fell back, his arms making an arc in the air. Campbell ran over, but realized right away that the man was dead. She put two in his chest. They were now down to three.

"She's on a boat, I need a boat!" Campbell screamed. He was running toward the dock and scanning the waters for a possible boat he could take.

"Sir, we have no jurisdiction here, this is unauthorized!" yelled McCarthy as he followed Campbell. Campbell stopped and turned, breathing heavily, eyes full of rage.

"I don't care, get me a boat!"

"Sir," McCarthy grabbed Campbell by the arm. "Call the Coast Guard, they'll get her."

"She took one of my own, she's going down!" Campbell snapped his arm away and continued to scan the waters.

"She took two, Tom was killed in the explosion," said McCarthy quietly. Red flashed in Campbell's eyes—he liked Tom. His nostrils flared as he turned to the water, and saw the Donzi disappearing down Biscayne Bay. McCarthy decided not to argue anymore.

Campbell found what he was looking for further down the dock. A fat man and a scantily-clad woman were disembarking a garish orange and purple cigarette boat. He ran down toward them and aimed his gun to the man's fat red face. The woman screamed.

"Key!" he demanded. The man extended his shaking fat hand toward Campbell. He snatched up the key, and pushed the man aside in order to jump into the boat. McCarthy and the remaining member of their team followed. Campbell was already at the wheel when they got in. The boat took off, making a wide arc turning in pursuit of Catalina. By this point she was far down the Bay.

48

Catalina lost them for a bit, but was sure that at this moment they were looking for a boat to continue their pursuit. She needed more weapons. Catalina tossed the now useless remote overboard, pointed the bow toward the Rickenbaker Causeway and abandoned the wheel in order to slip inside the cabin to grab more guns. She quickly emerged packing the Berettas under each arm and one more tucked into the back of her pants, pockets bulging with spare clips. She put a bag with machine guns by the door of the cabin. Catalina grabbed the wheel just in time, an ugly-colored cigarette boat gaining speed behind her.

Campbell was at the wheel. He had some water to cover, but realized that she was heading toward the Rickenbaker Causeway and figured that they would catch up to her since she would be forced to slow down in order to pass under the bridge.

"Shit!" spat Catalina. There was quite the boat traffic ahead by the bridge. She slowed down just a tad in order to figure out her best maneuver around it. The garish monster behind was getting closer. Suddenly she had an idea. She grabbed one of her machine guns, turned around, and unloaded a full clip toward Campbell's vessel. The men dropped on deck as the rounds hit the windshield. She didn't hit anyone, she had a different result in mind. The boats surrounding them were now either stopped or moving rapidly out of the way, which is what she wanted.

Catalina tossed the empty gun inside the cabin, dropped down the bottom on her bolster seat so she could drive standing up, firmly leaned against the cushions, and gunned the throttle. She was fully intent on maneuvering around the obstacles in front of her at full speed. The Donzi came really close to hitting a couple of yachts head-on with Catalina turning away at the last moment, spraying water all over. And every time she looked behind her, Campbell was not only able to keep up but was gaining.

"Bugger! They can't have bigger engines, can they?" she asked herself and made another heart-stopping maneuver. A whine of police sirens erupted on shore—her escapades at the hotel didn't go unnoticed. This might not end they way she planned.

Campbell heard the sirens as well. Soon, their boat chase would be noticed by the cops and the Coast Guard would get involved. Not what he intended either.

"Hey, someone get on the radio and make sure everyone stays out of it!" he yelled out over the noise of the engines.

"What am I suppose to tell them?" It was McCarthy who responded, as usual.

"Tell them we're in pursuit of a foreign national… Matter of National Security… Pretend to be someone else… Do you think I care at this moment? Just get them out of the way!" he yelled back and went around a small yacht with a frightened family on board. He heard the children crying.

Catalina flew under the bridge at full speed, with only the engines in the water. The boat landed hard back down and she jumped up feeling the landing in every bone in her body. *Pop!* Another hole in the windshield, this one really close to her head. Catalina turned to port, making a large circle as Campbell's cigarette boat cleared the bridge at high speed as well. She came up behind them, drawing her Beretta. The man standing next to Campbell turned and saw her. *Pop! Pop! Pop!* She fired three rounds into his chest. The man fell back onto the helm then slid down. Campbell dropped to his side, as McCarthy started shooting at her. He missed, she was a fast moving target speeding away from them and he was not a good marksman. They were now down to two.

"Mike!" yelled Campbell to his fallen friend but got no response. "Shit!" He turned to McCarthy, just in time to see him miss a shot, and yanked on his arm. "Get him down below... he's gone," and with that he returned to piloting the boat in pursuit.

She needed a plan B. Catalina realized that the Coast Guard was going to get involved at any moment and she'll never be able to get out of Miami. She needed a new plan and fast. She looked down at her bag full of weapons. A packet of C4 was peeking out from underneath all the guns. An idea came to her, and she franticly searched herself for her phone. It could work, but she would need help from Tyrone. She found the phone and dialed, while looking for a wide enough space to turn around without getting too close to Campbell's boat once again gaining on her. Her conversation with Tyrone was brief, he instantly figured out what she was intending to do and said that his team would be ready. Catalina dropped the phone back into her pant pocket and concentrated on turning around. She had to go back up the Bay, toward the marina where her Sanctuary was hidden.

49

"What the hell is she doing now?" Campbell asked when he noticed that she was making a wide turn.

"Turning, she's turning!" McCarthy stated the obvious. They just kept on following her. Catalina was heading toward the other Rickenbacker Causeway bridge between Virginia Key and Key Biscayne.

"Get the Coast Guard! She's heading out into the Atlantic! Tell them to block her, but not to detain," ordered Campbell to McCarthy.

"Sir?"

"You heard me, I'm taking her out!"

Catalina's intentions were to go around Virginia Key and Fisher Island, avoiding the Port of Miami with all the cruise ships, to get as close to her Sanctuary as possible. She was about to pass Fisher Island on the starboard side when she saw fast approaching Coast Guard vessels. They were trying to block her from entering the Atlantic. She cut to port, Campbell following suit. A Coast Guard vessel followed them as well. Catalina looked up, no helicopters yet. She was hoping there would not be any, otherwise her plan would not work. She was too occupied with looking for helicopters to notice that she was steering head on into a large yacht. But the yacht sounded a horn and Catalina managed to turn the Donzi away just in time. The maneuver left her exposed just long enough for Campbell to exploit the opportunity. He rapidly fired several shots, did not miss, and watched her fall on the helm of her Donzi.

The boat sped up however, she must have fallen on the throttle.

"Got you!" yelled out Campbell when he saw Catalina fall. McCarthy was surprised by Campbell's reaction, he didn't expect it.

Searing pain ripped through her left shoulder. She bit her lip, her training and discipline preventing her from screaming and panicking. There was pain in her back as well, but of a different variety. The slim design of her vest only protected her back, she took a round in the left shoulder which was left exposed. Blood was everywhere—it was a through-and-though. Catalina slid down to the deck. She had to stop the bleeding. Her right hand yanked on the pockets of her cargo pants, pulling out QuickClot pouches. She ripped them open with her teeth and slapped one on to her shoulder with as much pressure as possible. More sharp pain shot though her. She applied another pouch to the wound on her back, then pulled herself up. The boat was out of control and flying through water at high speed toward downtown Miami. Her left arm was now immobile, she would have to do everything one handed. She gritted her teeth and concentrated on controlling the boat, mentally blocking the pain from her shoulder. Her adrenaline was running high, providing temporary pain relief as well.

"Shit, she's alive!" Campbell could not believe his eyes. He noticed that there was something white on her shoulders. "I put three rounds in her back, how is she still standing?"

"I think she came prepared, because she's patched herself up!" McCarthy replied with disbelief as well.

Catalina finally got the Donzi under control and made a tight 180 degree turn back toward Fisher Island. She flew by Campbell's boat , maneuvering around them and spraying them with water. The two men were now soaking wet. Catalina pulled the bottom up on her bolster seat and plopped down. With her left arm out of commission, she would have to use her knees to control the steering wheel when she needed to shoot. She did it in a car lots of times, she figured a boat should not be any different. She pulled the bag full of weapons over with her left foot and positioned it between her feet. Catalina grabbed another sub-machine gun and put on her lap. No more precision shooting, she was mad. With her left knee holding the wheel, she pushed the throttle down to gain even more speed as she slipped between Dodge and Fisher Islands. She saw more Coast Guard vessels joining the pursuit now.

Catalina zigzagged around boats coming in and out from the numerous residential islands at high speed. The Donzi was going so fast it was almost completely out of the water, periodically crashing down then coming back up again. Every time the boat landed, Catalina winced in pain. She discovered that it was painful to breathe, she probably had cracked ribs. She unsnapped her Kevlar vest, in case she needed to ditch it quickly. Her pants vibrated—Tyrone signaling that his crew was ready. She turned her head to see how close Campbell and the Coast Guard were, and found them a lot closer than anticipated. She just needed to go under the bridge.

McCarthy was ordered to fire if he got an opportunity. Campbell was low on rounds, they didn't arrive heavily armed because he severely underestimated her. The men saw the Donzi turn toward the bridge. The boat was jumping in and out of water. McCarthy fired, hoping to hit one of the engines. But he missed and the bullet just nicked the hull. McCarthy decided to try again, he was now just as determined as Campbell to bring her down. They followed the Donzi under the bridge with the Coast Guard right behind them. The Coast Guard had the power and the means to take her out, but they were ordered not to unless she would fire directly at their vessels. She never did.

The Donzi flew under the bridge and came out the other side. McCarthy noticed that she was turning to port. He fired several rounds. And missed. Again. The bullets grazed the hull, but did no serious damage. To the boat at least. But they pissed off Catalina, who suddenly let go of the wheel, stood up, aimed a machine gun at both men, and pulled the trigger. They dropped on deck. The rounds ripped through the boat shredding everything. The men dove inside the cabin. The noise of exploding rounds was deafening. Her magazine held 40 rounds and she was determined to unload them all. Suddenly, it all stopped.

"She's out of ammo, let's get her!" Campbell said and drew his gun. He was out of the cabin and back on deck before McCarthy had a chance to stop him. *Pop, pop, pop, pop, pop!* Campbell screamed and fell down. She got him.

McCarthy leapt out of the cabin to help his bleeding boss. Campbell was alive, but barely. The air went silent, she stopped shooting. Campbell was trying to pull himself up. McCarthy popped his head above the shattered windshield to take a peak, and froze in terror at the scene unfolding in the water. The Donzi was now flying toward the pier out of control. Any second she would hit the timber piles. Campbell finally managed to get himself upright only to witness the Donzi lose control and realize with horror that Catalina was still onboard. The boat continued to careen from side to side. Suddenly, the Donzi jumped high out of the water. She spiraled in the air over the timbers and crashed down on the concrete pier. The boat exploded, sending a massive fireball into the air and spilling fire all around. McCarthy heard Campbell scream

"No!" before the shockwave of the explosion knocked both men back on deck.

Fire, he saw fire everywhere. Campbell was being bandaged up and lifted out of the cigarette boat by the Coast Guard guardians when he was able to look at the destruction. He was losing consciousness. He heard sirens of the approaching police and fire engines. The fire was so massive, he could feel the heat radiating from it even at a distance. McCarthy's face appeared in front of him, concern written all over it. The young man leaned in and started whispering something urgently into his ear.

"…Too much fuel on board… very hot… no way she survived…" that was all Campbell was able to make out. The realization that Catalina Bennett was dead finally hit him and he lost consciousness.

50

Washington, DC

It was too hot to be running outside, yet here he was, gracefully jogging by, his iPod strapped to his left bulging bicep, headphones in the ears. He jogged in place at intersections, continuing on when the lights changed. He was black, tall, well built, wearing an expensive watch and Nike athletic wear. If anyone paid close attention, they would realize that instead of running shoes he was wearing basketball ones. It was an uncomfortable choice of footwear for a run, but no one noticed. And so he continued to jog around Embassy Row, looking around at stately residences and cars going by from time to time. He was near Massachusetts Avenue when the lights changed at an intersection and he was forced to bob up and down in one place, waiting for the lights to turn.

Suddenly, he stopped. He reached into his shorts, pulled out a cheap phone, and yanked the headphones out of his ears at the same time. He didn't greet his caller, just listened intently. He hung up just as the lights changed. He ran across the intersection, still holding his phone. But instead of continuing on, he stopped and knelt down to retie his shoe. He fiddled with his shoelace, looked around, and started doing something on his phone. He was still preoccupied with his phone when, suddenly, a blast ripped apart a residence on Massachusetts Avenue. There was no fire, yet, but the debris flew everywhere. The pops of smaller blasts came from inside the building, then silence followed before the structure shook and collapsed onto itself. There was one more explosion, and fire engulfed the rubble.

The jogging man didn't watch the fire. He calmly turned around when the first blast ripped though the building and took off. He ran north for several blocks before stopping in a shade of a large tree to, once again, busy himself with his phone. *"Done"*, he typed with his thumbs. He sent the text and then watched the phone's screen to flash the word "sent" before continuing with his jog. He wanted to make sure that his message reached the recipient: Eddie Washington, his boss.

"Get out of the house and wait for the Boss to call you. She's in deep shit here," was all that Tyrone said when he called a couple of hours earlier. Diamond flipped on the switch of the last detonator and left the house. He spent the entire morning wiring the house to explode, using the precise plans he found taped to the back of a very large china cabinet in the dining room. He was following Catalina's instructions, it was her intent to blow up her Embassy Row house in case things went terribly wrong in Miami. The plans were designed by Frank years ago when the house was remodeled, she taped them behind the china cabinet before he left for Chicago.

Diamond drove around for a while, trying to find a good, but relatively far away, spot in order to watch the house. He couldn't. Not without being noticed. He finally pulled into a parking garage of a health club and changed in the back seat of the Lexus into some workout clothes he happened to have in his bag. He decided to pretend to be a jogger and just keep running in circles in the vicinity of Catalina's house until the Boss called with further instructions. It was late afternoon and hot but he couldn't come

up with any other options. He didn't have to jog for long—
he was on his second lap when he got the call.

————

Chicago's Western Suburbs

Jon Worthington waited until the evening news to
finally take his golden retriever out for a walk. It was still
humid and he was hoping to do a short route, but at the
last moment was ordered by Melanie to pass by Mark and
Frank's residences to see if there was any sign of Frank's
niece. The woman's sudden and quiet departure rattled
the women of the block and they spent every waking
hour gossiping about it. So Jon dutifully walked toward
the homes, hoping there would be nothing to report back
because he didn't want to get involved. He was wrong.

He heard loud voices coming from the house even
before he got close. The two men were yelling at each
other in Frank's living room. In some foreign language,
Jon couldn't tell which. He stopped in front of Frank's living room window, hoping the dog would pick a tree and
give him an excuse to stand there for a bit. He got lucky,
tonight his golden was in an agreeable mood. And for
once, Frank's curtains were open, giving Jon a view inside
the house.

They were having a very heated argument. Both men
were yelling at the same time, punctuating their yelling
with large arm gestures. At some point the baby joined
in crying. Jon could see a large TV on in the background.
CNN. Mark finally picked up the baby and stormed out,
leaving Frank pacing and screaming into the air. Jon heard
a phone ringing, then saw Frank yelling into the phone.
That conversation Jon could understand. Frank was yelling
at someone to skip the bullshit and give it to him straight

because as a father he deserved to know the truth. Jon guessed that the caller did not agree because the conversation ended when Frank threw the phone against the wall. Frank suddenly turned around and noticed Jon standing outside and looking into his windows. Frank marched to the window and shut the curtains with a snap. Jon tugged on the dog and hurried away. On the way home he decided to keep what he just saw to himself and never discuss it with his wife.

Frank was continuing his tirade, mumbling something about the neighbors, when Mark and Sofia appeared back in the living room. But even through all the mumbling, Mark was able to catch the news anchor coming back with breaking news. He grabbed the remote and turned up the volume. Frank, now attempting to put back together his shattered phone, was not paying attention. A gentle pull on his elbow turned him toward the TV. Mark silently pointed to the screen. They both stood motionless, Mark tightly clutching Sofia, as the news anchor continued to deliver the news.

"...high-speed boat chase that ended in a fiery crash of one of the boats.
Authorities deny any possible connection between several earlier explosions that ripped through downtown Miami and the boat chase. Contrary to eyewitnesses at the time of the explosions in Epic Hotel, only one casualty was reported. The man was identified as Jason Ellis, a Virginia resident. No names of the possible victims of the boat's explosion have been released yet. An unidentified source with the Miami-Dade fire department said that there are no survivors."

Frank fell on down on his knees and started to scream. Mark, trying to contain his emotions, squeezed Sofia so tightly the baby cried out in pain. He loosened his grip then turned away from his father and walked out of the house as fast as possible. Right now Frank needed to be alone. As soon as the door closed behind Mark, Frank got back on his feet and unleashed his rage onto his surroundings. When he was finished, the living room was completely destroyed. He looked around the room, collapsed on the floor and did what he never did before—started to pray, in Latin. He was begging for a miracle: for Catalina to survive.

51

Miami

The fire from the Donzi's explosion was still raging full force, painting the night Miami sky deep orange. There was unusually high drug-running activity that night as well. In the turbulent Atlantic waters, due to a developing storm, the US Customs & Border Protection could not keep up with the sudden onslaught of go-fast boat traffic. Someone commented that the fatal boat chase earlier in the day must have caused a panic within the Cartels. With all this activity in the water, the CBP was struggling to keep track of where everyone was heading.

With most of the traffic pointing toward South America, no one noticed a faint blip on the radar heading off to Cuba. If they were able to take a look at close range, they would have found out that it was indeed two go-fast boats, running really close to each other with one boat having a lead of only a couple of feet. The boats were identical to the one that blew up that afternoon. Each boat had a crew of two, heavily armed. They had no cargo, but a passenger, who was lying unconscious and barely breathing below deck in one of the boats. As they got within eyesight of Cuba, the lead boat turned off course and started heading back to Miami. The boat carrying the passenger continued on to Varadero.

A medical team and an old ambulance waited for the boat on a deserted beach. There was no dock, the crew had to stop several feet off and then carry their passenger to shore in their arms. The medical crew rushed in to help and soon the passenger was on a gurney. The trauma doctor, dispatched with the medical team, rushed over to assess the injuries while one of the medics started to insert an IV.

"She's got a through-and-through in the shoulder, several fractured ribs and burns. She had to take a swim and lost a lot of blood by the time she managed to get to safety," reported one of the men to the doctor in Spanish. "She was unconscious when we finally were able to get to her box." The doctor nodded, and the gurney was pushed into the ambulance. The doctor climbed in behind it. He was about to shut the door when a hand grabbed it and held it open.

"Is she going to live? We were ordered to ask," said the man from the boat, with an extremely concerned look on his face.

"I don't know. But we will do everything we can for her," the doctor answered. The door was released and the doctor shut it closed.

The men got back into the boat and watched the ambulance disappear into the night before turning on the engines and speeding back to Miami. When they returned, they noticed that the fire from the explosion was finally under control and was dying out. They could just make out an outline of charred remains of what once was a beautiful Donzi 43 ZR craft.

"Pity," said one man to the other.

"Hey that boat probably saved her life, man. Those pigs could barely keep up," said the other.

———

Mercy Hospital, Miami

Campbell was finally out of surgery. He was rolled

into ICU and McCarthy took a post in front of his room. At some point, several men in bad suits and flashing various badges came to talk. McCarthy had to leave his vigil in front of Campbell's room to try and explain, in a manner that would satisfy everyone, why CIA was operating domestically. He returned to his perch an hour later. It was several more hours before the doctors came to check on Campbell's condition and finally allowed the young agent to see his boss. And only for a minute.

Campbell was in a bad shape, but awake. His chest was bandaged, tubes everywhere. McCarthy leaned in and whispered: "I took care of everything. Ellis will be responsible, with ICtech denying any knowledge of his actions, of course. We brought our guys home. The Fire Captain said that the boat was loaded with ammo and C4. Coast Guard put divers in the water but they didn't find anybody. There was an explosion of a diplomatic residence on Embassy Row in DC. I don't have all the details yet, but I bet it's connected." Campbell managed to grab McCarthy's hand and squeezed it. "The doctors said that the bullets missed your heart, you'll live... I think she missed on purpose, sir." Campbell shut his eyes and turned away. The monitors over his head beeped suddenly. A nurse rushed into his room and shooed McCarthy out.

Epilogue

Somewhere near Palermo, Sicily, nine months later

The soft purr of the engine echoed through the streets of a small fishing village, as the gleaming Aston Martin V12 Vantage effortlessly glided down the winding road by the coast. The car slowed down before turning off on a side road leading down to a sea-front villa nestled within luscious vegetation and a multitude of olive trees and surrounded by a high stone wall. The Vantage rolled through a wide wrought iron gate guarded by large men heavily armed. The car continued past a long garage with glass doors revealing a small collection of performance cars including a black Audi R8 and a beautifully restored red Ferrari 250 GTO.

The British automotive beauty finally came to a stop in front of the ground floor terrace. The driver side door opened to reveal a beautiful young woman. She unfolded herself out of the car and, just as the car did a moment ago, glided down the graveled driveway and disappeared into the cool shadows of the villa. She flowed through the main floor's spacious and well-appointed sitting rooms, without noticing the priceless works of art on the walls or a large display case filled with Fabergé eggs. The rooms opened up to a shaded outdoor back terrace beyond which lay an infinity pool with stunning views of the sea. She finally stopped on the terrace to shed her clothes before diving into the pool. Her body was well tanned and flawless. After several laps around, the young woman finally stopped by the edge of the pool and turned to gaze out into the sea. She floated, looking at the sparkling water, for quite a long time.

Her solitude was interrupted by the butler announcing that breakfast was served. He handed her a cobalt blue plush beach towel and she got out of the pool. The woman wrapped herself in the towel, and headed toward a terrace table set with gleaming silver and fine china. She exchanged a small conversation in Sicilian with the butler about her morning drive and the pool's temperature. Once she was seated for breakfast, the butler disappeared into the house, only to reappear moments later with a silver tray laden with regional morning delicacies prepared by her housekeeper. He presented her with the food, a cup of cappuccino, a morning paper and a large manila envelope, and disappeared once again. She was left alone to enjoy the breakfast and soft sea breeze.

About half and hour later, the butler reappeared carrying a satellite phone. She frowned when she saw him, but he smiled and nodded. This caller was a welcome one. She silently extended her hand for the phone and once received, waved the butler off. She watched him leave and walked over to the pool before finally answering. In English.

"This better be good."

"It is. I'm happy to report that your lovely niece has finally gotten a molar! Molars, to be exact. Two on the bottom. And the top are not far behind."

"Great! Oohh, I can't wait to see them. Now get off this phone, bro!" she replied with a smile.

"Yeah, yeah. It's encrypted, they won't trace it. Daddy's doing fine, by the way, although I don't know how long he can last living in the Caymans next to Eddie's compound.

Says he's a noisy neighbor. We all love you and miss you. Take care, sis."

"Love you too. *Ciao!*" Catalina hung up the phone.

She stood for a couple more minutes by the pool, looking out at the sea. It was soothing to her, the hum of the waves healing. She listened for a while longer, reflecting on the wonderful news. She smiled, her cold steel blue eyes briefly warming with fond memories of her time spent with her niece. She hoped that soon she would be able to reunite with Sofia, Catalina had so much to teach her... She turned around and returned to her breakfast. Cappuccino in hand, she dumped out the contents of the manila envelope on the table. Surveillance photos and a dossier. She spread the pictures out on the table, studying them while sipping her drink. Once the cappuccino was finished, Catalina walked back into the villa. She stopped in the middle of her sitting room and yelled at the top of her lungs:

"Antonia! Where did you stash my guns?"

About the Author

Katherine Brankin grew up on Leo Tolstoy and Fyodor
Dostoevsky, but matured on Ian Fleming. Already being
an accomplished designer and blogger of Driving Master
Danny, writing fiction became just one more outlet for
her imagination. The characters and their incredible
stories just appeared in front of her one day and she
took a chance.

Katherine lives in the suburbs of Chicago with her family
and two nocturnal pets that keep her company when she
writes at odd hours of the night fueled by large quantities
of hot tea and antipasto platters.

For all things Catalina, visit www.whoiscatalina.com.

www.ingramcontent.com/pod-product-compliance
Lightning Source LLC
Chambersburg PA
CBHW020414110726
47899CB00006B/1982